THE LIARS' CLUB

THE LIARS' CLUB

JAMIE LEE FRY

THE LIARS' CLUB
JAMIE LEE FRY

Print edition ISBN: 9781737120230
E-book edition ISBN: 9781737120247
Barnes & Noble Edition ISBN: 9781737120254

First edition: October 2022
10 9 8 7 6 5 4 3 2 1

WWW.AUTHORJAMIELEEFRY.COM

FOR JEREMY, MY HUSBAND,
BEST FRIEND, AND RIDE-OR-DIE.

PROLOGUE

Sunday, October 17, 7:30 p.m.

I knew from the first second that I saw your face I couldn't be myself with you. I knew you wouldn't like the real me, and quite frankly, I'm not even sure *I* like the real me. But I'm working on it. That's why I have to pretend.

Aww, sweetie, don't give me that look—that you-are-sick-in-the-head kind of look. That's not very nice of you. Although, I do know that expression all too well. This isn't my first time, sweetheart. Go ahead, squirm all you want—I enjoy watching you struggle. I can't explain it. It's my malfunction. I simply can't help myself, and this is my favorite part: the moment of realization that you're screwed, there's no way out. The way your eyes flicker as you replay every misstep that led you to this very moment.

That look excites me.

Thrills me.

The reason I can't stop.

I crave it, over and over. . .

You don't want to be caught off guard like the last time. I don't blame you. You weren't expecting it. There was no way you could have known. I'm getting good at what I do, you see. I play the part well.

You're probably wondering if I'm going to kill you right now. And the answer to that question is no. I want to, but I have to wait.

What? Oh, I'm sorry, I can't hear you through your duct-taped mouth. Your moans do excite me, though. Your tiny body is quivering and I'm sorry for that, but just a little longer now, my dear. It's all part of the game—the mindfuck.

Do you know I chose you because of your profile picture? You were virtually begging for someone to treat you like this. But right now, you're a fucking mess with your cheeks all red and splotchy and your mascara running down your face.

See, sweetie, you made me do this. You made me choose you for the game. You were my pawn. And guess what, babe? I believe I won, but that means. . . Well, my dear, that means you lost.

SIX WEEKS EARLIER

CHAPTER ONE

Max
Friday, September 10, 11:59 a.m.

It's almost noon. Where is she?

My eyes are fixed on the door, but my foot taps impatiently out of my control, vibrating up to my hip bone. I need to calm down, but my body won't obey.

The door slowly creaks open. Could it be?

It's not her. A pang of disappointment punches me in the gut as a middle-aged man trudges inside.

"Welcome to Epic Records. Can I help you find anything?"

Keeping his head down, the man slowly shuffles past me, ignoring my greeting.

He has today's newspaper wedged under his arm. An all-too-familiar headline in bold print glares at me—*Local Woman Murdered. No Leads*—accompanied by a photograph of a homely looking woman in her thirties with long brunette hair.

"So sad," I say, following him and pointing to his paper, trying to get the customer to engage.

He lets out an annoyed gruff, then continues to the rear of the store, where he begins sifting through the used records.

"Jerk," I whisper under my breath, just quietly enough so he doesn't hear me. But do I really care? What's the worst that could happen? Kade fires me? I doubt it. I'm his best employee and I'd like to think I'm his friend. This place couldn't function without me, especially lately.

I lean down and reach into a newly opened shipment of inventory. I curl my fingers under a pristine stack of vinyl records and pull them carefully out of the box. I set the tall pile on the countertop, taking the top one. I unwrap the shipping packaging, careful not to ruin the intentional cellophane wrapping in the process, and scan the barcode into our computer system to create a new item. It's mindless work, really. I scan the second record from the pile and as my fingers hit the keyboard to type in the new listing, a breeze sweeps across my Birkenstock sandals. My toes curl in reaction to the cool air.

The door! I neglected my precious entryway for more than a few seconds. I must pay better attention, or I could miss my opportunity.

But it's still not her. Instead, a young girl and a baby-faced man casually stroll inside.

"Welcome."

Giggling to themselves and wrapped in each other's embrace, they walk past the counter, also ignoring my greeting while sipping on their pumpkin spice lattes. Everything about the pair screams "musical tourist"—the name I give to posers who buy records to feel hip. I can spot them from a mile away.

The girl pulls out her phone and begins taking selfies in front of the vintage posters, solidifying my assumption; they're not here for the music. They just want to *look* cool.

I'm slowly losing hope of ever connecting with others who have the same affinity for the history of music, as those genuine record-loving customers are few and far between. Darn musical tourists. They make me detest a job I should be enjoying. Luckily, I have Kade to chat with about my passion or I would go crazy. Another old soul trapped in a different time. However, we see and experience the "now" quite differently.

Where are the beatniks and the Grateful Dead fans? I want to chat their ears off. You'd think they'd be lingering around a record store, wanting to recall tales of the past with anyone who'd listen. I would love to hear their stories about what it was like growing up during that era. I really believe that I was born a few decades too late for the life I was meant to live.

Is it bad I don't understand my own generation and their dependency on technology? I just don't get it.

But *she* is different. I've never seen her pull out her phone in here. Not once. Plus, she's really cute. Where is she? My stomach churns in anticipation. I anxiously check my watch. It's now five past noon.

She always comes at noon.

Like clockwork; every Friday, midday. I imagine it's her lunch hour and Fridays are her payday. Although, I wouldn't know for certain because I have never actually spoken to her.

I walk up behind the young couple, catching them mid-pose. "Anything I can help you find?" The man barely glances in my direction and the girl doesn't look past her phone.

Am I invisible? I feel like it.

They resume their stance in front of a Led Zeppelin poster, the fake shutter noise of the phone camera sounding as I walk away. I highly doubt either of them could name one of their songs—not even 'Stairway to Heaven.' I'm annoyed, and yet I can't help but envy the young fools in love, and for this, I hate them.

I can't help but think about the first time she came into the store. That was six Fridays ago.

She walked in alone and went straight to a Bob Dylan record. I liked that she knew exactly what she wanted.

I continued to watch her from afar, mesmerized by her every move. From the way she wrinkled her nose as she read the back of the album, to her little content grin as she tucked the record under her arm. She appeared slightly younger than me, but not by more than a year or so. She was cute as hell, with a tiny little nose and eyes as blue as the ocean. Her hair an intentional mess of loose blonde curls, giving that I-don't-give-a-fuck impression.

Afraid to even say hi, in fear of doping up the conversation and starting off on a bad foot, I darted to the backroom, my nerves rattled by this beautiful creature along with a flurry of insecurities created by my old friends. They went so far as to use my name to coin a phrase for any time a guy messed up a conversation with a girl: Don't *Max it up*, they'd say.

I didn't want to *Max it up*. But that's what I do.

I want to be normal. Suave. Like Kade. I suppose that if I looked more like Kade, life would be easier. He's buff, bronzed, and starkly handsome. Every girl flounders at the sight of him. I, on the other hand, am much thinner, lankier, and paler than Kade. He has that effortless hair that can flop any which way and still look cool. While I have the kind of hair that looks like I rolled out of bed if I don't style my thick black birds' nest. I'm not the kind of guy girls swoon over; I'm the kind of guy who runs away like a coward when a girl finally piques my curiosity.

So, I peered around the corner as Kade rung up my new love interest while she was unaware I was admiring her from afar.

"Great album choice. One of Dylan's finest," Kade commented in a charming but know-it-all tone.

She smiled a wide toothy grin back at him, eager to engage. "*The Freewheelin'*, in my opinion, is the album that rocketed

Dylan's talent to another level. His sophomore album cemented his career. Don't ya think?"

"Absolutely," Kade responded.

At that moment, I knew she wasn't a musical tourist. She was like Kade and me. She then thanked Kade and left the building. My heart plummeted to my feet with the realization that I might never see this girl again. I'd messed up. I should have said hi, at least.

But the following Friday, she came back.

I watched as she thumbed through a stack of records, landing on a Janis Joplin album. She carefully pulled it out of the bin and did that same cute wrinkling of her nose as she read the back of Janis's second and final solo album, *Pearl*. It's such a shame Janis didn't live to see the success of her hard work—an early member of the so-called 27 Club. The list is long and sad. Too many immensely talented musicians gone too early. What I wouldn't give to live in a world that didn't take Jimi Hendrix or Jim Morrison during their prime—the curse of rock 'n' roll—and drugs.

My eyes stayed with her as she smirked and tucked the album under her arm, now making her way over to me. Her confident demeanor was sexy, but intimidating. Her appearance of black-and-cream checkered Vans, tight tapered black jeans, and a loose-fitting white T-shirt didn't scream *threatening*, but yet she was.

This time, I was the only one working. I had no choice, I had to ring her up. My legs went weak as she marched up to the register.

Her ocean-blue eyes stared wide-eyed at me, and all my courage abandoned my body. I couldn't even muster up a "Did ya find everything OK?" All I could manage was a smile and an awkward, "Hi." She must have thought I was such a dick. I'm not a dick, just a coward.

She slid her card into the card reader, and I handed her a receipt. I didn't even say thank you. Who does that? That's the minimum effort of customer service, and I failed. I failed at my job, and I failed at speaking to the woman of my dreams.

The following four Fridays, I took an early lunch and hung out in the backroom. I wasn't ready for her. I needed more time to gain my confidence. Perhaps if I knew more about her, I could make a better impression.

So, I listened around the corner and watched her every move. I made note of her purchases. She had a thing for sophomore albums, and I was intrigued. Over the next three weeks, she bought Grateful Dead's *Anthem of the Sun*, Creedence Clearwater Revival's Bayou Country, and Joni Mitchell's *Clouds*. Why was she only buying second albums? What was her reason? Was this something I could ask her if I ever got the courage to talk to her? I owned and enjoyed every one of those albums, so we already had a lot in common, if I could just open my mouth and speak to her.

I bet she didn't belong in this generation either—another soul destined for another time.

It's now 12:25. She's not coming today. My foot taps nervously again. I rest my hand on my leg, hoping to calm the sensation, but it doesn't help.

Dang it, Max.

Thoughts of never seeing her again whip through my mind, stirring up unwanted memories of my cowardice; a nagging reminder of my inability to just be a *normal guy*. The words that my ex-girlfriend used frequently. *Coward* and "Why can't you just be a normal guy?"

I know Kade doesn't have these problems. He leaves here every night, ready for a new date. Drinks, sex, repeat. That's Kade's motto. He might as well have it printed on a T-shirt. To be honest, we wouldn't be friends if the guy didn't have such a love for music. But here I am, working at Kade's store, Epic Records, and have been for over two years. Stuck in a life barely moving forward. Listening to Kade's heartless "sexcapades." His stories have been more frequent and, quite frankly, more scandalous over the last six months.

As the seconds tick on, I resign to the fact that she's not coming. I glance down at my outfit, feeling stupid. I picked every piece for her today. I even styled my hair. Well, I styled it more than I usually do. It's a considerable upgrade, nevertheless. My usual roll-out-of-bed-and-let-it-hang-wherever look wasn't going to work today. But it doesn't matter now. I missed out on my opportunity. She's never missed a day before. Perhaps she's sick? Or away?

I begin to worry about the fate that might have befallen my love, before I'm struck by the annoying idea that maybe I could find her on social media.

No, I can't do that. It should be a natural connection, not forced.

But what if she never comes in again? What if I've missed my chance?

Maybe I could try to look her up. But she might not be on social media—like me. Of course, that will make me like her even more, but that means I may never find her.

But where would I start? I don't even know her name. I could probably find her with a little bit of work. I don't even know what app to try first. Is Facebook still cool? I honestly don't know. Do I dare ask the musical-tourist couple what the hip app is these days? I know they'd know.

Screw it.

I shout over the counter, directing my voice to the aisle of new records where the couple has taken up residence. "Hey what's the best social media app? What are people using the most?"

The girl's eyes dart around the store before realizing the question is directed at them. She rolls her eyes but answers, "Socialite, duh."

"Thanks," I quickly respond, ready to end the awkward moment. The couple takes that as their cue to exit the store along with the middle-aged man. Neither purchase anything. How this store stays afloat is beyond me.

All right. Socialite, it is.

I reach under the counter and lock my fingers around my phone. A sick, queasy feeling weaves itself through my stomach.

Am I really going to do this? Social media is the downfall of our society. If I do, then I'm going against my own rules—my social morals. Who am I if I don't have rules? Just another poser?

Max, why can't you be a normal guy? My ex's words nip at me— Nag, nag, nag. I'm overthinking things—another one of my annoying downfalls that my ex pointed out before everything completely exploded.

But things could be different with this one.

If I could just find her.

I can do this.

Just download the stupid app, Max.

I let my finger hover over the Socialite app icon, but before I can even hit download, the door whips open.

In walks a man, perhaps in his mid-thirties. He appears out of place, with his tailored button-up collared shirt. His skin flawless, his light sandy-colored hair perfectly side-parted, tall but slender with perfect posture. I part my lips to greet him, but he gives me no chance to speak.

"Where's Kade?" the man questions. His face stern and serious.

"Um, he's not in yet. Is there something I can help you with?"

"Fucking Kade," the man says rubbing his temples. A word

I didn't expect from a man who looked like him. "I'll wait." He pushes past me and assertively walks toward Kade's office.

"Dude, you can't go back there!" I shout, tossing my hands in the air.

The man doesn't respond. An iridescent glow from the office light illuminates the room along with the rustling sound of papers being shuffled on Kade's desk. This jars me, but I'm not one to get involved, so I just let it happen.

Coward.

He reappears after a few moments, taking long strides toward me, only stopping once he reaches the doorway. "On second thought," he says, "have Kade call the second he fucking walks through the door. Here, as he seems to have forgotten who I am." He flicks a rectangular black card at me, but it misses the counter, landing on the floor.

"Um, yeah. . ." I say again but he's already on the sidewalk, turning left.

I bend down to retrieve the item. It's a shiny, black business card with a gold embossed border. A simple name is all that's printed on the first side.

Ben Matthews

Flipping the card over proves just as useless as the front.

30492

Noli pugnare daemonibus tuis, amplectere eos.

What good is this?

"Prick!" I shout to an empty store, shoving the card into my pocket. I check my watch again, it's after 12:30. She's definitely not coming in. I retrieve my phone and press the Socialite icon in the app store, going against my better judgment and breaking my own rules.

See, I'm no fucking coward.

CHAPTER TWO

Kade
Friday, September 10, 12:30 p.m.

Fuck! I did it again. I can't control myself.

My head throbs as I search the room for clues from last night. The biggest one is resting heavily on my bicep.

What's her damn name? Does it even matter?

Quick little flashes of an all-too-familiar sequence whip through my hazy memories. Little pieces of a story that needs to be shown. Then I can move on. My routine. Like clockwork.

Too much whiskey.

Alone in a bar until I wasn't.

Sleeping Beauty, whose real name I don't recall, taking a seat next to me.

Shots of tequila.

Kissing our way out of the bar.

Clothes torn off.

Wild sex.

Passed out.

Current situation.

Drinks. Sex. Repeat.

I smack my lips and the flavor of last night's events makes me want to vomit. I need to get out of here. I assume I'm late for work. I don't see a clock to confirm my suspicion, but the location of the sun shining through the window suggests I'm correct.

Dammit! I don't want any questions. I just want to grab my things and go. But Sleeping Beauty here is ruining my plan.

My muscle twitches from underneath her skull. I give her a soft nudge, careful not to wake her. She takes a deep, sleepy inhale and I slowly slither my left arm free, her hair tickling my skin. But before I can swivel my body off the bed, she reaches over and dreamily grabs my right hand, pulling it tight against her curvy and lengthy body. Her tanned skin sprinkled with freckles.

I'm stuck again.

Fuck.

The unnamed girl I would rate as a solid seven tugs my forearm closer to her naked body. I spoon her against my will.

Stuck, trapped, and alone with my thoughts.

I spot a coiled-up mess of my clothing along with my cell phone on the hardwood floor near the door. If only I could roll out of bed and quietly sneak over to my pile. I would be out of her house and safely in my car before she even notices that I'm gone. Perhaps she won't even remember me at all.

I'm an ass. I know it.

I don't need a therapist to tell me this, although they have, but I haven't needed them for a while. I have something better. Someone who encourages me to be me—to not feel guilty for my behavior—who doesn't judge. Although, I might be in a little trouble with him, but that's tomorrow's problem.

My impatience is intensifying. I need to go now. Plus, they always want to chat in the morning. I don't do that. The less attachment, the better.

Eh, screw it. In one swift movement, I tug my hand away from her tight grip, startling her more than I intended. She flops around like a dying fish, squinting her eyes, trying to recall the events of last night, I assume.

I'm almost free as I near the end of the bed when her sleepy voice calls out, "Hey, were you just going to leave here without waking me up?"

"Um." I stare coldly at her.

I got caught. That's all I care about. I ignore the question and continue over to my pile of clothes on the ground.

Her eyes blink rapidly. "Hey, I'm waiting?" she says, tugging a blue blanket up toward her torso, covering up her breasts and her shame. "So, all those sweet things you said to me last night were just, what? Lies?"

I don't respond as I slip into my jeans and slide my feet into my sneakers. I'm halfway out the door, still wrestling myself into my shirt, when a loud thud, which I can only a assume is a shoe or something smacks against the wall. "Do you even remember my name, asshole?" she shouts.

Joy? No, that's not it, but it doesn't matter, I'm free.

I rush out of her apartment, down the single flight of stairs, and into my car. I press the ignition and the clock flashes: *12:45*. Shit. I'm late. Again.

Drinks. Sex. Repeat.

I slam my hands against the dashboard, remembering her name, "Janice, her name is Janice. Ha, I'm not an asshole," I shout out to an empty vehicle. "Or maybe it was Joy." Oh, fuck it.

CHAPTER THREE

Max
Friday, September 10, 2:45 p.m.

"Rough morning?" I ask as Kade sluggishly makes his way into the store. His expression is flustered, and he ruffles his hand through his wet shaggy, brown hair. Even when he's a mess, he's still better looking than me on my best day.

"More like rough afternoon. Sorry I'm so late man." His voice is groggy. He's hungover. This is becoming a familiar pattern.

"Well, did you at least have a fun night?" I ask.

Kade rubs the back of his neck, letting my question linger for a moment. "I think so," he says with a hasty laugh. "How's the morning been?"

"Eh, a lot of shipment came in, but other than that, it's been a slow start for sales. You haven't missed much, except for this random guy that came in about an hour ago, demanding to see you."

Concern draws across Kade's face. "Who was it?" he asks while stroking the stubble on his chin—another indicator of his rough afternoon.

"Ben Matthews," I respond, recalling the name from the business card. "He went into your office but couldn't be bothered to wait. He was kind of a dick."

"You let him into my office? Max!"

"He let himself in. He seemed to know the place pretty well," I respond defensively.

Kade shakes his head. I've disappointed him.

"Who is he?" I ask.

"It's not your concern, Max," Kade barks.

"Well, you better give him a call." I slip my hand into my front pocket for Ben's card, but Kade's already stomping off to his office. He lets the office door slam shut, and it echoes through the store.

I know not to bother him.

He gets like this sometimes after a long night of drinking—moody and distant. And the mention of Ben has stirred something up.

"Whoa, what's crawled under his skin today?" Emmy says, emerging from the backroom. "It appears I didn't time my entrance all that well and missed something big." Emmy struts up to the register and punches in her employee number to clock in. "But wait! First, what is going on with you?" Emmy asks, motioning her pointer finger down the length of my body and back up again. Her hip sticking out and her full red lips pursing into a sassy pout.

"I don't know what you mean?" I respond, letting my gaze drop to the ground.

"Well, someone's looking fine today."

I give Emmy a cockeyed grin and shrug my shoulders, hoping to dodge where this conversation is heading.

"Come on, tell me. What's the reason behind your new look? Gotta hot date after work?"

Twist that knife, Emmy, keep making me feel worse—a sad reminder that Record Store Girl was a no-show today and my efforts went to waste. But Emmy doesn't know about my dream girl, so I can't really be mad at her. I could tell her, but I don't want to seem pathetic. Emmy's one of the few people who doesn't see me that way and I don't want to give her a reason to. I'd like to think Emmy looks up to me even though we are close in age. I took Emmy under my wing when she started here eight months ago.

"So? Hot date?"

"Nah, I just thought I'd put a little effort in today. Trying something new," I respond, walking away. I stop at a bin of new records to alphabetize them, but Emmy follows.

"Oh, I like it. Keep it up. It's nice seeing you care a little," Emmy replies, giving me a playful nudge on the shoulder.

I produce a half-ass smile.

"So, what's been going on today? Anything exciting?" Emmy asks.

"A whole lot of nothing. A few musical tourists and a butt load of shipment. Don't worry. I finished it all."

Emmy smiles. "Thanks for getting the new inventory sorted, but seriously, Max, you need to ease up on our customers. If they didn't enjoy music, they wouldn't be coming into a record store. Poser or not, they're still buying and hopefully enjoying the music and finding something new. A poser is only a poser until they fall in love with the music. Then they become a fan. Fans make bands—and stores like ours—money," she says, sticking her tongue out at me.

"But—"

"Max!" Emmy says, cutting me off before I can rebuttal.

"Fine." I frown, sticking my bottom lip out far for dramatics.

"And what's going on with Mr. Grumpy Pants? What's got him all moody today? Did you do something to piss him off?"

"Eh, kinda," I say sheepishly. "Has a guy named Ben Matthews ever come in looking for Kade while you were working?"

Emmy freezes for a moment; her eyes wander to the ceiling as if she's searching for the answer somewhere in the abyss. "I think I know who you're talking about. Really tall, good-looking, arrogant asshole?"

"Sounds like him, but everyone is tall compared to you."

"Hey, I can't help that I'm vertically challenged," she says with a stern pout.

Emmy must only be five foot two with shoes on. It's cute how she struggles to reach the top shelves in the store.

"But if we're talking about the same guy," she continues, "I can't stand him. He never acknowledges me when he comes in. He just goes straight to Kade's office like he owns the place. I don't get good vibes from him."

"Strange. I wonder who he is and what he wants with Kade? He was adamant that Kade call him immediately. I'm kind of worried about him. Do you think he's doing OK? He was late again today and totally hungover. I know you see him more than I do these days," I ask.

"Dude's been drinking a lot lately. Drinks, sex, repeat has been on nightly duty. Man should be tested weekly, if ya know what I'm saying. He needs to have some more respect for himself and those poor women."

"Yes, agreed. Let's keep an eye on him. We can't have him spiraling out of control or we will be out of a job. I don't know how he affords to keep this place running and pay his hefty bar tab at the Rose Tavern every night."

"Right. I'm sure he will figure his shit out," Emmy responds.

"Let's hope. But hey, I think I'm going to take off since it's so slow and I didn't get a lunch break since Mr. Grumpy Pants was so late. Let Kade know I took off when he finally emerges from his dungeon."

"Sounds good. Enjoy your night, Max."

"Hey, you too and be safe. Have Kade walk you to your car tonight. Did you see there was another murder?"

"Yes, I saw that. So sad. It seems to be getting closer too—the last three were found outside of town, near the reservoir, but this one was just a mile from here. Police think they're connected but no leads. How the heck can they have no leads?" Emmy says.

"Right! Either way, be careful."

"Thanks, Max, but don't worry about me. I will be safe, plus I don't fit the killer's MO—I'm not a druggie street girl."

"Hey, I don't know what you do with your nights," I taunt.

"Oh my God, Max, you didn't just go there. Get out of here. Go home." Emmy lets out a long-winded laugh. "Now, get," she says, shoving my phone and work bag into my hands.

As I walk out the store door, I smile at our exchange, but I couldn't tell Emmy the real reason I want to leave early—I want to search for my Record Store Girl.

***

The moment I walk into my apartment, hunger hits me. I mosey over to the refrigerator, pulling out a box of leftover pizza. I don't bother warming it up or even grabbing a plate. The sad simple life of a bachelor.

While I munch on the slice of pizza, I take a seat at the kitchen table, pull my phone out, and open the Socialite app.

I'm disgusted with myself as I click the icon to create a new profile. This is not who I am but what other choice do I have?

Plus, what if she's missing or dead? There is someone out there killing women.

You're overreacting, Max. Overthinking things—trying to come up with a reason to make yourself feel less like a stalker. Just like Emmy, Record Store Girl doesn't fit the killer's MO. She'll be fine . . . but better safe than sorry. I'm doing this for her. Maybe for us. Will there be an *us*?

I begin entering the essential information, typing in my email address, sex, location, and age. I leave the photo blank and type *Max Jennings*.

Although, do I really have to be honest? This is just recon. I won't connect with her on here unless I have to, and then I can change my information if necessary.

I repeatedly hit the backspace button, then retype *Matt Jenkins*.

Now the hard part, searching for a girl that I know nothing about. I don't even know her name. If I was smart, I should have taken her credit card the one time I rang her up, swiped it for her, and checked out her name.

Well, hell, I shouldn't have been a coward and just talked to her like a normal person! Then I wouldn't be sitting in my lonely apartment on a Friday night searching for a girl that was right in front of me on multiple occasions.

I start with a wide search of women in Clear River, Oregon, then narrowing it down to women in their twenties and thirties. I begin scrolling through an endless sea of locals, some even looking familiar. My heart yanks for a minute seeing that poor girl from the newspaper earlier—as Emmy mentioned a druggie street girl, but she didn't deserve what happened to her?

I shouldn't be doing this.

But my fingers don't obey and I keep scrolling. I can see why this is so addictive.

"Emmy!" I shout. My coworker's face appears in the middle of my screen search.

Should I click on it?

I feel like it's an invasion of privacy.

But that's what it's there for, Max, to be clicked on.

Before I allow myself to second- and third-guess my decision, I press on the image, pulling up a full profile.

Emmy Malone
Age: 26
Location: Clear River, Oregon

I click on the tiny profile picture to enlarge the image. A wide-eyed Emmy fills my entire screen, drawing my attention to her thick lips painted in her signature deep-red lipstick. Her shoulder-length copper-brown hair with red highlights shimmers in the sun in its natural tight and twisty curls. Her round face is pink and sun-kissed. A stage and crowd are blurred behind her—presumably at a concert. This photo describes Emmy perfectly. It even showcases her fun, bubbly personality. She chose well.

I stare at her photo a little too long. I begin to feel arousal in my pants.

No, that's Emmy.

My friend.

Calm yourself down, Max.

Fucking social media getting in my head.

I get up from the table and grab a joint from the drawer next to the sink. I light it and take a few puffs. I let the high take over and allow my unwelcomed thoughts to leave my body before returning to my phone.

Max, if you weren't such a coward, you wouldn't be sitting here, creepily searching Socialite for a girl who couldn't give two shits about you.

My ex's words sting me.

Flashes of her tossing my belongings on the front lawn.

"Coward. Max, you're a fucking coward."

My fingers started tapping out letters on the keyboard faster than I can process my wild thoughts.

Chrissy Parker.

I click on it. My ex's profile loads. I'm nauseous but I don't stop.

Chrissy Parker
Age: 28
Location: Tillicum Valley, California

There she is.

Living the perfect life she's always wanted, but without me. Seeing this is like a big "Fat fuck you, Max Jennings."

I click on her photo, enlarging it.

Does she really look that good now? She was always pretty, but this photo looks a little too perfect. No flaws, except too much makeup. She's let her hair grow long—something I always suggested. It's blonder than before too.

I exit out of her photo and begin the endless scroll on her feed. It's been two years. I have a lot to catch up on.

I know I'm just torturing myself, but I keep dragging my finger and scrolling down.

An announcement catches my eye.

Don't fucking stop, Max. Just keep scrolling.

The red flags are there, but I can't control my finger. I click the post, enlarging it.

A wedding announcement.

Chrissy's getting married.

I was never good enough for her to marry, but this guy is? I wonder if she calls him names. I wonder what damage she's done to him. I wonder if he's a coward and an overthinker. Probably not. He's probably brave, and I bet he checks all the boxes for her that I couldn't. I can't help but glower at the photo of them. I pinch the screen to zoom in closer, their happiness staring me straight in the face.

I run over to the cupboard, pulling the door wide open, and scan the lower shelf, where I keep the booze. I need something to take the edge off, weed won't fix this problem tonight. My eyes land on an old, dusty bottle of cheap rum. I don't waste any time pulling it from the shelf and I twist the cap off and take a long pull and then another.

My lips pucker as the liquor stings my tastebuds. I can't even afford the good booze. I bet Chrissy's new beau drinks the expensive liquor. I'm such a failure.

What was I thinking going down this rabbit hole? Why did I look her up? I can't unsee this news. I can't unsee the happy couple sharing their joy with the world.

Fuck you, Chrissy. Fuck you! If you only knew . . .

CHAPTER FOUR

Max
Saturday, September 11, 9:22 a.m.

Emmy's eyes widen, a puzzled look spreads across her face. I accidentally let her gaze catch mine, and she stops counting the cash midway through the ones—half a stack of singles hang limp in each hand. "Whoa, dude, you look like hell. What happened to you?" Emmy shouts.

"Hey, could you tone your voice down a notch? I had a rough night."

"You think. What happened, Max? I've never known you to be late for work."

"It's only twenty minutes." I frown.

"Twenty-*two* minutes." Emmy says, pointing at the time on the register. "So, what's the story? Are you going to tell me why you look like death warmed up?"

"Eh, I did something stupid last night. Remember, I vaguely told you about the last girl I dated? How she was horrible."

"Yes." Emmy nods, encouraging me to continue.

"Well, I just found out that she's getting married."

"And let me guess, it sent you running for the bottle?"

"Yep, pathetic, I know."

Emmy sets the cash back in the drawer and reaches out toward me. She begins to softly rub my arm. "It's not pathetic, Max."

Her touch stirs up the unwanted memory of seeing her photo last night and the feelings that came along with it. I take a shy step back, no longer within her reach.

"From what you told me, it sounds like she wasn't very kind. But it's normal to have those kinds of thoughts when someone moves on. So, how'd you find out? Someone call you and tell you?"

I tuck my chin into my neck. "No, I found her on social media."

"Dang, dude, what were you thinking? That's never a good idea. Especially for you, the guy who doesn't condone the use of these social sites—it's the downfall of our society. Blah, blah, blah," Emmy mocks me. "Seriously, Max, what were you thinking? Why, after all this time?" Emmy's big, brown eyes lock on mine.

I turn away to avoid her accusatory stare.

Emmy is right.

I shouldn't have done that.

I somehow went two years without knowing what was going on in Chrissy's life. I told myself I wouldn't look back. I couldn't. I had to keep going forward.

So why did I have to torture myself last night?

I couldn't tell Emmy the real reason that I was on the site. "I don't know why—it was a huge lap in judgment. I'll delete the app. It's none of my business what she and her fiancé are up to."

"I think that's a good idea, Max. No good can come from online stalking your ex-girlfriend."

I nod in agreement, but I'm not going to delete the app. I still need to find Record Store Girl, but I won't look at Chrissy's profile again. I can't do that to myself.

"Oh, hey. Sorry to change subjects while you're all sulky and stuff, but you know that guy you were asking about yesterday?" Emmy asks, tugging at her twisty tendrils.

"Ben?"

"Yes, that guy. He came back in last night."

"Is that right?" I ask, my interest piqued.

"Yes, and he was hollering at Kade in the office. It got pretty heated. Customers were giving me concerned glares, Max, and I had to give them some lame excuse," Emmy says, biting at her bottom lip with her two front teeth, resembling a little rabbit; it's a habit that she has when she's uncomfortable.

"Really? Could you tell what they were arguing about?"

"I couldn't hear much, but it didn't feel right. I think Kade is in trouble. I mean like if this Ben character was a friend, why would he come to his place of business to yell at him, why not meet him at the Rose Tavern after his shift or something like that? Whatever he wanted with Kade, it felt urgent."

"Wow. That is super strange. Did Kade say anything to you? How was he after Ben left?"

"Nope. He didn't bother to come out of his office until we closed. He left me on the sales floor alone on a Friday night and we were pretty busy too," Emmy says, folding her arms across her chest, and pursing her lips into her classic Emmy pout.

"I'm sorry, Em, you should have called me. I would have come back in."

"I didn't want to go above Kade's head like that," Emmys says, shifting her pout to a frown.

"I get it. Kade is still the boss, but he's not acting like it right now. I guess all we can do is keep an eye on him and see if things improve. I know he doesn't like it when we butt into his life, but we might have to if he's really in some kind of trouble."

My phone vibrates in my pocket. I pull my phone out and a text from Kade flashes across my screen. "I think we have our answer, Emmy." I respond, showing Emmy my screen.

Kade: *Hey Max. Not coming in today.*
Jake will cover my shift. Not feeling well.

CHAPTER FIVE

Kade
Saturday, September 11, 9:35 p.m.

I park my car outside the club, but I can't bring myself to exit the vehicle. Thoughts of shifting back into drive and getting the hell out of here cross my mind, but I know I can't.

It's not an option.

Ben's words slither through my thoughts. *"I haven't given up on you, Kade, but I'm very disappointed."*

I've slipped back into some old habits, and Ben's not pleased. He's the one who taught me to stop caring and to act on my instincts.

Ben found me a year ago, passed out in my drink at the River's Edge Saloon. He offered to help me. He saw how I was hurting, but I didn't realize how much this man would become part of my life—part of my every decision.

And now I owe him. He needs a favor. He needs a new recruit.

I told him I don't know anyone. That answer angered him. Poor Emmy could probably hear the random outbursts from across the store last night; I closed the door, but Ben's voice can carry through a building.

"What about one of your employees?" he'd asked, and I responded with a hard no.

But Ben pushed. "The loner hipster one will do."

I have three loner hipsters working for me: Jake, Jed, and Max. But I knew he was talking about Max. He saw him that morning. He picked up on Max's vulnerability. It's what Ben does best. He wants to fix people.

When I didn't respond, he said, "The dark-haired one that looks like he has a chip on his shoulder. He will be a perfect candidate for the club."

Poor, damaged Max. I can't do that to him.

Sure, he'd be a perfect candidate. A single twenty-eight-year-old who works at a record store. An awkward dude whose ex dismantled his self-confidence. A guy who has potential but doesn't see it in himself. He's slender, but in that hip sort of way. A lot of chicks dig guys like that. He's casual, always wearing jeans, Birkenstocks, and a band tee with a flannel thrown over top. He's Max. The shut-off, awkward guy. Yes, the perfect candidate, but I can't do that to him.

Plus, I'd rather not have Max know what I've been up to. I don't want him to judge me. He looks up to me like I'm some kind of god to him. It's nice having someone admire me. I don't want to ruin the illusion he's created of me.

No, I can't do that to Max, nor my ego.

So now, I'm sitting here in my car without a recruit.

Ben will not be pleased.

CHAPTER SIX

Max
Saturday, September 11, 9:40 p.m.

Another Saturday evening spent alone.

Normally, I would read the next book on my TBR or bum around my apartment, listening to records, but tonight is slightly different.

I have my little projects. I need to find Record Store Girl, and I need to figure out who Ben Matthews is and what he wants with Kade. I know Kade wasn't sick today, so what has him so out of whack lately?

Selfishly, I prioritize finding Record Store Girl first and set Ben and Kade on the back burner.

I had a slight detour last night with Chrissy, but I can't—I won't—let myself go down that rabbit hole again. It's been two years; I must move on. I can't dwell on the past, even if it completely ruined me.

Things will be different once I find Record Store Girl. I must stay focused on her. I will man up. I will approach her. Meet her. I won't be a coward.

With my phone in hand, I take a seat on the couch. I open Socialite and once again I narrow down my search.

Location: Clear River, Oregon
Age Range: 20–30
Sex: Female

A few more familiar faces appear in my search, but I still don't see my cute blonde with the messy curls. The more profiles I pass by, the sicker I feel. I'm resorting to the very thing I can't stand. So many fake profile pictures. The perfect lighting. The perfect filter. No one looks this perfect in real life.

Fake. It's all fake.

We're teaching society to act this way, to create a profile just to hide behind. We are creating a world that I don't recognize.

When I think about how much the world has changed in such a short time, I feel ill. If you took someone from 1850 and dropped them into 1930, they could probably manage. It would be overwhelming, sure, but they would figure it out. If you dropped someone from 1940 straight into 2020, they would run for the hills and never look back. Things are strange and complicated. It's more than overwhelming. Teens are killing themselves over keeping up with online expectations. It's sad and unnecessary. Bullies twenty years ago were so different from the bullies today; it's one thing to be blatantly mean to a kid's face and another to hide behind a computer. It's much easier to throw insults when you can't see their face.

Even with all these angered thoughts racing through my mind, I keep flicking my finger and scrolling through profile after profile, but none of them are hers.

I let out an exasperated sigh. I will never find her. Maybe it's better this way. I'd "Max it up."

It's useless, so I switch my search to the man that has Kade all riled up and missing work lately. I clear the search bar and type in *Ben Matthews.*

A few suggested profiles load, but I'm instantly disappointed when his face doesn't immediately appear. I thought this would be easier since I at least have a name. It's more info than I have for Record Store Girl and I'm still failing. I hate this app.

I start my search over and type in the following information.

Location: Clear River, Oregon
Age Range: 30–40
Sex: Male

After spending a good ten minutes of scrolling through faces of men in my area and feeling like a creeper, I'm shocked when his photo appears. It's him. He's unmistakable in his pompous white collared button-up shirt, his hair parted perfectly with that Ryan Gosling classic side-part. His name is simply his initials: *BM.*

You clever little shit. You don't want to be found, do you?

His profile is about as generic as his business card, lacking nearly all information. There is nothing in his feed, no current posts, not even a repost of a meme. Nothing.

I close the worthless app and open Google. I type in *Ben Matthews.* But nothing worthy of a click populates.

I pull his card out and flip it around my fingers a few times.

Who are you, Ben Matthews? What is your deal?

The phrase on his business card gives me pause. I didn't pay attention to it at the store, because it didn't seem important, but now it's the only thing I haven't tried. I google the meaning.

Noli pugnare daemonibus tuis, amplectere eos.

Don't fight your demons, embrace them.

CHAPTER SEVEN

Kade
Saturday, September 11th, 9:45 p.m.

I close my eyes and inhale deeply, letting my fingers curl around the steering wheel. I squeeze tight, holding my breath for ten seconds before exhaling, letting all the air vacate my body. I repeat this five more times before dropping my hands in my lap.

It's game time.

I push the door open, and a brisk wind whips through the car, reinvigorating my mood. I scan the parking lot for other members. Did Ben ask them to bring a recruit too? Or was that just me?

Letting that thought linger, I take my time walking to the back side of the building—an old strip mall where Ben rents a room in the basement.

I spot Jordan, Ben's first club member, leaning casually against the wall near the doorway, a cigarette resting in his right hand. Jordan catches me staring at him as I get closer.

"I know, I know. Bad habits die hard," Jordan says, extinguishing the butt of the cigarette against the brick wall behind him. He slides the remaining portion into a nearly empty pack, then shoves it into his back pocket.

"Hey, I'm not here to judge."

Jordan's brow creased slightly. "That's true. You have no room to judge, Kade."

An uncomfortable silence fills the space around us. I'm not sure how to respond. I know to watch what I say around Jordan. I like Jordan, I do, but sometimes, things have a way of getting back to Ben.

"So, are you just going to pretend like you haven't missed the last two meetings? Ben's pretty pissed about that," Jordan says, fidgeting with the collar on his shirt, which looks like something straight out of Ben's closet. If Jordan's brown hair didn't have a natural wave, I'd say he's even tried to mimic Ben's classic hairstyle. He's turning into a mini Ben.

I let my hesitation to answer linger a tick too long. Jordan clears his throat, bringing me back to our conversation. "Oh, I know," I say. "He came by to see me last night. He let me have it, along with an odd request."

I pause to see if Jordan will bite at my subtle hint.

He runs his tongue over his top lip and lets his eyes turn up before responding. "He asked me too."

"So, I guess he will be pissed at both of us. Meeting's about to start—we should probably get inside."

Jordan gives a snide grin. He opens the door, and we walk down the concrete steps in silence. I let Jordan get the club door and we file inside. I quickly scan the room for new faces, but it's our regular crew.

Jordan makes his way over to the usual spread of hot wings, nachos, and mozzarella sticks. With a hot wing in hand, he effortlessly inserts himself into Bobby and Decklan's conversation over at the pool table.

Ben must still be in his office, so with the extra time, I avoid the food table entirely and head straight for the bar. I pour myself a glass of top-shelf bourbon—neat. The club's bar is only stocked with top-shelf alcohol. Ben always says, "If you want to be successful, you act successful." Another one he likes to use is, "If you ain't lying, you ain't trying." And of course, "Fake it until you become it."

The club was started to help us act on our truest instincts and never feel bad, to lie until we become everything we are supposed to be. No regrets, no compromises, and no guilt. It felt good for a while and was fun, but things are changing. I can feel it. Ben is changing.

I relocate to the other side of the bar, taking a seat at one of the high-top leather stools. I swivel my chair around, noticing that Bobby, Decklan, and Jordan have moved to the lounge area. It's a simple corner of the room, with leather recliners and a large screen TV that is always on a sports channel. I'd much rather have music on, but I usually lose that debate.

The room is long and spacious, with only two rectangular frosted windows high on the wall that meet the street level. From the outside, you'd hardly even notice them.

I take a slow sip of my drink, letting the taste linger on my tongue, feeling briefly at peace. That is until I hear, "'Sup bitches?" Owen's deep voice reverberates off the walls. Must he always be so loud?

Owen is a simple-minded attention-seeker, and the other guys love him. I don't get it. Owen was the last member to join the club, shortly after me. Bobby and Decklan idolize him. I suppose Jordan would do the same if he wasn't so preoccupied with Ben's every move. Owen has that military-style haircut that's naturally platinum blond, a strong boxy jawline, and an unhealthy addiction to the gym. I'm muscular, but Owen is jacked. Steroids would explain his intensity, but I shouldn't judge; we all have our vices and mine is resting in my right hand.

The three guys get up to meet Owen, greeting him with fist bumps and high fives. Owen has a way of elevating the energy when he enters a room. In my opinion, it's a good thing he's usually the last to show up. The group engages in macho chatter, but I manage to block it out.

I glance at the large clock on the wall, and it's a few minutes past ten; the meeting should be starting soon. I join the four members standing around waiting for Ben to make his entrance. As I approach the guys, Owen cups my shoulders, giving them a tight squeeze, pulling me further into the group. "Missed ya, bro."

I simply nod.

Everyone knows not to ask where I've been. They know it's not the time because Ben is listening. He's always listening. Owen, Bobby, and Decklan would never throw another member under the bus like that.

The hinges on Ben's door creaks.

Everyone falls silent, and a veil of obedience coats the room. Ben emerges from his office, he struts down the narrow hallway and into the open space. Ben walks in with a confidence most can never procure in a lifetime, and yet, Ben, a man in his thirties, has mastered it already. Before our paths crossed, I'd never met someone so self-assured. It's an attractive quality. One that I admire.

"Good-evening, men," Ben says, his voice cool and calm.

The group takes a few steps forward, forming a half circle around him.

I catch Jordan rolling his shirtsleeves up to his elbow, mirroring Ben's look tonight. Both wearing straight-leg jeans and dress shoes. I fear Jordan is taking his admiration a little too far now.

Ben strokes his smooth face, letting his finger rest in his dimpled chin as he intensely gazes at the five of us. His golden eyes lock on mine for a moment. He takes a sharp breath, then clears this throat.

"I'm very disappointed in all of you. Not one new recruit stands before me." Ben shakes his head, keeping his eyes straightforward.

He must have visited all of us yesterday. Five recruits seem excessive, especially all at once. He was the one who organically found each current member, so why now does he want us to recruit more? Is he done with us? What's the rush? This feels forced.

"What's up with the changes? Aren't you happy with the OG five?" Bobby asks. His round face slowly shifts from confidence to apprehension. Ben doesn't like pushback. I know this too well. Bobby slowly tucks himself behind Owen, turning his head to the ground, giving his coarse hair an awkward tug.

Ben raises his left eyebrow, pondering Bobby's question.

"Don't you all agree you are more satisfied with your choices and your life is better because of this group—because of me?"

"Yes," we all respond in unison.

"And haven't I been generous of my time, money, and advice?" Ben asks.

"Yes."

"So, when I come to you, asking a simple favor, I would expect you to do as asked without questioning. I feel like this is a slap in the face. That you don't appreciate all I do for you. I give two nights a week of my time and all this free of charge," Ben says, gliding his hand out before him, showcasing the nice club he's created.

"I-I'm sorry Ben," Bobby stutters. "I didn't mean to disappoint you. I just like how things are and I didn't understand. I apologize."

"It's OK, Bobby, I know change is hard on you. But change can be good if used correctly. You've all changed since you've been with me. I found each of you at the lowest point in your life. Owen, remember how you nearly beat your best friend to a bloody pulp for sleeping with your girlfriend while you were on active duty, serving your country? I taught you how to channel and redirect your rage, how to manage and manipulate your trust issues?"

"Yes, sir," Owen responds with perfect posture, his right arm nearly jumping to a salute, but he quickly catches himself and subtly lowers it back to his side.

"Jordan, you'd just got divorced and your cheating vindictive wife took everything from you, including the business that you built from the ground up. Your wife didn't appreciate who you are. She didn't understand you. But I get you. I see you."

Jordan nods, giving Ben a sly grin.

"Bobby, you were in such a depression that you tried to kill yourself. And all over some stupid woman. You didn't think the world needed you. But I showed you a new path, and we got you out of your slump. Isn't that correct?"

"Yes, Ben. That is correct," Bobby responds, a sadness layered in his voice.

"Oh, and Decklan, you wouldn't have had the guts to get away from your controlling mother if it weren't for me. You now live on your own and I'm helping you, so you never have to be controlled again."

Decklan nods.

"And, my dear Kade, you were a lousy drunk with a sex addiction and your business was failing. But I gave you a plan to get back on track, we saved your business, and I've helped you see your vices differently."

"Yes, Ben, and I'm grateful for that," I say.

"Well, if you're so grateful, then why did you miss the last two meetings? Care to share?" Ben asks, locking his gaze onto mine.

Wow, he's calling me out in front of the group. I thought we put this conversation to rest yesterday; this type of stuff should be reserved for our private sessions.

"I'm sorry, I thought I was doing fine, and I could skip a couple." My response is generic, but it's pretty much the truth. I know I was wrong; I can't leave, nothing is free, and I owe him.

"Kade seems to have lost faith in the system. But the system only works, when you stick with it."

"Yes, Ben, sorry. I made a mistake," I reply, maintaining eye contact.

"You are all capable of greatness and you've come so far but you're still not where you should be. I know I've told you this before, but let me remind you where I came from, let my story re-inspire you." Ben reaches up and casually releases the top two buttons on his shirt. "I came from a broken home, just like most of you. My abusive mother cared more about meth than her own son, and she often left me alone at a young age, leaving me, in turn, to take care of my even younger brother. I felt unwanted and discarded. I knew from the time I was five years old that this wasn't a life I wanted to live. When I started school, I got a glimpse of a life outside my home. I made friends with a well-to-do kid and would weasel my way into dinner and sleepover invites for my brother and me. It started as a need for a hot meal and warm bed, but turned into something so much more. I wanted my friend's life so badly that I pretended his life was mine. I faked it. I mirrored his life until it became my life."

Ben lets a pregnant pause loom over his admission before continuing. "Fast forward to college, where I created an app and later sold it for millions. My life is golden and blessed. Don't you want that for yourselves? I had demons, but I used them to change the trajectory of my life. I used them drive me to become the person I was always meant to be. I couldn't allow my life to be an outcome of my earlier circumstances. It just wasn't on the cards for me. I've turned my struggle into something positive. And now I'm here helping you work with your demons, not against them.

"Don't fight your demons, embrace them!" He shouts.

We mirror his chant, "Don't fight your demons, embrace them." Pumping our fists into the air.

"Don't fight your demons, embrace them!"

"Don't fight your demons, embrace them!"

"If you embrace the demons that make you who you are, then you can fight to create the *lie* you want your life to be," Ben shouts. "So, shouldn't you all want to share this knowledge to help another lost soul embrace their demons, to fight for a life their meant to live? To use their demons to become the person they were meant to be."

The five of us bow our heads in agreement.

"Now, the hard part. I don't want to be like this, I want you to have free range over your instincts, but this is nonnegotiable. I suppose it's my fault, I guess I didn't make myself clear yesterday when I visited each of you," Ben says, rubbing his temples. "A new recruit. That was it. Simple."

"Ben, I tried, but no one wanted to hear my pitch. I need more time," Jordan pipes in.

"Jordan, Jordan, Jordan, what have I told you about excuses?" Ben demands.

"That you don't tolerate them, and it makes us weak as men when we use them," Jordan dutifully responds. I secretly wonder what Jordan's private sessions are like with Ben that causes him to feel the need to emulate him so much. Ben is Jordan's god.

"Exactly. You appear weak when you use an excuse. It means you aren't man enough to face the task at hand. No one is privy to excuses in this club. We teach confidence here and excuses are taking you backward."

"But isn't lying like an excuse?" Decklan poses.

Ben shakes his head, rubbing his fingers through his perfectly coiffed hair. "Have you not been listening to a word I've said tonight, Decklan? Lying is the vehicle to get you what you want; faking the very thing you seek. Whereas giving an excuse is like a stutter. Nothing about an excuse is confident."

"Oh, sorry. That makes sense. I get it," Decklan responds.

"All right, I'm done listening to your nonsense tonight. You all failed me. I will give you one more week. And trust me when I say that I really hate to do this, but if you don't bring a new recruit next week, you are out, as well as. . ." Ben lets his words trail off, his face stern and eyes cold. "Let's just say that you all know what is at stake if you don't comply. Now get the hell out of my club."

CHAPTER EIGHT

Kade
Sunday, September 12, 10:00 a.m.

Fuck, I did it again.

I should have gone home last night, but instead I went to the Rose Tavern. This time, a redhead is curled up next to me. She's a six and a half on my scale. I know this is my demon, and I'm allowing it to play, but I have other things on my plate now. I need to deal with Ben's demands.

This should be an easy escape, at least. I spot my clothing next to the bed and slowly get up, moving delicately so I don't wake her. I quietly slip into my jeans and T-shirt. I pick up my shoes and carry them with me out the door.

In my car, I bang my hands against the dash.

"Fuck."

I'm so fucking screwed.

Bring a new recruit.

I can't do that.

Ben has his eye on Max, and I can't drag him into this.

Especially not now with the club shifting like this. After last night, things still aren't sitting right.

Do I come back empty-handed? Let the dice roll and see what happens? But I know what would happen. I know what is at stake if I don't do as Ben asks. He knows things about me.

Things that can't get out. Things I've done. People I've hurt. Money, I owe.

I have six days to figure something out, but I don't have many options.

Drink. Sex. Repeat is the only thing that makes sense right now.

CHAPTER NINE

Max
Saturday, September 18, 11:57 a.m.

I'm busy ringing up a customer when the back door slams shut. I quickly turn around, shocked to catch a glimpse of Kade sliding into his office—the first glimpse I've had of him in a week. His hair is a disheveled mess, his clothes wrinkled, his skin pale.

He's avoiding me.

Is he afraid I will call him out on his behavior? Because I should, but Kade doesn't respond well to that. Plus, he's the boss, and I need this job. I did it once about a year ago, though. I was concerned, and he shut me out, making things worse. But then he got better. He started AA or something, but I knew he didn't truly give up drinking, but just got better at masking his problems. It didn't interfere with the business, so I let it be. That is until recently.

I don't want Kade to fire me for sticking my nose where it doesn't belong. Drunks can make rash decisions, and I don't want to be his punching bag. Although, Kade has never been a cruel drunk, just a shut-off one. But one thing I do know is that everything has been a mess since Ben Matthews came into our store just over a week ago. Stirring up Kade, making him miss work, and presumably causing him to drink like a fish.

What if Kade owes this mysterious man money? Is he a loan shark, like the kind you see in the movies? If Kade needs help with money, that's one thing I can't help him with—I'm broke as fuck.

But whatever it is, it has Kade all out of sorts. This is the most work I've ever known him to miss, and it's made for a rough week here, leaving me to manage the store. I've had to do all the ordering, payroll, reporting and everything else. Things Kade usually takes care of. Luckily, he showed me the ropes early on in my employment in case of vacations or emergencies so the wheels are still moving, but we can't keep patching up the leaks forever. Emmy's shifts moved around, and the part-time guys, Jake and Jed, had to pick up more hours. I spread them through the evening, so Emmy had overlap for closing—I can't let her close alone, with a killer on the loose. I've already called Jake in as a backup tonight.

And to top off this already stressful week, I'd hoped that perhaps Record Store Girl had been too busy on last Friday to come in, and so maybe she would pop by sometime during the week, but nothing. And then another no-show this Friday. Plus, Socialite has proved useless too.

What a shitty fucking week.

I catch sight of Emmy across the street. She jumps into the coffee shop. Perfect timing. I need someone to uplift my spirits and Emmy always seems to be able to do that.

A few minutes later, she emerges from the café, two coffees in hand as she crosses the street. A smile forms across her face when she catches me staring at her from the register. "Max, long time no see. What a week, huh?" Emmy says, shoving a cup of hot coffee into my hand. "Thought you could use this."

"Thanks, Em. I really did need a pick-me-up today."

"Let me drop my stuff first, then we need to talk."

Emmy takes her time in the backroom and reappears a few minutes later. She clocks in and leans across the counter toward me. Her voice hushed, she says, "He's so much worse, Max. Kade came in last night, right before closing, and locked himself in his office. Jed tried knocking and asked if he was OK. Kade was clearly drunk and told him to fuck off. This is not normal behavior, even for Kade." Concern coats her voice.

I run my fingers through my hair, thinking, pondering what to say. I mean, what can we do? I know this song and dance with him, but this is the most extreme I've seen him, and Emmy has to work with him tonight, that is, if he's actually going to stay for his whole shift. I suppose he's the boss and can do what he wants, but he still has commitments he's made to his staff.

"I'm genuinely worried about him, Max," Emmy says, tugging on her curls. "I know Jed tried to ask him last night, but do you think we should try again? He's here, isn't he? Should we just go and ask him if he's OK, or if he needs someone to talk to? We can ask him together."

"Yes, he just got in, but I don't think that's a good idea. Kade can get distant and that could make it worse. If it's something he wants to share, he would have already. Let's just keep an eye on him and make sure he's OK. We will know the right time to intervene," I reply, but I fear right now is the right time, the only problem is, I don't know how to provide the help he needs. He's Kade, he doesn't operate like a normal person.

"OK, Max, you've known him longer, so I trust your judgment."

I smile a kind smile at Emmy to ease her worries. "No worries, just make sure you keep me posted. You see him more than I do. If you need anything, always know you can call me."

"Thanks, Max. I just hope he snaps out of this. He's a good boss, even if he's a little off the wall sometimes, and his behavior can be a bit out there, but that's why I enjoy it here so much. You guys are all fun, and I actually look forward to coming to work."

"I know what you mean, Em."

CHAPTER TEN

Max
Saturday, September 18, 7:00 p.m.

After my conversation with Emmy, I decided to stick around downtown after work. If Kade blew up at Jed last night, who's to say Emmy won't press his buttons tonight and he'd do the same to her. I know I told Emmy not to push him but sometimes she doesn't realize what she's saying until it's left her mouth. So, if she needs me, I will be close. Plus, it's not like I have anything better to do.

The Rose Tavern, just down the street from our store, is where Kade finds himself most nights. I may as well give it a try and possibly gain a little insight into my boss's world outside of work while I wait out the night.

When I walk in, I immediately see why he likes it here. It's an upscale tavern with a relaxed vibe. The bar is off to the right and has a long hand-carved wooden bar top with bluish-purple epoxy running down the middle and matching handcrafted barstools. It's not as dark as most taverns, but still dim enough to create a casual ambiance. The bar is well stocked with a selection of expensive liquors along the top racks, and the beer taps are labeled with craft beer from all the well-known breweries around the state. Of course, Kade loves this place; it's great. At least he's not spending his time at a dingy, dark dive bar.

I snag a seat toward the window, overlooking the river that runs through town.

"What can I get for you, man?" the bartender asks before I can even remove my coat.

I glance at the taps before responding. "Boneyard's Hop Venom, if it's on."

"Perfect choice, my friend. That one is my favorite." He walks over to the tap and pours my beer. He grabs a coaster and sets my drink down in front of me. "Name's Mark. If you need anything, just holler."

"Thanks, will do," I say.

As I spin back to face the window, I whack my knee against what appears to be a walking cane that's leaning up against the bar.

"Ouch! Actually, Mark, wait," I call out. "Is someone sitting here? They've left a cane."

"Oh, he's gone. It belongs to one of our regulars. I'll take it." Mark tugs it from my hand as I pass it over the bar. "He tends to leave this behind from time to time when he's had a few too many," he responds.

Mark seems pretty cool, and I want to ask him if he knows Kade, but I don't want my boss to know that I'm snooping in his life. Emmy and I might be overreacting, and Kade might be OK, but what if he's not? What if it's something serious that he can't handle alone. I take a long chug of my beer, and heavy foam rushes against my upper lip.

I gaze around the bar, realizing that I'm the only person alone in here. I pull out my phone and let my finger hover over the Socialite app, a little freaked by how natural it feels. I want to search for Record Store Girl again, but I stop myself. I'm just not this type of person. I can't let myself become that type of person.

***

It's nearing closing time at Epic Records. Emmy didn't call, everything must have gone smoothly. I flag down Mark to pay my tab. I only planned on hanging out for one drink, but that turned into two, and now I'm a little buzzed. I shouldn't have opted for a double IPA. It's stronger than the stuff I'm used to drinking. I wince as I lay down a twenty to cover my drinks and tip. Twenty bucks doesn't go far these days.

Maybe I should bum around downtown for a bit to knock my slight inebriation. I can't help but wonder if this is what Kade ends up doing every night.

A silly drunken idea keeps nipping at me. Why don't I find out what he gets up to? I know where he is right now. I'll follow him.

Have a little adventure, Max. Do something fun.

I've already taken a small step into his world, why not another?

I run down the side street and cut behind the store. I wait for Kade out back, tucked into the back entrance to the men's clothing store next door. I check my watch for the time. It's after nine. I bet he's about to leave, if I haven't missed him already. If I have, my silly adventure is over.

I pull myself further into the doorway as I catch a glimpse of Jake and Emmy walking out. They don't lock the door, so Kade must still be inside. The pair takes off to the right, toward the parking garage.

Do I stay and wait?

I decide to give it a few minutes, and to my dumb luck, Kade emerges. He pulls his key out and turns the lock.

This is the pinch point. Do I really follow him? I'm already being weird and sneaky, and it might be fun to see what he does on a nightly basis, and just maybe I can get some answers to his current state.

Screw it. I'm here already, and if he ends up at Rose Tavern, I will turn and go home. But to my surprise, Kade heads right, away from the tavern.

I feel super creepy right now, but I'm also exhilarated. I never do anything exciting. I haven't had this kind of excitement in a long time. It's sad how I find stalking my boss alone on a Saturday night fun.

I toss my jacket hood over my head, staying far enough behind while also avoiding lingering under streetlamps in attempt to go undetected. If he happens to spot me, I will act normal. I'm just out and about, sick of being at home alone. It sounds like a believable excuse for a guy like me.

He turns into the parking garage, taking long strides with each step. The brisk air punches me in the face as I pick up my pace to catch up, careful not to lose him.

He turns into the stairwell, allowing me time to dash to my car on the first level. It would be easier if he'd stayed downtown, so I didn't have to drive, but against my better judgment, I slide into my car.

Keeping my engine off, I wait until Kade circles down to the first level. I watch as he swipes his parking pass at the gate before starting my engine. I flip my headlights off and creep up to the exit. I quickly swipe my card while eyeing up on Kade's direction.

He turned right, so I turn right.

I keep a close distance for a couple of blocks without Kade making a single turn. This is easy.

I'm glad it's dark, less chance of him spotting me. I decide now is a good time to flip my headlights on. I can't have a cop pulling me over.

Kade pumps his breaks, slowing down. His blinker flashes left as he pulls his car toward an area known for eclectic shops and funky fashion. Where the heck is he going?

Then he takes a sharp right, pulling into a strip-mall parking lot with only a few cars scattered throughout. I quickly maneuver past the lot, parking on the side street where I can keep an eye on him.

This can't be right. Is he picking someone up here?

No, it looks like he's getting out.

Kade trudges through the parking lot, kicking at rocks as he slowly makes his way across.

I exit my car and stay behind him.

He turns to go behind the building. He tugs on a door and disappears inside. Perhaps he's heading to a cool underground club or a hip speakeasy. That would make sense, but seeing him creep into the back side of a closed shopping area makes no sense at all. This is strange, even for Kade.

But now, I'm even more intrigued. As I hang back, I notice a few other guys approaching from the far side, opening and then vanishing through the same door.

I pick up my pace when a figure causes me to pause.

"Ben," I yelp, my voice startling me. My hands jolt up, covering my mouth. He doesn't turn around, so he can't have heard me, but I know, even from this distance that it's Ben Matthews, the man of mystery. This must be the place where Kade knows him from, but what is this place?

Ben confidently struts toward the door, tugging it open and disappearing inside, just as the others did before him.

Once no one else is in sight, I jog over to the door and let my hand rest on the handle, ready to pull it open. But I hesitate.

What am I doing? This is insane.

If it's a bar, Kade and his friends will wonder why they've never seen me here before. If it's an exclusive social club, then they will wonder how I know about it.

I have a solid mix of alcohol, adrenaline, and boredom now combined with a large dose of curiosity driving me. There is nothing rational about what I'm about to do. But I'm gonna do it anyway.

My heart begins thumping recklessly within my chest as I yank on the door, ready to expose myself to everything inside.

Disappointment bolts through me like a lightning strike.

All of my courage wasted on a dimly lit stairwell leading down to another door.

Now what?

I could give up and go home, but I've come this far. I take a deep breath and wait for my adrenaline to come racing back, but it doesn't. This decision has to be pure Max.

I take one step, then another, letting my hand glide down the narrow railing. By the time I reach the landing, the light from above is nearly nonexistent. My only source of light is the dingy light coming through a tiny frosted-glass window at eye level. The images on the other side are blurry, but there are people behind this door. I hear them.

Mustering up the last of my forced courage, I yank on the final door. My swift movement doesn't propel me through the entryway as I expected though, instead I'm rocked backward.

It's fucking locked.

In the darkness, I let my hand graze against the door in search of a latch or something, but there is nothing.

This little adventure is over.

I pivot my body, ready to leap back up the stairs, when a distinctive voice fills the room behind the door. The words are muffled but I know it's Ben Matthews. I lean my body against the wall and press my ear against the door. Something nudges against my stomach. I back up and run my fingers over the item. It's a keypad. A lot of good this will do me. It is an exclusive place. I know I'm not welcome, yet Ben's voice lures me back to the door. I strain my hearing, listening for clues to unravel this mystery, nervously shoving my hands into my pocket.

Ben's words curiously strike me. "Wow, this is an exciting night! I couldn't be happier to see all your faces. If you're new to the club, I welcome you with open arms. A new season is upon us and you're all in for a special experience. One that will change your lives forever. You may be wondering why you're here and I will get to that momentarily, but first I have some business to take care of. Kade, will you see me over by the door?"

Oh shit. Oh shit. Are they coming outside?

I yank my hands out of my pockets and something comes up with my right hand. Ben's business card floats down to the ground. If this isn't a sign that I should run, I don't know what is. But my feet don't move. I bend down to retrieve the card, letting it rest in my hand.

"Kade, you have failed me and this club." The voice is close, practically right on top of me. I can hear him clear as day. "I'm very disappointed in you. All you had to do was bring a recruit, it was that simple. I really hate to part ways like this, but——"

"Ben, please, don't," Kade pleads, his words stacked with fear. "Ben, no."

Recruit? For what? If it's just to join a posh members' club, I could be his sign-up, if that's all he needs. But how? Wait for him to open the door and jump out? Surprise! I'm here.

Don't be an idiot, Max.

"Ben, it doesn't have to be like this. Can't we at least discuss things?" Kade begs. "You can't do this to me."

"Kade, it was a simple request. One recruit. You can see yourself out," Ben says. "Of course, we will have to discuss some unfinished business, but I will find you later."

Shit. Shit. Shit. My palms are sweating. I glance down before wiping my hands on my pants. The numbers on the back of Ben's card are staring at me.

30492

What are the odds that this is the keypad code?

My stomach churns as I punch each digit carefully into the keypad. And like magic, the door clicks and the pressure of the lock releases. I push through and into the middle of Kade and Ben, facing a group of guys who are staring at me, dumbfounded.

Kade's mouth drops open and his eyes fill with confusion. I give him a nod, accompanied with an uneasy grin.

"I'm here, Kade. Sorry, I'm late." The lies stumble out of my mouth surprisingly fast.

What on earth am I doing? But it's too late, so I must continue with my "excuse."

"I got stuck behind an accident on my way here. Thanks for texting me the code so I wouldn't make an entrance. Apparently, that didn't work." I let an uncomfortable chuckle release from my belly. "Hello, everyone, I'm Max." The words come out more confidently than I feel. My knees quiver below me, as if they might give out.

Ben turns his head sideways, his golden eyes narrowing in confusion. It feels like he's never going to speak. Do I say something or just keep my mouth shut?

Finally, he takes a step toward me, extending his hand out. I meet him in a firm handshake that lasts longer than necessary. "Well, welcome, Max. Nice to see you again. Join the others, won't you? Next time, don't be late. I don't like tardiness." Ben gives me a million-dollar smile before turning and walking to the front of the group.

Kade wraps his arm around my shoulder, pulling me tight against his body. His eyes filled to the brim with fury, but then slowly soften in what appears to be relief. He pulls my head close to his mouth, his breath hot on my ear. "I have no idea how you knew. You saved me, buddy, but you just fucked yourself."

CHAPTER ELEVEN

Max
Saturday, September 18, 10:03 p.m.

Holy hell. I'm literally shaking in my shoes. Sensory overload! What is this place and what did I just do? It's like I just had an out-of-body experience. Did I really just follow my boss and burst into a club with a secret code? That doesn't sound like me, but it was me.

See, I'm no coward.

I saved Kade from being ousted from his club.

Which is a good thing, right? With Kade's words still hot in my ear, I really don't know what to think.

I follow Ben and Kade and take my place with the group of men gathered in the middle of the room. All their eyes are fixed on me and Kade and growing more curious with every second. Can they see I'm a fake? That I'm not his recruit?

Who are all these guys and what kind of club is this? I should have thought this through before I barged in and generously offered myself as Kade's recruit.

Ben positions himself in front of the group, but rather than starting an address, he says calmly, "Please be patient. I need a moment." Then he begins taking deep mindful breaths.

I decide to use this time to check out my surroundings. I let my eyes bounce around the area. The room is quite spacious, much bigger than I assumed from the other side of the door and much nicer than I expected. It seems like a place Kade would enjoy spending his time, especially with the well-stocked bar to the left of us. The room is painted dark blue with framed pictures of local landscapes and motivational quotes hung around the room. Leather recliners, a big-screen TV, massage chairs, and a pool table make up the area behind us. This place screams luxury. It's everything that I am not. I wonder why Kade has never mentioned it before. How did he find it? Although, I still don't fully understand what exactly *it* is.

I let my eyes linger on Kade. He's staring straight through me. I'm sure he's still processing my unannounced entrance. I'm so nervous about having that chat with him. I have no idea what I'll say. *I've been worried and bored with my own life, so I dove headfirst into yours?* Nope, I can't say that.

Ben shakes his hands out at his side, as if he's shaking off some bad energy. Is that because of me? Am I the bad energy? He makes direct eye contact with each person before letting his steely eyes lock in on mine. Chills flush my body.

Here we go. I'm about to get some answers.

"Welcome to the Liars' Club, gentlemen. This is the first day of the rest of your life. You are all here because you need something. A piece of your life is missing, and I, Ben Matthews, can help with that."

The Liars' Club. That's interesting. I'm listening. Sure, he's still the arrogant guy that came into the store, but what is he offering? I guess I don't have anything to lose by being here. But if this place has membership fees, I'm broke and I can simply walk away. But Kade's words are still there: *"But you just fucked yourself."* I want to ask Kade what he means by "fucked myself," but there is no opportunity. Everyone is watching. Is this place the reason Kade's been so off this week? But it seems so nice. Or maybe this is the place that gets him back on track after he gets fucked up.

Ben glides the length of the room, his movement controlled and effortless. "So, you've all been chosen to join my exclusive club. You've either been handpicked by me or one of my trusted club members."

Well, that's not true for me but he doesn't know that.

Ben stops directly in front of me. He places his hand on my shoulder. "Max, have you heard of the phrase, fake it until you become it?"

"Um, I've heard of 'fake it till you make it.'"

"Yes, Max, it's pretty much the same thing, but I put a nice twist on it. 'Fake it until you become it' means more to me. It's heavier. It carries more weight in my opinion. This phrase will be your go-to mantra. My goal is to help you fake the life you want to live until it becomes your reality. You will lie to others to gain the confidence to become the very thing you're seeking."

"Whoa, that's intense," someone mutters from the back, but Ben either ignores him or doesn't hear him.

But I agree, it does sound intense, but, then again, I could use some help. I haven't been in a good headspace mentally for a while. Of course, there are reasons for that: Chrissy's words always badgering me and banging me over the head. It's so loud sometimes that it takes over my thoughts. Her voice strong, as if she's standing right behind me: *"Come on, Max, why can't you take the help? It's standing right in front of you. Do you want to be a loser forever? Come on, Max. Jump in feet first for once.*" I can almost feel her blonde hair tickling my face as the image of her steps out of sight and I push her out of mind. I'm not living the life I want, but this could be the changing point, the time to prove Chrissy is wrong. A new Max: one who doesn't run away from the girl of his dreams. The one who struts up to her and confidently strikes up a conversation. To be more like Kade.

A smile begins to form across my face. Yes, this could be good.

"Who is excited to be here? Who is excited to change their lives for the better?" Ben asks, his voice exhilarated.

Two younger guys standing near me give a shallow, "Whoop!"

Kade stays silent, his arms folded tightly across his chest.

"Come on, men, you can do better than that. I don't think you understand how special you are to be here in this very room. I'm offering you a chance of a lifetime," Ben says, his voice full and confident. It reminds me of the day I met him in the record store. I see now that I took his confidence for arrogance. A confidence that's now quite alluring. Maybe Emmy and I were wrong about him. Emmy's not going to believe this shit.

The entire crowd erupts in hollers, and "hell yeahs." Except for Kade.

"Yes! This is what I'm talking about. I want this club to change your life, I will be personally invested in your journey. Think of me as your life coach," Ben says, his smile widening, his teeth whiter than fresh snow.

"I'm a broke college drop-out. I don't think I can afford your club, Ben." The voice comes from a handsome guy behind.

"That's the best part of the club. It's free."

"Free?" the guy questions.

"I'm a generous person, what can I say?" Ben responds, his

expression flat. "But seriously, I want to help as many people as possible to succeed and find themselves. Most men aren't living a genuine life. They've either been hurt by someone or told by others what they're worth. Some are even told to not be themselves altogether. So over years of being directed to act a certain way, people start to believe the lies they have been told. But I'm here to tell you how to flip the system. I want to unwind everything you've been told until we get to the bottom layer of who you really are or want to be. Then, we will rebuild you from the bottom up. Yes, that requires faking it, but if you've been living this false life all this time, why shouldn't you take charge of that narrative and empower it into who you really want to be, then you will find contentment in yourself."

Everyone glances around the room, questioning if this guy is for real. It does sound good to me. Maybe he can undo Chrissy's damage. I'm buying his pitch. But when will Ben find out that I'm a fraud? That Kade didn't handpick me. Will they kick me out?

"I was once discarded and told that I was worthless, but I'm not and I wasn't. I took that as a challenge, and I was only five years old. Imagine a five-year-old being told he wasn't worth anything. Most kids would have agreed, but not me. That was where my journey started. I lied to get to the top, and I wasn't going to look back. I have everything I've ever wanted. Money, success, and this club."

Well, I guess he has the right to his arrogance; he's built himself from the ground up.

"Hey, Ben, what does that phrase on the wall mean?" one of the guys next to me asks.

We all turn around, seeing the Latin phrase from Ben's card painted high on the wall above the TV.

Noli pugnare daemonibus tuis, amplectere eos.

"That's a conversation for another meeting," Ben quickly responds.

I'm a little confused because I already know it's meaning: Don't fight your demons, embrace them. What does that have to do with faking it? What does that have to do with lying your way to happiness?

"So, what do I expect from you?" Ben pauses. "I ask that you join us for our weekly meetings every Saturday night at ten p.m. On top of that you will also have one-on-one sessions each week where we will discuss your issues and how to envision the life your lie will help you become. Don't worry, it will be fun, and, of course, you will get free access to my club. Just not on Wednesdays and Saturdays, during meetings and one-on-one times. Sounds pretty great, doesn't it?" Ben asks.

"Yes, it does," I respond and a few others nod in agreement.

"Good. Now, let's get some introductions going. My original five, Bobby, Decklan, Jordan, Kade, and Owen," Ben says as each guy makes a slow movement to indicate who they are. Kade simply nods, appearing more standoffish than the other four.

"Now, the newbies. Let's start with Max since he made quite the entrance." Ben chuckles.

Not me, not first. I can't go first. I begin to recoil into myself, shrinking back as I always do. The high from my entrance has worn off. I'm back to being Max, king of the cowards.

"It's OK, Max. Now is not the time to be shy," Ben says calmly.

Great, he can sense my fear. I'm not masking it well.

"Um," I stutter, shoving my hands into my pockets. The sharp edges of Ben's card cuts along my pointer finger. "Um, hi. I'm Max. I work with Kade. I'm not sure what else you want to know?" I respond, tilting my head toward the floor.

"Hello, Max," the group replies in unison, as if it were a rehearsed response. I slowly lift my head; Ben's eyes lock in on my discomfort. He tilts his head up, raising one eyebrow, studying me.

"Max, what is your malfunction?" Ben asks with a straight face.

"My what?"

"Your malfunction. What is it? What is the one thing that is wrong with you, or so you've been told? The thing that others would see as your damage."

Holy hell, is this a rhetorical question? I don't want to answer this in front of a group of strangers and my boss. I'd prefer to keep my insecurities tightly tucked in their own little box, with the key hidden safely out of reach.

"Max, everyone has a malfunction," Ben continues. "Something that doesn't tick right inside your head because of what others have told you about yourself. Your boss, Kade, his malfunction is his sex addiction and alcohol consumption. But Kade's not a bad person because of it. He's actually quite the opposite. It makes Kade who he is."

Kade hangs his head. I know Kade's malfunction already, but I can feel the sting of the blow.

"Come on, Max. This is a safe space. Nothing you say here will leave this room." Ben coaxes as his face hardens. "I'm dead serious. You are not allowed to talk about anything in connection to this club outside of this room. Everything you hear here stays in this room. I mean it. We will be discussing some sensitive things and it needs to stay within these walls. Trust me when I say that I have a way of knowing."

The vague threat in Ben's words is hard to miss. Now I'm questioning if it's OK to tell Emmy. I feel that the answer is no.

"Max, I shall repeat my question. What is your malfunction?"

Record Store Girl and Chrissy both zig-zag through my mind. My legs begin to shake as my heart races. "I can never act when I need to. My mind gets jumbled, and I overthink everything, especially when it comes to girls. I haven't had a healthy relationship in over two years." The words roll fast off my tongue as my breath catches, leaving me feeling faint.

"Thank you for sharing, Max. This is where your journey begins. Your malfunction is safe here," Ben says. "OK, who is next?" he asks, his palms out, gliding his hand toward one of the younger-looking guys next to me.

"Hi, name's Ethan. I have a hard time committing to one girl, and apparently girls don't appreciate that. Owen said I'd have fun here," Ethan responds.

He's chilled and laid-back. Maybe I could be more like Ethan.

"Owen is right—you will have fun here. Owen has come a long way with his malfunction. He has some rage, but now he's channeling that into MMA training, right, Owen?"

"Yes, sir," Owen responds, his posture assertive, his chin up and chest puffed forward. He's too intense. I don't want to be like Owen.

"Ethan. You have a baby face—might I ask how old you are?"

"Twenty-four," Ethan says.

"I think we can work with that. We can build on this." Ben claps his hands together. "Good. OK, let's keep this introduction train moving along." Ben nods to the kid next to Ethan.

"I'm Mateo. I'd rather not say my thing if that's OK."

Good, another coward like me.

"Don't be shy, Mateo. Just spit it out. You will feel better."

Mateo shuffles his feet and kicks at the carpet below him.

"Come on, Mateo. It's OK, just say it." Ben asks again, his voice patient. He reaches out and lets his hand rest on Mateo's arm. "Anything you say here, stays here."

"It's porn!" Mateo shouts, as if he were being tortured, tossing his hands in the air. "I love porn. I'm addicted to it."

I snicker at his admission. Thankfully, no one hears me.

"Bobby, Mateo here must belong to you," Ben says.

The older members all laugh. An inside joke that we new guys don't get. Bobby must enjoy porn too.

Mateo lowers his head. His chin tucked down into his neck. I almost feel bad for Mr. Porno and the fact that I laughed at him. He or any of these guys could have laughed at me and they didn't. Bobby walks up to Mateo and pats him on the back while Ben reassures him, "Mateo, you are fine, and you have nothing to be ashamed of."

The next guy jumps in without any direction from Ben. "Word, I'm Ezra. People call me Ez. I'm a DJ. I failed out of college; now I'm back. Deck told me to come tonight, so here I am. I'm game for anything. Don't have much going on these days. So, yep. That's me in a nutshell. Pretty easy-going," Ezra says. He's unapologetic about who he is as a person. He's by far the best looking of the newbies, with his dark, thick, and wild hair perfectly contrasting against his olive skin. His wide, deep-set eyes are darker than the night. I imagine he has no problem with the ladies.

"Well, all right, Ez. Glad you're here. Not sure that's a malfunction, but we will talk more later," Ben says with a smirk. Ezra is too confident for Ben. I wonder if Ezra needs this club.

"You in the corner. What's your story?" Ben says, pointing to the far-right side of the room.

A mousey guy steps forward. This is the first time I've taken notice of him. He's pale as a ghost and looks like he just rolled out of bed in his unkept T-shirt and messy hair. He doesn't look like the rest of the guys in this group. Hell, I don't look like any of the guys in the group either, but I fit in more than this dude.

"Well, I'm here because Jordan said I had to come," he says, his voice quiet and feeble. "I'm Jordan's brother, Hudson."

Jordan gives his brother a snarky grin, probably for calling him out like that. Hudson nervously tucks his messy, dark-brown hair behind his left ear. One curled lock finds its way back to his pasty white forehead. He's more uncomfortable than me, and that's saying something.

"And your malfunction?" Ben questions, his brows eagerly raised.

"I don't like groups. I would rather be home playing video games or sleeping. I don't do well with girls or crowds. People tell me I'm awkward."

Ben gives Jordan a concerned side-eyed glare. "OK, Hudson. I will get you to change your mind about groups. How old are you?"

"Twenty-eight."

"Have you ever been married?"

"No." He hangs his head low, avoiding eye contact.

"Long-term girlfriend?"

"No."

"OK. We will fix that, Hudson. We will fix *you*. Mark my words. We will fix you," Ben says confidently.

Hudson retreats back into the shadows. To be honest, I don't think he wants to be fixed.

My hand jolts straight into the air, like a little kindergartener needing to be called on before speaking.

"Yes, Max. Do you have a question?" Ben asks.

I don't know what's come over me and before I can give thought to my action, I respond, "Um, yes, I do. Um. What's your malfunction, Ben?"

I don't know what's come over me, but I feel compelled to know this answer. If we are all broken, then he must be too, or he was once.

"I have no malfunction, Max. I have no need for a place such as this, but I'm here to help you. I want you all to achieve greatness."

"What makes you qualified to help us, then?" I ask.

Ben turns his head up, his jaw shoots forward. "Max, this is a system of trust, and you must trust me to move forward. If my story of spinning myself from worthless to gold isn't enough to inspire you, well, then maybe this isn't the place for you, and you can see yourself out. Take Kade with you too."

I've angered him. I didn't mean to go that far. I'm curious and I want to see what he's offering, plus I did this for Kade. Kade needed me and I may as well have just gone home like the piece of shit I am and not have saved Kade. I hang my head. I open my mouth to apologize. I want to stay. "Ben, I, I, I'm. . ."

I feel a hand on my shoulder pulling me back into the group. It's Kade. "Let it go, buddy."

JAMIE LEE FRY

CHAPTER TWELVE

Kade
Saturday, September 18, 10:35 p.m.

I'm sweating through my shirt. My pulse is racing, and I need a drink—badly. I feel like I'm in a dream. No, a nightmare, where everything is distorted. There is no way Max is really here, there is also no way in hell my shy employee just called out Ben on his malfunction.

But I'm not that lucky. It's not a sleepy dream, but rather my unwanted reality. I'd much rather be drinking; things feel right when I drink.

I let my eyes wander to the bar. The bourbon on the top shelf is calling my name, ready for my lips to meet it again. I can already taste it on my tongue. But right now is not the time.

Ben quickly regains his composure, taking one of his calming deep breaths as the group waits in silence. The new members look unnerved and totally unaware of their damnation.

I tossed myself to the wolves tonight; I was at the mercy of fate. I played the shitty hand that I had but it felt better than bringing someone I knew into this club. I felt almost honorable for my decision, that is until divine intervention, or pure dumb luck had other ideas.

Now a piece of Max Jennings belongs to Ben. But how big of a piece, well, only time will tell. He's now part of the so-called Liars' Club. Before, it was just the club. Now, we have an official name. I let the word *liar* sit on the edge of my thoughts as it processes. I suppose it's fitting and a little catchy.

Ben clears his throat, bringing the attention back to him. "I have a fun surprise for all of you next Saturday—even the old members don't know what it is—I can't wait to share it with you all. But before I dismiss you for the night, let me roll out the schedule for the Wednesday one-on-ones. Ethan, seven p.m.; Max, seven thirty; Hudson, eight; Mateo, eight thirty; and Ez, nine. The original five, you guys get the night off. Well, kind of. You just need to make sure your recruit attends. That's it. Simple."

Ben pauses, then walks into the group. He reaches out and shakes Max's hand, pulling him into a bro hug. "I'm glad you're here, Max. You made the right decision to stay."

Max doesn't even realize he ever had a choice.

Ben moves on to Mateo, then Ethan, Ezra, and Hudson, doing the same thing with each new member. Making them feel welcome and special.

"Newbies, normally, I would enjoy it if you stuck around, but I have old-member business tonight, so you are free to leave. I hope you're excited about your new possibilities. And remember, not a word about the club outside these walls. Bobby, Decklan, Owen, Kade, and Jordan, won't you please stick around? We have a few things to discuss."

"Kade?" Max questions, nodding his head toward the exit. Does he expect me to follow him? I can't, Ben won't let me. Of course, I want to follow him and ask him what the hell he was doing here, tell him to not come back, that this isn't the place for him, but I can't. He's trapped. Just like me… "Max, I will catch you later, bro," I quickly respond, ignoring his other attempts to capture my attention.

Right now, it's Ben's time.

As soon as the door latches with the last of the newly appointed members safely on the other side, Ben's face shifts. "All right, men, I appreciate you all following instructions. Kade, I'm sure glad Max showed up for you. Jordan, your brother? Couldn't you have at least found a stranger on the street? I don't like it, but it is what it is. He's here now. Bobby, Decklan, and Owen, good job. I like your guys. I can work with them." Ben gives a hearty laugh, patting Owen, who is the closest to him, on the back.

I've had enough of Ben's bullshit for one evening. "What is your plan here, Ben? I'm truly confused by tonight."

"That is not for you to worry yourself with, Kade," Ben responds.

"Well, it now involves my employee, and I feel responsible for what happens to him," I push back.

"Exactly. You are all responsible for your recruits. If they fuck up, miss a meeting, or go against my wishes, you are all held accountable. So, make sure they stay on task. Got it?" Ben says. He takes a deep breath and then adds. "To be honest, Kade. It's nice seeing you care about something for once."

I know it's true. I lack empathy under normal circumstances, but when it comes to my business, it means a lot to me, and Max has been loyal to Epic Records since the day he arrived. I bite my tongue, deciding I'm already on thin ice.

"I also don't want you guys putting ideas into their heads." Ben cautioned. "They are all in the club now, just like you guys. If you say anything to them, I will know, and I will hold you responsible. Don't even think about giving them any advice that I would consider ill."

The weight of Ben's words hangs in the air until he breaks it with his kilowatt smile. "All right now, you guys are dismissed. Make sure they all show up for their one-on-ones, and I will see you all back here next Saturday. Big things are about to happen. Big. Huge." Ben says, throwing his hands up in the air, before turning and walking into his office, slamming the door behind him.

CHAPTER THIRTEEN

Kade
Saturday, September 18, 11:35 p.m.

I grab my usual barstool at the Rose Tavern and I order bourbon: neat, two fingers.

I thought Max would have waited for me, so I was surprised when he didn't rush me as I left the club. I could call and check in on him, although there isn't much we can discuss at the moment, so I will do it tomorrow. But right now, I need my routine more than anything and I need it badly.

A beautiful girl with caramel-colored skin takes a seat next to me. My mind immediately rates her on a scale that I've been using since I met Ben. Eight and a half.

"Hi, I'm Kade. Can I buy you a drink?" I ask, giving her my devilish smile.

Miss Eight and a Half gives a blushing grin, responding, "Vodka tonic."

I'm digging her edgy short, twisted curls that leave her long kissable neck exposed.

Mark, the bartender, hears her request and begins mixing her drink.

She shifts her torso to rummage through her bag that is hanging off the back of her chair and pulls out a tube of red lipstick and applies it. She replaces the cap, then shoves it back into her bag, letting it fall against the back of the stool.

Miss Eight and a Half crosses her long, sexy legs that go on for days and swivels her chair in my direction. Leather boots climb up her thighs, where they are met with a tight black skirt, revealing just enough of her skin to make me want to see more.

I do a quick assessment of her. It's a little too cold for her attire. I can't help but think she carefully curated an outfit that would get her this exact result.

"How's your evening going?" I casually ask, without reacting to her unequivocal sexual invite just yet, keeping my head forward as Mark slides her vodka tonic toward her on a red napkin. She smiles. Mark looks back at me and winks. He knows my game. I've been coming here too long. I can always count on Mark to make things go smoothly for me.

I thought about asking Mark to come tonight before I decided to go rogue and fuck myself, but Mark seems pretty pleased with himself and his life choices. So, I didn't bother. Now, instead, I have to deal with the consequences of tonight's events. But that is a tomorrow problem. Tonight, I have Miss Eight and a Half to ease my worries.

She carefully picks up her glass and raises it to cheers the random guy, me, who bought her the drink. Her red lipstick leaves a print on her glass. She doesn't wipe it off, leaving it there as a reminder of her pouty, kissable lips. Well played, Eight and a Half.

"Thanks for the drink." She ignores my question. She doesn't want to talk about her night. That's OK.

I give her my best grin. The one I worked out in front of a mirror. The one that says I'm nice but not too nice. Girls aren't looking for nice guys at a bar. They're looking for a guy like me.

Miss Eight and a Half extends her body along the bar with her left arm inching closer. Another open invitation. "So, what's a good-looking guy like you doing all alone in a bar like this?" She laughs flirtatiously, retracting her body back to her seat.

Tease.

She thinks she's being clever. That's a pickup line that's reserved for guys, not beautiful women. She satisfyingly curls her lip, grabs her glass, and rests back comfortably in her chair, leaning against the back. She takes another sip of her drink and crosses her arms, letting her vodka rest in her right hand directly below her breasts. Is she trying to draw my attention to her chest?

I give her a sultry grin, so she knows I'm into her game. I divert my attention back to my drink. Nearly empty now. Taking the final sip, I have a feeling tonight's going to be just what I need.

I raise my empty glass to Mark, and he brings over the bottle of whiskey and pours me another one. I can always count on Mark to give a little longer pour than he should.

I grab a glance from my side view to make sure I've rated her correctly. Her long legs are still crossed. Her tiny waist and perfectly perky boobs that I've been invited to glance at are slowly making me think that perhaps she's a nine. Once I rate someone a nine, things change. I have different rules for nines. My ex-girlfriend, Whitney, was a nine and a half but that was a lifetime ago. I've never conquered a ten. That's my unicorn. My mythical creature. My goal. But sadly, she is not a ten.

"It's been a long day. Just needed a drink, you know?" I raise my glass toward her and then lower it to take a drink. The bourbon hits my lips, and I'm reminded of all the reasons why I enjoy sipping on the expensive stuff. I enjoy the bite. It reminds me that I'm alive.

"I'm Evie, by the way." She extends her dainty hand out toward me. I grab it and give it a playful shake. Her skin is soft against mine as I slowly release my grip, gingerly letting her hand slide along mine.

"Would you like to talk about your long day? Maybe somewhere a little more comfortable? I live a few blocks down. It's walking distance."

Wow, this girl moves fast. Sure, she's a nine now. Game on.

"Evie, dear, you read my mind."

CHAPTER FOURTEEN

Max
Sunday, September 19, 10:29 a.m.

I'm surprised to see Kade this early in the morning. He's approaching the back door to Epic Records as I walk up behind him. Seeing him at this time has caught me off guard. I wasn't expecting him yet, if at all.

If he shows up on Sundays, it's usually to file week-ending paperwork, but lately he hasn't cared about that, so I thought I'd have more time to prepare my story. He will want to know why I barged in on his club. Plus, I have questions that I'm dying to know the answers to. Like, what the hell did I walk into last night? Is Ben Matthews for real? I thought about all that he said last night, and it seems too good to be true. I haven't made up my mind if I'm coming back.

Kade reaches into his pocket for his keys. His hair is a mess, and he's wearing the same clothes as last night.

"Kade, we need to talk," I demand, coming up behind him, unaware of my obtrusive volume until I see Kade taking a step backward. I've startled him.

Kade's eyes blink rapidly as he runs one hand through his wild hair while messing with his keys in the other. He frowns before letting his mouth drop open, ready to speak.

The sound of feet shuffling through the gravel in the alleyway behind us gives both of us pause. Kade and I abruptly spin around to see Teddy, the manager from the men's clothing store adjacent to Epic Records. Nice guy, but a little bit of a gossip if you ask me.

"Hey, Teddy," I yell out, waving my hand.

Teddy continues in our direction, shouting. "Oh my gosh, have you guys heard what happened?" His voice higher pitched than normal.

Like I said, a bit of a gossip.

"No," I respond, shrugging my shoulders, taking the bait. What? I'm buying myself time before Kade's inevitable inquisition.

Kade produces a blank, I-don't-give-a-shit look as he continues to struggle with his keys.

Neither of us really buy into Teddy's attention-seeking gossip normally, but I need time before I tackle the other things on my agenda this morning.

Teddy stops, placing his right hand on his hip, his hawk-like nose turned up. "Seriously, you guys, this is bad. You haven't heard?" he says in his know-it-all tone.

"OK, what—?" I attempt to ask, but Kade rudely cuts me off.

"Oh my God, just spit it out, Teddy!"

Teddy raises his eyebrow, giving Kade a snide glare. "Well, I thought you guys would want to hear this. Another girl was murdered last night. They found her body a few blocks from here. She was propped up against a tree, facing the river. Her throat was slit."

"Oh, man, that's horrible." Nausea makes my stomach twist. "Do they know who she is? Have they released her name yet? Is this connected to the other murders?" I ask, concern choking my voice—that poor girl.

"No name released yet. Police aren't saying anything, but my friend Rachel is roommates with a girl who thinks she knows who it is, and if she's correct, this girl doesn't fit the other killer's MO."

He pauses, taking a deep, dramatic breath, before whispering his unproven gossip. "Her name is Evie Simmons."

Kade's keys fall to the cement slab below the door, jingling as they smash against the pavement. He frantically reaches down to scoop them up. When he stands back up, it's as if all the color has left his face.

"You OK, man?" I ask Kade. "Do you know her?"

"No, the name sounds familiar, but I don't think I do. It's just awful." Kade shifts his body away from me, turning into the door. His hand shakes as he struggles to jam the key into the hole.

Once he's successful, he unlocks the door and enters the building, shutting Teddy and me out.

"That was odd," Teddy says, ruffling his hands through his blond hair. "Don't you think that was strange? Did you just see how he reacted. You don't think he really knows her, do you?"

"I wouldn't put too much thought into it. Kade's been in one of his moods lately. He doesn't mean to be an ass. I promise."

"Poor girl," Teddy continues. It's clear that Teddy wants to keep talking about this, and quite frankly, I am a little interested... Another girl found murdered. This time downtown. I think that makes it four since the beginning of summer. This is huge news for our midsized town. Everyone is going to want to chat about it today. News spreads like wildfire around here, and if this is the same killer, he's switching things up.

"If it is Evie Simmons, my friend said this girl was pretty and most definitely not one of those druggies. And the other girls were just dumped, not propped up—staged—for everyone to see. And the throat slicing is new too," Teddy replies, disgusted.

"Do you know what happened?" I ask.

"Rumor is, she went out last night, and then this morning her body was found, that's all I've heard so far. That poor sweet girl. She had no idea that it would be her last night out. I'm just sickened," Teddy says with deep concern, as if she were a dear friend of his.

"I'm sure we will find out more soon. So sad. Do they have anyone in custody yet, if they don't think it's in connection to the other killings?"

"I don't think so. It's all so horrible. I hope they catch the person who did this, along with that other monster, and I hope it's sooner rather than later. We can't have a killer—or killers—lurking in these streets any longer. This needs to end. Hey, if Emmy needs someone to walk her to her car after her shifts this week, will you let her know to call me?"

"Absolutely, I'll tell her. Kade closes with her most nights, but if not, I will tell her to call you." I smile at Teddy's thoughtfulness.

"Well, if I hear anything else, I'll let you know. I gotta get to my store—we open in fifteen!" Teddy says as he hurries away.

"OK, see ya around. Be safe, buddy," I say, then I abruptly turn to rush inside the building.

It's now time to face Kade.

CHAPTER FIFTEEN

Kade
Sunday, September 19, 10:45 a.m.

Evie.

The girl from last night.

Her name was Evie.

The girl with long legs and silky skin.

Evie.

The girl I fucked last night in her apartment.

Evie.

The naughty girl who bit her lip and told me to spank her.

The girl that screamed my name so loud that her neighbors banged on the wall. The beautiful girl I left the Rose Tavern with. The girl Mark saw me walk out of the bar with last night.

Evie.

Fuck. Fuck. Fuck.

I don't need this right now.

I need a drink. No, I shouldn't—it's not even noon. I bang my fist against my desk. The vibration causes my cup of pens to crash onto the floor. I bend down to retrieve them. My head is level with the bottom drawer of the filing cabinet. The drawer that's reserved for my stash, not paperwork. I slowly extend my arm, ready to pull it open, but my eyes catch Max's feet before I have a chance. His toes wiggling free in his Birkenstocks. Christ, it's only forty-five degrees out this morning.

"Crazy about that girl, isn't it?" Max says, shifting as he speaks.

I quickly gather the pens scattered all over the floor, scooping them into the holder. I carefully place it on the desk, but my hand is shaking. I hope Max doesn't notice.

"Yes, it's so sad," I say, quickly realizing there wasn't much sympathy in my response. It's one of my malfunctions. I shake my head to add something to my words.

I need to shift the subject. I can't let Max linger on this topic. I can't talk about Evie right now.

"Did you follow me last night? I'm not going to be mad. I just need to know why you were there at the club."

Max reaches up, scratches the back of his dark hair that appears more styled than usual. Is that some kind of gel or pomade? Is this Ben's influence? He is already rubbing off on him. Sure, Max's still wearing his normal clothes, but his shirt is wrinkle free and he's freshly shaven. Is that the musk of cologne I smell too?

"Yes, I might have followed you," Max says, his eyes shifting focus to the floor, losing any confidence he gained last night.

"Why the hell, Max?"

"Well—"

"For fuck's sake, Max. Just spit it out already."

"Emmy and I were worried about you."

Shit, I didn't think my choices through. I honestly didn't think my employees would care or take notice. I thought I disguised my "excuse" just fine. I figured they would be happy the boss wasn't around, and they could pick up extra hours. I guess my alcohol-infused choices were not good ones. I never wanted to alarm anyone. I just needed time to think about Ben, the meetings, and my recruit, or the lack thereof.

"OK, that's fair. I was a little off last week. But to follow me? Couldn't you have just come to me, Max?"

"No, because you were a wreck last week. You yelled at Jed and told him to fuck off. We were all afraid of you."

"Well, I've been under some stress, and as you saw, the club can be a little intense, and well, sometimes, it gets to be a lot."

"Um yeah, Kade. What the heck is that place? Is Ben for real?" Max says, demanding a simple response, but it's not that easy.

"It's for real, but we shouldn't be talking about the club. Ben has rules for a reason. You're a part of it now, so that comes with the weight of secrecy. You can't tell anyone you're a member. Not even Emmy. You got that?"

Max's brown eyes widen. "Sure, I understand." He shifts the weight of his feet onto his heels and tugs at his flannel shirt.

"I don't love the fact that you felt you needed to follow me, and seriously, bro, how did you know the code to even open the door?"

Max shoves his hands in his pockets. "As I said, we were worried about you. I'm sorry for following you and not asking you straight out what was going on. Honestly, I hadn't really seen you all week, and Em was worried. And then there was this." Max produces Ben's business card from his pocket.

"Where did you get that?" Did I leave one of Ben's precious business cards lying around? That's a huge club no-no. Ben only hands out his cards to potential members. The night Ben found me at River's Edge Saloon on the east side of town, face down in my drink, he paid my bar tab, took me out for greasy breakfast food, and got me an Uber home. The next day, he showed up at Epic

Records. I don't even remember telling him where I worked, but he was there waiting for me, with a coffee in hand as I arrived to open the store. He produced his card, black and shiny with gold embossed lettering. He told me where to find him if I wanted a different life. I was at rock bottom, so I took the bait. But why Max?

Max clears his throat, bringing me back to the business card. "He gave it to me when he stopped in to see you. I didn't think anything of it, and I slipped it into my pocket. The number on the back just so happened to be the door code. I took a chance when I heard you needed a recruit, and I thought I could be that person for you. Kade, I honestly just wanted to help."

"Max, you violated my privacy."

"I'm sorry, man. I just wanted to help," he repeats.

"I wish you hadn't done that. I was fine."

"Well, I did, and it happened. Hey, what did you mean last night when you said that I'd just fucked myself?"

Ben's words slice through me. I know I can't warn Max. Max is now my responsibility. "Oh, never mind that. I was just in the midst of the moment. I was pissed. Forget I said it."

"OK, I'm not sure the club is the right place for me, anyway. I like what Ben had to say, but I'm not a club type of person. I don't need to go back."

If I had just played my hand last night, left the club, that would have been my cross to carry, but now Max is involved. We are both fucked if he doesn't come back.

"I think you should come back. It's actually a pretty cool club. I think Ben could really help you."

Max leans into the doorframe. "No one can help me."

He's sulking. It's what Max does. He wants to be pushed.

Think, Kade. Push him or we will both pay for the consequences of his actions.

Ah, the girl. That's it. That's the carrot to dangle. "I see how you looked at that girl a few weeks back, the funky one with curls. You like her, and you haven't even been able to speak to her—don't think I haven't noticed. She is cute, and I bet she would like you."

"You know about that?"

"Yes, Max, it's pretty obvious."

"Do you know her name?"

"Nope, sorry. But I do think Ben can help you work on yourself. If not for this girl, then for the next one. Trust me. I got your back, bro. We are in it together now."

CHAPTER SIXTEEN

Max
Wednesday, September 22, 7:30 p.m.

"Welcome, Max. Take a seat," Ben says, indicating toward a leather barstool with his hand. His voice is gentle, almost hypnotizing. I obey and hop up on the seat closest to the wall. I wait, but he doesn't offer me a drink. Not that I really want one, but the gesture would have been nice.

Ben rests his right arm on the bar top, leans in. "Max, why do you think you're here?"

That's a good question, why am I here? I suppose I'm here for Kade, it's important to him, but also what if Ben can really help me with Record Store Girl like Kade suggested? "I dunno. I just am, I suppose." My answer is generic. I need more time to formulate my thoughts about Ben and this club.

Ben shifts, resting his left elbow on his knee, hand cupping his chin. "Max, my new friend, I want you to tell me what you hope to get out of our meetings." His eyes are more golden than the Rolex wrapped around his left wrist, and they lock me into his stare.

What is this? A court-ordered therapy session? Perhaps the man does have a superiority complex, but he seems to have earned it. This is his club, after all. He makes the rules.

I need to speak; I've let too much time linger. I motion my pointer finger in the air, indicating I need another moment to gather my thoughts, but really, I'm studying him. If I'm going to trust this man with "my malfunction," as he calls it, I need to know more. He's a hard one to gauge as far as age goes. He presents himself well: his skin's flawless, hair well-groomed without a hint of gray or discoloration. Perhaps thirty to thirty-five. There is no way he's my age, but he could have that Paul Rudd effect going on; he could be in his forties but forever look like he's in his twenties. Once again, he's wearing a tailored white collared button-up shirt. The top two buttons undone, letting his strong chest show. Fitted denim, with black dress socks and shoes.

Ben gives up waiting for my response—after all, he only has thirty minutes with me. Hudson should be arriving in around twenty-four minutes—not that I'm paying attention to the clock beyond him.

"You said you're having a hard time talking to girls, and you haven't had a real relationship in nearly two years. Is that correct? Isn't that what you said at our meeting?"

I nod. Yes, but only because I was forced to say something.

"Max, I'm really good at reading people, and I suspect there is more to this. We will peel back the layers and get to the bottom of your insecurities, so we can build you back up."

I don't know if I'm ready to pull back any layers.

"So, what's her name?"

"Whose name?" I ask.

"The name of the girl that's got you all twisted up inside. It's always a girl."

I hang my head so far, it's nearly in my lap, "I don't know her name."

"Not all is lost my friend," Ben says, giving me a reassuring squeeze on my knee.

Ben's head jerks back to the clock; time is spinning by and he's barely gotten anything out of me. I almost feel guilty for wasting his time.

"Max, as you know, we don't have long, but I honestly feel that when we are pressed for time, we work harder. We push things out that could take years to uncover in traditional therapy. Have you ever noticed that you find yourself working harder to complete something when a deadline's nearing? If you put something off for so long and then it's due, you will work all night to get it done. Why do you think that is?"

I shrug my shoulders.

"It's the same thing here. You've put off discovering what's wrong, and now we only have a short amount of time during these sessions to figure it out. I want to help you, Max. I truly do, but I need you to work with me here. This will be a weekly thing, but we will continue to push through your layers and break through the boundaries you've set for yourself. I will fix you, Max."

I have a hard time finding words. I don't know what to say. Can I really be fixed? Can he help me undo the damage that's been done? I can't tell him everything though. There are some things I need to keep secret.

"Tell me about your last relationship. What was her name?" Ben asks.

A direct question that expects an easy response, but I really don't want to let Ben into that world. I say nothing.

"Come on, Max, work with me here. This is all part of the process. A name is not so hard, unless you never got her name either?" Ben lets out a controlled laugh.

Not funny, dude.

"Her name was Chrissy," I respond, giving Ben a crooked smile.

"Tell me about Chrissy."

I'd rather not.

A loud rumble of thunder claps outside. I let my attention drift to the droplets of rain that begin to ping fast against the frosted window panes at street level. Shadows of people quickly rush by.

Ben snaps his fingers, drawing my attention back to the topic I'd rather avoid. "Focus, Max. Tell me about Chrissy."

I begin to shift in my seat. My palms are sweating. "There isn't much to tell. It didn't work out."

Ben leans back, crossing his long legs. "Max, buddy, you got to work with me. What's with the resistance? I'm here to help."

"Nothing against you, Ben, but I don't know you, so why should I trust you?"

"That's fair. I get it. But I just want to help. This isn't my first club, Max. I've been doing this for a long time and have helped many men over the years become the truest versions of themselves. I helped Kade, Owen, Bobby, Decklan, and Jordan. Do you think they would come back week after week if they weren't getting the help they were seeking? I want to push them even further now, but they are all better because they met me. Don't you want that for yourself?"

"Are they? Kade's drinking more than ever. Plus, maybe I don't need any help, and I'm fine how I am." I respond with more cockiness in my voice than I intended.

"Kade just had a minor setback, but that is his journey, not yours. Kade trusts me. If he didn't, you wouldn't be here."

I need this conversation to be over. We don't need to talk about Chrissy. "Did you hear about that poor girl that was found murdered downtown on Saturday night? They still haven't caught the person. Newspapers don't think it's connected to the other murders. Isn't that wild?"

Ben frowns at me. I'm not sure if it's because I'm changing the subject or if he's genuinely sad about the dead girls. "Yes, so tragic, but Max, I know what you're doing. Let's not discuss that right now. We are in the middle of something. Come on, get back to Chrissy. Why didn't it work out? Who ended things?"

Annoyance is pulsating from my toes to my fingertips. I don't want to talk about this.

"What happened?" Ben asks again. "You can tell me. Remember, this is a safe space."

My fingers begin to tingle, I feel a sliver of sweat beading down my back. I don't want to talk about it.

"You can tell me."

More sweat runs across my upper lip. I know Ben sees it. This is my hot-button issue. This is the one that messed me up. Ben reaches out and grabs my arm. He squeezes gently.

"Chrissy fucking ended things." I leap up, letting my chair bang against the bar. "Is that what you want to hear?" Huge tears begin to well up in my eyes. I blink rapidly, trying to dismiss them before Ben notices.

"Max, it's OK. Things we discuss here will stir up emotions, ones that you've buried deep down. This kind of reaction is normal. Please, come back and take a seat."

I let out an exasperated huff, but I do as I'm asked. Ben gives a kind smile. "So why did she end it?"

I draw in a long breath—the kind I saw Ben do Saturday night—and I'm surprised by how it calms me a little. On the exhale, I spit it all out. "She thought I was a *coward*, and she wanted me to be more like her friends' boyfriends and husbands."

"Good, good, we're making some progress. Why do you think she used the word *coward* to describe her feelings for you? You emphasized *coward*. It must be a trigger for you. I know it would be a trigger for me if someone called me that."

"I don't know. Probably because she was a selfish bitch, and she wanted me to feel bad."

"OK, if you don't want to tell me the real reason for her calling you that word, then we can move on. It will come out later. How serious was this relationship?"

"We lived together and dated for nearly two painful years. She hated me in the end. She wanted me to be normal. Fuck. What even is *normal*?"

"Did you feel like you were a coward? Did you feel like you weren't normal?"

"Maybe, sometimes. I never stood up for her and gave in quickly to others, and I always gave in to her. Maybe she was looking for more of an effort, or a fight. I really don't know. I don't think she ever really understood me. We didn't even have the same taste in music. I mean, how can you be with someone who doesn't love what you love?"

"I think there is more to this story than you're telling me, Max. Did she cheat on you? Did you cheat on her? What was your sex life like?"

"Well, there was this incident—" My words shock me as they tumble out of my mouth without hesitation. I quickly freeze up in my seat. "I'm not ready to talk about that, actually. Not with you."

Ben takes my body language cue not to press me on this.

"What about now?" he says instead. "You said you haven't dated anyone since Chrissy, but is there anyone that has caught your attention? The girl you mentioned earlier?" Ben says with a devilish grin.

"Yes, her. I can't get this one girl out of my head. She is a customer at the store. She is my dream girl, and I feel connected to her even if I've never spoken to her. I have Chrissy's words in the back of my mind with every girl I've ever attempted to talk to. Well, except for Emmy, but we work together, and we are just friends."

"Kade has mentioned Emmy before. She sounds like a *lovely* girl."

Strange, because every time you've been in Epic Records, you've never even said hi to this 'lovely' girl.

"What else do you know about your so-called dream girl?"

"Well, she used to come in every Friday around noon, but I haven't seen her for a few weeks. I think I missed my opportunity to talk to her."

Ben leans in close. "Trust me. These things have a way of working themselves out. I know you will see her again," he says, patting me on the knee.

A repetitious pounding rattles the coded door. "Give us a second, Hudson," Ben softly calls out.

"Looks like our time is up. Your homework before Saturday—" Ben pauses, cocks his head, his smile tugs upward toward his narrow nose. "I need you to create an account on Socialite."

My face begins to tighten and my brows crease in confusion.

"And this time, Max, use your real name and add a photo, will ya?"

My heart is racing up my throat. I swallow hard, pushing it back into place.

Nope, that's not my heart.

Chunks begin to rise, lodging in my esophagus. I swallow hard, choking, coughing. I feel ill. I can't speak. I'm at a loss for words.

"Oh, and Max, your dream girl's name is Jovie."

CHAPTER SEVENTEEN

Hudson
Wednesday, September 22, 8:00 p.m.

I hesitate before I rap my knuckles against the club door. My brother Jordan gave me the code, but Max's one-on-one is still going on, and I don't want to barge in.

"Give us a second, Hudson," a muffled voice calls out.

Fuck. I don't have a second. In a second, I might change my mind and chicken out. Fuck. What do I do? Sweat beads its way down my back, and with the fall chill in the air, I shiver.

I twist my foot and pivot my body, lunging back up the darkly lit stairwell. My fingers quickly glide up the handrail, guiding my path. I let my sweaty palm meet the door, ready to shove it open, but a gush of heat blows up toward me. I glance down to where a little bit of light is leaking through. The door is opening.

I have just moments to decide my fate. Should I run out the door and never come back?

Yes, that's what I'm going to do.

But as I push on the external door, Max shoves past me,

knocking the door wide open, rocking me off my balance. With my body contorted, trying to steady my feet, I regain my balance. I'm about to follow Max, when—

"Hello, Hudson," Ben calls. I slowly turn to see him standing on the landing, his arms crossed and his brows pinched tight. He caught me.

I slowly shuffle my way down to greet him. His hand is extended outward, but his eyes are cold. His manly hand encompasses my weak and clammy grip as we meet in his expectant handshake.

I'm trapped. There is no way out.

Why did Jordan involve me in this mess? Brothers need to look out for each other, even if we are total opposites. None of this is me. This place is not for me. Jordan should have known that.

Ben pulls my arm in toward his body in a bro embrace, locking his arm around my back. I don't do bro hugs, not even with my own brother. I feel his body against mine, the tension in his body dropping, but I can't let mine go.

"It's OK, Hudson. I forgive you for trying to leave. It's a natural instinct to run from things that frighten you."

I freeze in his arms. My belly twists into a pretzel.

"I was, um, I was just getting the door for Max," I stutter.

Ben shakes his head. "We both know that isn't true. I'm sorry I had to see you so late on Saturday night, but I appreciate what you did for the group." Ben moves his arm gripping me around the shoulder as he guides me to the bar. "Hudson, don't worry, everyone will have a task to complete, such as the one I gave you. Normally, I would wait until after our first one-on-one, but this task was very important, and it couldn't wait. I just knew you were the right man for the job. I appreciate what you've done. I knew I could count on you. I sensed something special in you, and I was right."

Tears begin to flush my eyes, covering them like a blurry veil before slithering their way down my face.

"Ben, what the hell did you make me do?"

CHAPTER EIGHTEEN

Max
Wednesday, September 22, 8:01 p.m.

I fly past Hudson on the stairs. With a quick glance, I notice he's pale, almost sickly. He could probably say the same about me right now; I feel white as a sheet.

My breath is a choppy pant by the time I slide into my car.

How did Ben know about my impostor Socialite account? Was he looking into me like I was looking into him? How could he have found that account? I made sure it had no connections to me. I was careful.

I shove my hand into my pocket and slide out my phone. I'm tempted to toss it out the window and drive over it, but instead I open Socialite.

I click the "remove profile" button on the settings screen.

I feel nauseated.

How on earth did Ben know about my Record Store Girl—Jovie? Her name is Jovie. Of course, it seems that Kade knew of her and my crush, but would he give that information to Ben to help me? Or perhaps hurt me? Kade didn't even know her name, so Ben must have done some homework, if that's the case. He could find her, but I couldn't.

No one knew of my fake account and my endless nights spent searching for her. The only evidence of that is on my phone. The one I'm holding in my hand, the one I never let out of my sight, except when I'm at work occasionally and when I'm asleep. Both thoughts disturb me. No, I will not let that paranoia in.

I'm excited I know her name, though, but I'm rattled by this information. Privacy is the strongest pillar of my life—for a reason.

Who are you, Ben Matthews, and why go to this length to 'help' me? Ben didn't even know I existed until two weeks ago.

I'm half tempted to stick around and wait to see what he throws at my new pale counterpart. Does he have something he wants to toss at him too? But somehow, I don't think the guy has any secrets.

I throw a quick glance over my shoulder to make sure no one is watching me. Anything is possible right now.

My phone buzzes in my hand. A text flashes on my screen from an unknown number.

Unknown: *Good chat tonight, Max.*
Don't forget your task and use your real
name this time. We still have some work
to do before you are ready for Jovie. Don't
go and search for her just yet.
Patience, my new friend.
Ben

Holy hell. I don't understand this dude's endgame. Helping me or stalking me? I honestly don't know. He has my emotions all over the place.

The only good that came out of this is that I finally know her name. I don't have a last name, but a first name is a start.

Do I actually create a new account—a real account?

Do I come back on Saturday?

I decide not to wait for Hudson. It's pointless. I'm probably overthinking things as I always do. Maybe this is Ben's way of helping me with Jovie.

I lean forward to press the ignition button on my car. My phone vibrates again before I shift into drive.

I reluctantly glance down. It's from the unknown number. Ben.

Max, I know what really happened with you and Chrissy.
Keep coming back. It's for your own good.

CHAPTER NINETEEN

Max
Wednesday, September 22, 9:00 p.m.

I feel instantly better the second I step foot into my apartment. My safe space where everything feels normal. Well, except for the sword of Damocles hanging over my head—Chrissy.

Does Ben really know what happened?

He has to be generalizing. Like, he knows I got my heart stomped on and he wants to fix me.

There is no way Ben could know what really happened.

I moved here to Clear River two years ago, because no one knows me here. People only know what I tell them.

There is no way he could possibly know about. . .

No, there is no way. I was careful.

I'm overthinking it. It's a text. People always misinterpret text messages—another reason to hate technology.

I need to shake these thoughts and move on. I'm being silly. Ben just wants to help me.

I pull my phone from my pocket and open Socialite. I stare

angrily at the blank app. I deleted my impostor account, and I don't know what good will come from creating a 'real' account. I don't see the point. But I could try and find her. I have her first name. But Ben said not to. That I am not ready. Do I trust that he knows what's best for me? I only just met the guy. Fuck. My mind is twisting all over the place. But what if he genuinely wants to help me prepare myself for her—Jovie.

Enough of this. I wedge the phone into the cushion of the sofa. I'm done with this shit for the night. I walk over to my record collection and yank Grateful Dead's *Anthem of the Sun* from its place on my shelf. It's easy to find as all my albums are in alphabetical order—a habit that's carried over from work but comes in handy with my large collection.

I carefully place the album onto the turntable.

Thinking of Jovie, I smile with a little bit of hope. This album reminds me of her. It was one of her purchases before she stopped turning up to the store. I let the music play and wash over me as I drift back to the couch, wondering if she's listening to the same record at this very moment; our souls connecting on another level greater than we could ever imagine.

I let my thoughts follow me to the kitchen where I pull out my Rasta-themed bong from the top shelf of my cabinet. I load the chamber with the sweet, sticky kush that I picked up on my way home from work a few nights ago. Tonight's problems call for a hit or two from Bong Marley. Not beer, or rum, but some good ol' reliable ganja.

I can't help but wonder how much Jovie and I would have in common. Does she smoke weed? Would she find it funny that I named my bong Bong Marley? I sure had a good laugh when the name came to me. She seems pretty chill. I bet she would.

If I had just asked her out, I would know the answers to all my questions, and perhaps we would be sitting here together on my couch, listening to Jerry Garcia, smoking together. I wouldn't have followed Kade or needed Ben.

"*Coward. You will never be a normal guy, Max Jennings.*" Chrissy's words are omnipresent. But she is right. I am a coward. But Ben Matthews is going to help me with that. Right?

I take one long hit from Bong Marley and then another and another until I feel all my insecurities and tension release from my body, slowly removing itself from each appendage. My shoulders relax as the rest of the stress disappears and I melt into the couch.

Everything else is tomorrow's problem.

CHAPTER TWENTY

Max
Thursday, September 23, 3:00 p.m.

This week has been nothing short of insane. How is it Thursday already? Kade's in his office, his door closed, shutting Emmy and me out. Again. He's barely said two words to me since Sunday. He only checked in to make sure I was going to the meeting last night. He hasn't bothered to ask me how it went. I did all this for him, and last night, I could have used a friend, but he didn't care enough to pull himself away from the bottle.

"Oh my God, Emmy, today is so boring. I would even be glad to help a musical tourist at this point. Anything to get this day moving."

"Max, you're so dramatic. Come help me sort these new records. That will get the day moving and get you to stop bitching."

I mosey over to Emmy, where she has a box of records scattered across the counter. "Do you want to take M to Z?" she asks.

"Sure," I respond. I start to gather them up when Emmy begins to fiercely shake my shoulder, her red fingernails digging into my skin.

"Max, Max. Look!"

With one hand still on my shoulder, her other hand points toward the large display window. It takes a second for my brain to register what Emmy is pointing at. I squint to focus through the large window decal announcing our buy-two-get-one-free sale. Two nicely dressed men in suit jackets are strutting across the street. The sun reflects off a gun that's holstered to one of the men's belts. Two armed detectives are making the turn into our entryway.

The door flings wide open, ushering in an invasion of crisp fall air and a burst of newly fallen leaves. The foliage dances in the wind and floats effortlessly down to settle on the carpet like a fall blanket.

My stomach churns.

Detectives.

Why are they here?

Everything seems to slow down, like watching them in slow motion. The men kick up the leaves with their shiny dress shoes as they march into the store. They make a direct path to the counter.

"Hi, I'm Detective Henricks," he says, tucking his suit jacket back and flashing the badge opposite his holstered gun, his voice husky and deep. He's a bulky man with sculpted muscles accentuated by his tight jacket. "And this is Detective Clemens." He points to the thin man with a long face and thick black-framed glasses standing next to him. "We are looking for Kade Kinzinger."

Emmy gasps. "What on earth do you want with Kade?"

Emmy's big brown eyes widen, her head rocks slightly back as she quickly covers her mouth with her hand, as if to take back the words that have already flown out.

My heart drops to my stomach.

"What is this in reference to? Is Kade in some kind of trouble?" I ask.

The thin officer turns his lip up, giving an annoyed glare and completely disregarding my question.

"Mr. Kinzinger. Is he here?" Henricks asks again.

"He's in his office," I say, pointing to the back of the store.

The officers don't respond to either of us as they brush past us toward Kade's closed office door.

"Emmy, what the heck?"

Emmy and I lock eyes. Her expression is concerned and uneasy.

"I have no clue. What could they want with Kade? With everything going on in town with the murders, it has my mind going to a bad spot. Do you think something has happened to someone he knows?" she says.

Emmy leaps past the counter without another word. She subtly leans an ear against the door of Kade's office, now shut.

I begin to follow her, but she puts her palm out, indicating that I stop.

I retract my steps, moving back toward the front door.

Thankfully, there isn't anyone in the store. I flip the open sign to closed and lock the front door. Kade would be embarrassed if anyone saw him in this situation. Whatever this situation may be. The whole town is already on high alert with everything going on, but I bet the damage is already done, though. Teddy probably already spied the out-of-place cops and is already spreading the gossip.

When I turn around, Emmy is flagging me down, waving me over. "It's about that dead girl, Evie," she whispers, her breath warm in my ear. I'm stunned, shocked. I know my mouth must be hanging wide open. I stand next to Emmy, and we both carefully stretch to hear through the closed door.

Luckily, Henricks's voice is husky, making it clearly audible through the wood. "Mr. Kinzinger, you were the last one to be seen with Evie Simmons the night of her murder. We need your help to rule you out as a suspect and figure out her timeline."

Kade's voice is too low for us to hear. Either that, or he's gone quiet.

Emmy's eyes flicker. She reaches out and grabs my hand, squeezing it hard. I squeeze back, not letting go.

Kade can't have something to do with that girl's death. No, I can't believe it. But I can't dismiss his reaction when he first heard the news of Evie Simmons. The mention of her name caused him to drop his keys. He looked like hell and showed up wearing the same clothing from the previous night. Could Kade really have had something to do with this?

No, he couldn't. He wouldn't. He's not capable of something like that—of murder. The man I've known for two years has his problems, sure, but murder is not one of them.

Emmy drops her grip, swatting my leg to move. "They're coming."

Kade walks out of the office first, his face expressionless. The two detectives follow behind him. A sigh escapes me when I see he's not in handcuffs. That's got to be a good sign.

The trio walks past us, avoiding eye contact. When they reach the door, Kade looks over his shoulder, his hair wispy over his right eye. "Hey Max, let's lock up for the day. Find Ben. He will know what to do." His voice is too calm and collected for what just happened in his office. My voice would be shouty, high and choked up.

Kade pushes on the front door, but it's locked. I was one step ahead of him. He twists the lock and pushes through, the two men right on his heels. I rush over to lock it again. Sure enough, I spot Teddy on the sidewalk, camera in hand, photographing Kade's humiliation. "Dammit, Teddy," I whisper.

I turn around, Emmy's staring at me. Her mouth contorted into a stretched-out frown, showing her two front teeth. Her big, brown eyes are tight and drawn upward. "Max, tell me that didn't just really happen?" she cries. "They can't think Kade had anything to do with that girl's death. Can they?"

"I don't know, Em, but Kade seemed calm, so that's reassuring, right? Or really scary?" I respond, my mind reeling, trying to replay every event since Saturday. Where did Kade go after the club? How long did he stay at the club? Did he really know Evie Simmons? Was he drunk? Why was he in the same clothes? Why did he react the way he did when Teddy said the victim's name?

Emmy interrupts my thoughts. "And what's up with you knowing Ben?" Emmy asks. "I feel like I'm missing something here?"

"It's a long story, Emmy. I can't get into it right now. Can you lock up here? I honestly don't think Kade had anything to do with that girl's murder." I hope Emmy can't read my face right now. I'm uncertain about everything. "Teddy is just outside. Have him escort you to your car. I need to know you're safe. But don't give into his incessant questioning."

Emmy's eyes plead for me not to leave her, but I have to deal with Ben Matthews, and I'm not sure Ben would want Emmy hanging around.

"I'm sorry, Emmy. Kade needs me right now. I need to go."

CHAPTER TWENTY-ONE

Kade
Thursday, September 23, 3:40 p.m.

"I had nothing to do with that girl's death. I swear," I shout, pleading to the detectives from the back seat of their unmarked patrol car.

I know it's not smart to say anything until a lawyer is present, but I'm innocent. I have nothing to hide, plus I can't afford a lawyer right now. I don't want to rely on Ben—it's going to put me further in his debt—but I have no choice. Another thing to owe him—to hang over my head. He's the only person that can help me. Max better know how to get a hold of him.

"Am I under arrest?" I ask, noticing they didn't read me my Miranda rights, nor did they handcuff me. I wonder if I could have asked to drive myself, now that I'm thinking of it.

"No, Mr. Kinzinger, we just have a few questions for you," Detective Clemens responds.

"So, that's your record store, huh? How long have you owned it?" Detective Henricks asks from the passenger seat, trying to make small talk like he's my buddy. Not so fast—I see what you're doing here.

But still I answer. "Five years or so." My voice is quiet and hushed.

"Does it get pretty busy this time of year?" he asks.

"I'd rather not chat, if that's OK?" I respond.

"Yep, sure thing. We will save the chitchat for the station."

I stay quiet the rest of the ten-minute ride. I can't risk accidentally saying something that might implicate me, but soon I won't have a choice.

* * *

When we arrive, they guide me inside to an interrogation room—an empty white room with a long table. Two chairs are set up on one side and one on the other. I take the single seat.

"Can I get you a coffee or water?" Detective Henricks asks me.

"Coffee," I respond without making eye contact.

Both men leave the room. I know someone is probably watching me and my every move. I'm trying to be honest with my emotions and actions, but also cautious. I don't want to seem disingenuous. Yes, this is a sad thing, a girl is dead, but I didn't know her that well. Some therapists have told me I'm borderline sociopathic and disconnected from emotions such as fear and love. My erratic behavior sometimes makes me believe they are right, but that's not what Ben has taught me. Maybe I do need the group after all. Otherwise, I would be sitting in the psychologist's office having him tell me all the things wrong with me and trying to change me. But I have Ben, and that's all I need.

God dammit. I'm just me.

I feel the rage rising and my lack of care floating to the surface. No, I care a little—after all, she was a borderline nine. I squint my eyes, trying to muster up some tears to look the part.

The door slowly opens, and only Detective Henricks reappears. "Here, I hope you like it black. We just ran out of cream," he says, setting the cup on the table in front of me.

I'm sure they didn't just run out, and just beyond that door, there is a carafe filled with milky creamer. Joke's on him—I don't care. Instead, I avoid his remark and reach for the Styrofoam cup and take a sip. It's lukewarm, but that is what I expected. I don't show any emotions, but instead keep the tear-filled eyes and sullen face turned toward the table.

I hope he doesn't see through my act. The act of caring, that is, not the act of innocence. I am innocent, I just have a hard time with emotions, but that could fuck me. You know those guys who say they didn't kill their wife, but they look guilty as hell? That's me, but really, I'm being honest, and those guys usually end up on the electric chair.

Detective Henricks takes a seat opposite me, leaving the second chair empty. I wonder if he's the good cop or the bad cop. They're usually one of each, but why aren't they both in here? I bet the other one is on the other side of this mirror. Watching me, studying me. I can't be myself. Act like you care, Kade.

"I swear to you that I didn't have anything to do with that girl's death," I plead, letting my fake tears rush down my cheeks—a feeling that I'm not familiar with.

"Hey, we are just here to ask you a few questions. You're not under arrest but I do need to read you your rights since you're here.

"Whatever."

He begins to read me my Miranda rights, then slips me a card to sign. "Do you understand everything I just stated and that you're waiving your right to a lawyer, and you want to speak to us now?"

"Yes," I quietly respond, sinking into my chair. "Why not? I didn't kill that girl."

I pick up a pen and quickly scribble my name on the card.

Henricks doesn't waste any time. "We have witnesses that put you and Evie Simmons leaving the Rose Tavern together around midnight. What can you tell us about that, Mr. Kinzinger?"

Hmm. I bet it was Mark or one of the barstool regulars, perhaps that jerk with the cane, that gave them my name. I thought Mark was a friend.

"Yes, I met Evie that night at the Rose Tavern. She was a pretty girl, and we chatted, and then she asked me to come over to her apartment for a nightcap."

I decide to leave out the part about how she was dressed slightly inappropriate for the weather, and she was the one who came on to me first because that won't matter to them. She is the victim here.

"A nightcap? Is that all, Mr. Kinzinger? Because we also have neighbors saying they could hear you and Miss Simmons having loud intercourse."

"Just say *sex*, officer," I taunt. But he ignores me.

"They even said they heard her scream the name *Kade*. Well, isn't that your name?"

"Obviously, that's my name, and yes, we left the bar to hook up at her house and take in another drink. There is no law against two consensual adults having sex, is there, Detective?"

I can feel myself beginning to lose control. I want to lean over the table and punch him in the face. I need to calm down before I do or say the wrong thing. Come on, Kade, keep your shit together.

"Well, no. But the girl you had sexual intercourse with ended up dead sometime before six a.m., with you being the last person to see her alive, as far as we know. I need to establish a timeline here. You left the Rose Tavern at midnight after paying your bar tab—both yours and Evie's drinks on the bill. Then what time would you say you got to her place? Did you go straight there?"

"It was a quick walk to her place, maybe ten past."

"Then you got that nightcap?"

"No. She began kissing me, so we completely forgot about it."

"Then what?"

"We had sex."

"And that was around twelve thirty, according to the neighbors' account."

"I suppose if that's what the neighbors said."

"Then what happened?"

"I waited for her to fall asleep, and then I snuck out."

"Well, that was a jerk move, don't you think?"

"I doubt she wanted me to spend the night, Detective. She knew what this encounter was."

"Well, she ended up dead. So perhaps she didn't."

"Are you saying I'm guilty because I had sex with her? Because I'm not. I left and went home."

"OK, if that's your story. What time did you leave Miss Simmons's place, Mr. Kinzinger?"

"I left her house around one thirty, if I remember correctly. She fell asleep and I left. That's all. She was alive when I snuck out of her apartment. I swear." I try to turn the waterworks on again, but I'm all dried up.

"Do you have anyone who can corroborate your story?"

"It's not a story. It's the truth. And no, I went straight home and fell asleep."

"You didn't stop anywhere, catch a cab or call a friend?" he presses.

"I wish I could say yes, but no, I simply left Evie's apartment then went home."

"How drunk do you think you were? On a scale of one to ten, ten being the drunkest."

"I don't know. Maybe a three or four when I got to her house, but a one when I left. We didn't end up having that nightcap, as I said earlier. And I worked off my buzz during that wild sex," I say with snark in my voice, but immediately regret my tone.

"So would you say that you were inebriated enough to forget some of the events that conspired that night?"

"Absolutely not. I was tipsy, sure. Evie was too."

"Have you ever met Evie Simmons before the night of September eighteenth?

"No, I've never seen her before."

"Are you sure of that?"

"Yes."

"So, you mean to tell me, you met a girl for the first time, went back to her apartment, and had sex with her. You snuck out, and sometime shortly after, she magically ended up with her throat slit downtown and propped up against a tree near the river, and you had nothing to do with that?"

"Respectfully, this all seems like circumstantial evidence. I was simply at the wrong place at the wrong time. I swear to you."

"Can you tell me where you were the night of September ninth?"

"I don't know. I'd have to check my calendar, but I'm pretty sure I was at the Rose Tavern."

"What about the nights of July tenth and July third?"

"July third, night before the fireworks, I know I was at the Rose Tavern. July tenth, I was at the store doing inventory."

"Were you alone or with your employees?"

"Alone."

"Do you have security footage?"

"Yes."

"We will need that. I will send an officer over to get it now. Can you text one of your employees and let them know to have it ready?"

"Um, sure. I can text Emmy."

I pull my phone out and send Emmy a text, hoping she's still at the store. I type slowly as I question the other dates. What does it have to do with Evie?

Think faster, Kade.

Wait! These can't be the dates of the unsolved murders, can they?

Before I set my phone down, I quickly google *July 3, Clear River, Oregon.* I give a quick glance at Henricks; his eyes are focused on the mirror. I casually gaze down at my phone; an article comes up about a Clear River woman murdered with no leads. I quickly shove my phone back into my pocket. My heart is thumping so loud I swear it's going to leap out of my chest and land on the floor.

The other dead girls.

No, I can't be a suspect for those murders too. I understand why I look guilty because of Evie, but these? No fucking way. I need to shut my mouth.

"I would like to call my lawyer if you have any further questions. I know what you're insinuating, and I had nothing to do with this. With any of this. You've got the wrong guy, man."

"Sure, we just want to rule you out. If you wouldn't mind sitting still for a bit while we check that footage and a few other things. You can call your lawyer if you'd like. I don't have any further questions right now."

"Whatever, sure." I don't have anything to hide.

The detective gets up to leave the room as my phone vibrates.

"It's Emmy. She says your guys are at the store, grabbing the footage."

"OK, we will know soon," Henricks responds and exits the room.

An hour passes by as I try to remain calm and collected, knowing darn well they're watching me. They want to see me panic, but I'm not going to give them the satisfaction.

Detective Clemens and Henricks enter the room. "Looks like you're free to go, luckily your stories check out for those dates." Detective Clemens says, almost disappointed.

My stomach churns. Thank God.

"Do you need a ride back to work?"

"No, I'll find my own ride," I say.

"Oh, and, Mr. Kinzinger, please don't leave town. We will have some follow-up questions. And if anything comes flooding back to your memory, something you forgot, please call," he says, giving me an icy glare.

I reciprocate his stare and add a cocky smirk. "Yep, Detective. If I think of anything that will implicate me, don't worry, you'll be the first people I call." I get up, slamming the chair under the table. "Assholes," I say under my breath.

* * *

Ben is waiting for me when I get outside the police station. Right now, I'm glad I didn't leave the group. I would have no one to call but my employees and they wouldn't have the resources to help me right now.

Ben confidently strolls up to me and pats me on the back. "Max came to the club and told me what happened. I told him to go home because there wasn't much he could do. I sure hope you didn't say anything that could get you in trouble. I know how you can run your mouth sometimes."

"They just had questions about that girl's death. Evie Simmons. I fucked her that night, but then I left. She was alive when I left, in case you were wondering." I leave out the part about the other girls. It seems moot now.

"Oh, buddy, I believe you. Someone killed her, and it seems that you're the only lead. They would have arrested you already if they had anything on you. I will call my lawyer and get him on a retainer in case they pick you up again. If you really didn't have anything to do with her death, then you should have nothing to worry about."

"I fucking didn't have anything to do with her death, Ben."

"Yeah, yeah buddy. I believe you," Ben says, squeezing my shoulder.

"Ben, you know I can't afford your lawyer."

"Hey, let's not talk about that now. I got your back, but you will need to have mine if the time ever comes."

My stomach plummets as the gravity of his words hit home. But I have no choice.

"I understand, Ben."

CHAPTER TWENTY-TWO

Max
Saturday, September 25, 9:55 p.m.

I'm back at the club. Since Wednesday, I've been tossing and turning about what Ben said in our one-on-one, and I'm pretty sure he's just trying to help with Jovie and he was generalizing with Chrissy. I want to believe Ben is good. I mean, look he helped Kade without a second thought the other day.

When I found Ben at the club on Thursday, he was very calm and knew exactly what to do. Just as Kade said he would. I asked him if I needed to come up with bail money or a lawyer, but Ben said he would handle it. I was relieved. I didn't want to step foot inside the police station. Kade trusted him in that moment of crisis, so I think I owe a little blind faith to Ben and his club.

Jovie missed another Friday, so my organic opportunity has evaporated, leaving me little hope. So, I'm going to trust that Ben knows what's good for me. If he says I'm not ready for her yet, I will trust him. I want to be the best version of myself for her. I didn't create a 'real' profile. I don't see the importance yet. Ben hasn't followed up with me, so I'm going to see how long I can let that slide. I need a break from that stressful environment of fake people.

Kade walks into the club. This is the first time I've laid eyes on him since he walked away with the detectives. He texted Thursday evening saying he was let go but that he needed some time to regroup and I should get his shifts covered for the rest of the week. He'd be back on Sunday. With Kade taking some time off, Emmy and I didn't overlap shifts; not once. I was relieved it worked out that way because she'd have so many questions and I'm not sure how to answer. Emmy said the police wanted footage of Kade at the store.

He must be innocent if the cops didn't keep him, right?

Kade hastily walks to the bar and pours himself a drink. His gruff appearance is unsettling with his five o'clock shadow. His shaggy hair is wild, hanging over his sunken and tired eyes. He's crossed the line of attractive and went straight to messy. He leans his back against the bar, his arms crossed over his chest, only moving to bring his glass to his mouth. He's created an uninviting stance, and it appears to be working. Everyone is leaving him alone, including me.

I do a quick head count, and all ten of us are here again. Even pale Hudson, but he does have a little bit of color back today. Less white, more pinkish-red in his cheeks. His jet-black curly hair is still a disheveled mess with the same straggler hanging over his eye. There is very little chatter; no one is playing the games or watching the TV. Only a couple guys have touched the food, and no one besides Kade has a drink. I want to sneak some of the nachos but for some reason I feel that I need to be invited to have some. I don't want to be rude.

Ben's door squeaks, alerting us of his arrival. Everyone, including Kade, quickly gathers to the center of the room. The energy shifts drastically when Ben appears. Smiles begin to form across the faces of the men around me. Owen lets out a holler with Bobby, Jordan, and Decklan quickly joining in. The other newbies, minus Hudson, eagerly look around for approval to join the hoopla. I bet Ben loves this. We begin to cheer and clap.

Ben takes his place in front of the crowd. "Wow, thank you, guys, that was such a warm welcome. I'm so happy to see everyone here tonight. You have no idea how much this club and these meetings are going to change your life. I promise that each week we will do the work and we will make you all better! I hope you can feel the energy of this club. It should inspire you. It's going to be a great night for all of us! I promise."

I can't help but smile, and a tingle of excitement begins to stir inside of me. I glance over at Kade, who's standing on the outside of the group, arms still folded tightly across his chest. I can't let Kade get me down. Not tonight.

"I enjoyed all of our one-on-one sessions, and I found out a lot about our new recruits. We are all going to get along just great, and I'm now more excited to announce the big surprise. Everything I learned about the new guys confirmed my idea and how much you will all enjoy it. I'm stoked to have you all here, joining me on your new journey. This is truly going to be amazing."

"So, what is it? What's the surprise?" Owen asks.

"My eager Owen. Patience, my dear friend," Ben says in a soothing voice.

"Come on, tell us!" Jordan begs, a sly grin sweeping across his face.

"Fine, fine, you twisted my arm." A smile begins to tug at the corners of Ben's mouth. "A game."

He pauses, taking a deep breath, leaving us in suspense.

"I love a good game, that primal need to win. Every man craves to be the best. Who doesn't love a game?" he asks.

I catch a glimpse of Hudson taking a shy step backward, his gaze at his feet. This is not sitting right with him. Jordan, his brother has an eagerness about him. I never paid too much attention to him, but I can't help but notice how much his appearance resembles Ben's. Not his looks, but his style choices. I guess he wants to dress the part—fake it until you become it, right? My Birkenstock clogs and basic long-sleeved Woodstock peace-love-and-music T-shirt doesn't scream confidence, but I like my style. It's who I am. I don't want to dress like Jordan, successful or not.

"You might all think you're fine being mediocre. Jerking off to porn to avoid the real thing, playing video games to suppress your violent nature, avoiding conversations that make you uncomfortable, or just simply skating through life. But there is more that you want to feel. I will tap into that feeling. You will become addicted to that sensation. It will be the rush you never thought you needed. Last week, one of you asked about my phrase on the wall. *Noli pugnare daemonibus tuis, amplectere eos.* Well, it means, don't fight your demons, embrace them. This game is a play on that phrase. Please stick with me while I explain." Ben takes another long, deep, controlled inhale and a long, mindful exhale, once again leaving us hanging.

"So, your demons and malfunctions are as much a part of you as anything else. These are the hot issues that drive you away from happiness. But they shouldn't; they are a part of you. You should embrace them without letting them ruin you. There is a place for all your vices if you find a sliver of enjoyment from them. People, society, women; they make you feel bad and tell you that there is something wrong with you, but I'm here to tell you that's not the case. I'm here to tell you to stop lying to yourself and lie to everyone else. You will be assigned a weekly task to test your ability to lie to others, to fake it until you become everything you should be for yourself to succeed and find happiness."

Ben walks over to a chalkboard on wheels, blank side facing us, and pulls it forward toward the group. He dramatically flips the board over, and on this side is written:

THE LIARS' CLUB
RULES TO THE GAME

1. Create a fake profile (liars) on Socialite.
(Use your real name and photo but that is it.)
Everything else is a lie. Get the attention of
your target. Slide into her DM's.
2.
3.
4.
5.

"Tonight, as you leave, I'm going to pass out an envelope with your target." Ben continues. "I want you all to create a new Socialite account. Use your real name and photo but everything else will be a lie, and don't be afraid to have a little fun with it. Once you feel satisfied with your account, reach out to your target. Make sure you catch her attention—keep her hooked guys. If you fail at this task, you won't be able to move on to the next one and you will be out of the game.

"What's the incentive to play?" Ezra asks.

"Ezra, please, this is not the time to ask that. Just play and see."

My brow raises in suspicion. I don't want to play a game, especially one that has to do with Socialite.

"Before I hand out your envelopes, we need to discuss something serious. As most of you heard by now, our fellow brother, Kade, was questioned about the murder of Evie Simmons that happened one week ago tonight. We know our brother Kade would never do something like this."

The older members nod in agreement. The newer members, who haven't seen Kade in the best light yet, so they have no reason to trust his innocence, shuffle awkwardly in place. Jordan slides over to Kade and rests his hand on his back. "It's all going to be OK. I trust you had nothing to do with this."

Bobby, Decklan, Owen, and even Ethan, Ezra, and Mateo crowd around Kade, offering positive appeals. I know Kade doesn't like the attention, so I hang back. Hudson is the only other one who doesn't come forward.

"We will do everything we can to prove Kade's innocence if it comes to it. Luckily, they don't have anything concrete on him. But if anything changes, we will be prepared. Kade, my brother, I need your head clear for the game. This will be a good distraction for you. I think you may get the most enjoyment out of it."

"About that," Bobby pipes up. "Well, shouldn't Kade be lying low? You know, so it doesn't look like he didn't care about that girl. I mean, we all know how Kade operates—he moves on faster than a bullet."

"I understand what you're asking, but it would be out of Kade's character if he didn't move on to another girl. It's what Kade does. I honestly don't think Kade has anything to worry about with that girl. It will be yesterday's news."

"A beautiful young girl is dead. I doubt this will hardly disappear!" I jump in. "I think Kade needs to watch his back until they catch the real killer because right now, he's suspect number one."

Kade's eyes meet mine, giving me a thoughtful nod.

"I understand everyone's concern, but trust me, I know what is good for Kade and this situation. OK, guys? Kade will be

OK. So, I'm ready to get back to our little game," Bens says, cupping his hands together. "All I need by next Saturday is a trail of messages proving you're on the right path. One-on-ones will continue on Wednesday for the newbies. I want to track your progress, so please have something started with your target."

Ben pulls ten tiny little red envelopes from his back pocket. "Please don't share your target with your brothers. After all, this is still a game, and you want to win, don't you?"

Ben places the red item in my hand. I carefully open my envelope, unsure what to expect.

*Ivy Peterson – Don't forget I know what
happened that night with Chrissy. Play
the game and your secret will be safe.*

CHAPTER TWENTY-THREE

Hudson
Saturday, September 25, 10:30 p.m.

I want to vomit each time Ben opens his mouth. The very sight of the man makes me sick. My body shrinks into itself each time he steps even an inch closer to me—a visceral reaction.

I know only one person in this room knows what I've done, and it's probably my overactive imagination, but I swear every single guy in this room is looking at me and judging me. Would they have done what Ben asked me to do? Am I just too weak? I guess I deserve the stares and judgment if it's not all in my head. I did something so horrible that I can't ever forgive myself.

I know that I'm not imagining my brother giving me the death stare right now. I catch a glimpse of Jordan out of the corner of my eye. I try not to make eye contact. His glare is shooting directly toward me like little laser beams. Jordan knows I'm not paying attention and his nonverbal cues are shouting, "Pay attention, Hudson. Don't fucking act like this." Jordan is right and I need to act the part, so I don't get called out. That Max guy sure got on Ben's bad side the first night when he talked back to him. I thought it was funny—I seriously thought I was going to keel over from shock when he asked him about his malfunction. Maybe Max is someone I should befriend. He might be just the person I need on my side.

I can't help but wonder if Jordan has been asked to do something for Ben before. Something unforgivable. He's not said anything, but Ben said everyone would have a special task. No one looks like how I feel inside right now, so I doubt their time has come yet. So why me and why so soon? I just met the guy, but he already knows so much about me. Did my brother sell me out? I doubt it because Ben knew things that I have never even told my brother.

I can never forgive myself for what Ben made me do. All I can hope is that I never get found out. The only way to do that is to keep coming here and keep my secrets safe with Ben and this club. At my one-on-one, Ben promised that everything would be OK and that he had everything worked out, but how could he?

Either way, I know very well what would happen to me and Jordan if I never came back. Ben made sure of that.

A mere week ago, my life was normal. Well, maybe not normal but simple. I honestly didn't have much going for me. A twenty-eight-year-old slacker who skated through life primarily undetected by the opposite sex. Except for that fling with Nadia, that shouldn't have happened, but it did. No real goals or ambitions. I lived in my brother's shadow, that is, until his world fell apart, and now my parents look at us with the same sorrowful shame. There is sadness there. We both failed them.

I glance over to Jordan, who is still occasionally giving me a look to ensure I'm engaging, otherwise, he will wrestle me to the ground like he did when we were kids. He was always stronger than me.

I'm mad at him, but he doesn't know it. He brought me here to suffer and I can't even tell him that. He has no idea.

Saturday night, exactly one week ago, was the night everything changed. Jordan literally broke into my house. I was sleeping, and I missed his several phone calls and text messages. He was frantic and scared as he shook me awake. I've barely seen him over the past year—he's been so distant—so I was shocked to see him standing over me.

I remember I went to bed early that night because I had nothing else to do. I seriously went to sleep out of boredom. If Jordan hadn't broken my damn window and first begged me, then bribed me to come, I'd have never known about this club. He seriously offered me a thousand dollars that I wasn't even sure he had at the time—turns out, he did—but he bribed me to come, so I knew it must have been serious. He simply told me he needed someone for a meeting that he'd been going to. At the time, I didn't understand what was so important that it was worth breaking my window, pulling me out of bed, and paying me one thousand dollars, but I caved, and now I wish I hadn't. The look of desperation in his eyes should have been a red flag that this wasn't going to be OK. Jordan was in trouble, just as Kade would have been had Max not shown up. Thinking about it, Kade looked stunned to see Max that night. I feel there is a piece of the story missing with that one. I wonder if anyone else caught on to that.

Jordan gives me the look again, and I realize I really haven't been paying attention to the room, but Ben has given us our first club assignment. I quickly read the board to catch up.

Ben places a tiny red envelope in my hand. I don't smile or meet his eyes. I know this is no good. He gave me a similar red envelope last Saturday with my instructions for my task. I'd got a text on my way home. It was from an unknown number, but I knew it was Ben. He needed a favor, so I turned around and came back. Biggest mistake of my life.

I look around the room, everyone has theirs open. Max has a flat, unreadable expression, but no one else seems to be freaking out by what's written on theirs, so I quickly open mine. I feel somewhat relieved when I see a name. A simple name of a girl I'm supposed to find on Socialite and befriend. OK. I can do that. I already updated my profile, and my pic is an older one of me back when I cared more about my looks. In my early twenties, I was much better looking, and in a lot better shape. Ben also said I should work on that. Fuck this guy.

Ben rudely interrupts my thoughts. "Points will be rewarded as I see fit. If you don't comply by next Saturday, you will. . . Let's just say, it won't be good, so please do this simple task. Now that we've got the business part out of the way, why don't we spend the rest of the time getting to know one another? Remember what happens in the club, stays in the club."

Almost everyone takes off toward Kade, the sullen member of the group. The one who's been scorched.

He looks like a murderer if you ask me.

CHAPTER TWENTY-FOUR

Kade
Saturday, September 25, 10:36 p.m.

Everyone is wondering whether I did it. Did I fucking kill Evie Simmons? Did I slice her throat and leave her for dead like some kind of roadkill? I would like to think the original members know me better than that, but I can't be sure. And the new members have no reason to trust me.

I bet half are thinking, *Yes, that son of a bitch did it*, and the other half isn't sure. Even Max looks at me differently, and I've known him the longest. Max saw how I reacted when Teddy told us about Evie, but he hasn't brought that up. He was also there the day the two detectives picked me up for questioning. Emmy is probably scared of me too, even though she comes across as sincere and worried. No matter what happens, my name will always be associated with Evie Simmons. The beautiful slut who ruined my life.

Is Ben out of his fucking mind, asking me to try and get a girl on Socialite? But the almighty Ben has spoken, and what he wants, he wants, and I can't argue with the man who will help me prove my innocence. The man who is going to front my legal bill if things go south.

Fuck, fuck, fuck. This is not how I saw my life going.

Maybe I should run away.

No. That makes me look guilty.

I'm so screwed.

Ben's envelope is safely in my pocket. I need to play the game. Ben says so.

He dismisses the meeting and allows for social mingling.

Everyone begins to lunge at me, like I'm a freak show they want to prod and poke at. They want to see what I will say and do. They want to observe me, ask me questions, and offer their unsolicited advice.

I can't take it, not today. I catch Ben's attention, giving him an annoyed grin. He nods in understanding. I take off for the door and don't look back at what I know will be disappointed faces.

CHAPTER TWENTY-FIVE

Max
Saturday, September 25th, 11:30 p.m.

Back at my apartment, I feel like I can finally breathe. It's like I've been holding my breath since I opened that little red envelope.

I slip my bag off my shoulder, letting it crash to the floor, and dizzily walk down the hallway, tossing my keys to the table, but hear them jingle as they miss. I spot Bong Marley at the end of the table and swiftly grab it on my way. I need this.

Chrissy. . . There is no fucking way he really knows.

Don't forget I know what happened that night with Chrissy. Play the game and your secret will be safe.

The past few days I thought he was generalizing about our relationship ending, but this is too specific. He must know something. Could he know everything? No—there is no way.

Every part of me is vibrating with anxiety and stress. I need to relax. I need to calm down.

I take my lighter from my pocket and light the sticky goodness, and instantly the earthy aroma begins to fill the air. The bowl of cannabis cherries, and I hear the water bubble as I take a deep suck of the chamber, filling it with smoke. It's a soothing sound. I pull the stem out and take a deep, long inhale. I blow the smoke out of my lungs a little too soon, and along with it, an irritated, raspy cough. I repeat the process again, only coughing less this time.

I feel the effects already working through my body, calming me, but not clearing my mind.

How does he know?

What does he know?

All I do know is that if I don't play the game, my secret could be released into the world.

I plop down on the couch. My head is feeling heavy, but the good kind of heavy. The right amount of indica mixed with a dash of sativa for stimulation. I'm looking to be couch-locked, but still semi-productive. My worries begin to release, and my shoulders start relaxing before I decide to pick up my phone. I only have one week to complete the first task of the game.

I reach for the envelope and read the name several times before comprehending, the fuzziness already setting in from the weed.

"Miss Ivy Peterson. Who are you?"

I didn't even know about Socialite before this month started and now my whole life seems to revolve around it. I reluctantly open the app and begin to create a new profile. I pick one of the few photos I have of myself, which is an old one taken over three years ago at my friend's—well, not friend anymore—wedding. I'm in a gray suit and my hair looks good and styled nicely. It's not a true representation of my current looks, but a much more attractive Max.

Mission one accomplished.

Ok mission two. My age. I lie. I say I'm 26; for some reason it seems more appealing.

Mission three. The hard one. The about-me section. I can't say the truth here. No one would friend me if I did. *Twenty-eight-year-old record store employee who rents his apartment and has about one and a half friends and zero social life.* Instead, I opt for a more enticing lie. Plus, Ben told us to lie. It's easier to do so when you're given permission. I can't help but feel a little slimy, but Ben will know. I'm sure he's keeping tabs on all of our accounts. Christ, he knew what I was doing before I even met him.

I start typing:

Hello, I'm Max [The little wave emoji to seem approachable]. I'm a music-loving, book-reading kind of guy.

I backtrack and take out the book-reading part. I don't want to seem like a loner. I need to sound more appealing and less intellectual. Perhaps something more superficial will work.

Concert-going, coffee addict, craft beer connoisseur, and above all, life-of-the-party kinda guy. I'm always down for a good time.

I feel satisfied and I can't think of much more to add to my already overwhelming set of lies. I can't believe I'm doing this. I hit "Submit" and publish the profile.

My stomach gurgles. The munchies have officially crept in. I'm immediately craving a cheeseburger. I'm too fucked up to drive, and the convenience of ordering food from one of those stupid food service apps seems like a likely option, but I can't. I'm not that guy. I don't use these stupid apps to order food, meet girls and friends. I'm Max Jennings, the guy who hates technology but who's been forced into this world by Ben, the club, and society.

No, I won't give in to this one. I'm the guy who has no problem getting my own food and avoiding these apps that make people lazy and, ironically, antisocial. But I'm starving and I want food now. I could order pizza the old-fashioned way like a normal kid of the nineties. Call it in and have it delivered.

I place calls to three different pizza places and the first two simply keep ringing. On the third one, I finally get a person.

"Hi, I'd like to place an order for delivery."

"Oh, I'm sorry. You have to place the order through one of the food-delivery apps. We don't have delivery drivers anymore."

"That's stupid." The rude words slip across my tongue. I hang up the phone in defeat. This world is changing too fast—I can't even order pizza anymore without using an app.

An app for dating, an app for friends, an app for food, an app for a driver, an app for groceries. We can't do anything for ourselves anymore. What the fuck happened to us as a society? I sulk to my bedroom and forget about the food and looking up Ivy Peterson.

* * *

The next morning, I wake up with a bad feeling looming over me.

Oh crap, I forgot to look up Ivy. I had one task last night, and I forgot to do it. I now have one less day to lay the groundwork. What if my profile isn't good enough for her attention? What if she doesn't accept my friend request? I quickly run my hands through my blankets to try to locate my phone, barely remembering the moments leading up to my crashing out here. I was pretty high last night.

My stomach grumbles again. That's right, I didn't get any food last night either. I must seek out some breakfast, but first, Ivy. I need to see who I'm dealing with here. My fingers finally stumble upon my phone that's hiding between two blankets. Once I retrieve it, I open the app and type in *Ivy Peterson* and narrow the search to Clear River, Oregon. The first result is the only one from Clear River, so she must be my target. I click the little circle with her image.

Ivy Peterson is a beautiful girl with long, wavy, blonde hair. She reminds me of a surfer girl. She has that laid-back vibe going on, that I'm-too-cool-for-you grin. I quickly scroll through her other photos. One shows her flipping the peace sign, and in another one she's flipping the bird. She's always in the middle of her friends in group photos and she's much prettier than all of them. Maybe she surrounds herself with uglier people so she is prettier by comparison. If I'm assessing her correctly, she's shallow and curating an image for social media—just a typical girl, these days.

Why her, Ben?

I head back to her feed.

Age: 26

About Me: I love hiking, biking, and a good challenge. I love my friends more than life itself, and you can usually find me in a local coffee shop consuming copious amounts of this magical brown elixir.

We don't have much in common. Real Max and fake Max both only have coffee consumption and that's hardly a deal maker. I close my eyes and unwillingly press the "Add friend" button.

I flip back over to my profile, noticing I don't have a single friend. No one is going to add someone who doesn't have friends.

I look like a loser. I quickly add to my about-me section. "New account." Hoping that will explain the lack of friends. Ivy can assume that I haven't had time to re-add all my friends from my "old account." I hear of people doing shit like this all the time. The endless chatter I hear at work from customers is enough to drive me mad. But just in case that doesn't work, I quickly try to add about one hundred people or so from the quick-add section. I make sure I don't really know them because, after all, this isn't supposed to show the real me. Now, I have to play the waiting game. Let's see if Ivy bites.

Ben gave her to me for a reason. What reason though, I have no idea. If I could read Ben better, I might not be in this situation right now.

Surprisingly, my phone starts buzzing, and I get a slew of "Your friend request has been accepted" notifications. These poor souls. I don't know a single one of you and you don't really know me, but if you denied my request, you could be denying someone you thought you knew or thought that you might have known from a long time ago and that would be rude. You wouldn't want someone that you haven't seen in ten years to think less of you, now would you? Robots. All fucking robots.

Well, I thank all of you mindless robots and I appreciate your neediness, it's doing me a solid. Helping me look more legit.

I eat some breakfast. Eggs and toast. Nothing special. Then I shower and get ready for work.

I almost forget about my special little friend, Ivy, when my phone tings again on my way to work.

Ivy Peterson accepted your friend request.

CHAPTER TWENTY-SIX

Max
Sunday, September 26, 10:59 a.m.

I switch my phone over to vibrate and open the store for my shift. I'm surprised to see Emmy this morning as I flip the sign over to open. She shuffles over to the register, barely picking up her feet.

"Did Kade call you in?" I ask her as she clocks in on the register.

"Yep. He sent me a text last night, so I don't think he'll be here for paperwork today either," she responds.

She is silent for a moment. But Emmy doesn't know the meaning of silence. The girl always has something to say. She inches closer to me like she's about to tell me a secret. I can feel her desperation in the air. Finally, she cracks.

"Seriously, Max, I don't think Kade could kill a woman, but why haven't they found a second suspect? I feel like Kade is the only person they're looking at, and it's causing me to wonder. I don't want to be that person who doubts him, but it's not looking good for him. I see all the stuff online and it's terrible. Everyone in town thinks he's guilty."

"People feel safer having someone to blame, and right now, that person is Kade. The police wouldn't have let him go if they had anything on him."

"I know. It's just hard to look past all the negative stuff."

"Em, are you afraid of Kade?" I have to ask. I have to protect Emmy, even if I don't doubt Kade's innocence.

"No, I don't think Kade would hurt me, even if he is capable of what they say he did." Her voice is quivering.

I give Emmy a nudge. "You know you can always call me if you're ever scared. Just get out of the situation, even if that means just leaving work and going somewhere safe. I don't think Kade would ever hurt you either, but just stay aware of your surroundings at all times. I worry about you, and I would just die if anything ever happened to you."

"Oh, Max, you are just the sweetest. Thanks for always caring so much." Emmy turns her body into mine and reaches up on her tiptoes to hug me. The hug lingers longer than it should have, or perhaps it's all in my head. The intoxicating scent of her shampoo wafts into my nose. She smells like coconut. I feel myself getting aroused, and luckily, Emmy is already backing away. She gives me a light punch in the arm. "OK, enough sappy shit. Let's get working." She smiles and trots off to the stockroom.

I turn back to the store area, but my mouth drops when the front door slowly opens.

It's Hudson.

I'm stunned to see him outside of the club. What is he doing here? Does he realize this is where Kade and I work?

He looks cautiously around the store before clocking me at the counter. "Max, I was hoping to find you here. Is Kade here too?"

I expect he's hoping that I say no. His eyes ping on every corner of the store while nervously awaiting my response.

"No, it's just my coworker and me. Why? Are you looking for him?"

"No, I'm here for you," Hudson says, brushing his straggler curl out of his eye—I'm amazed because it actually stays in place. This is the first time I've really looked at him for more than just a couple of quick glances. He's actually a decent-looking guy. Maybe if he saw the sun a little more, he would be less ghostly looking, but the potential is there. But who am I to talk? I do see more of the resemblance to his brother now, though. Jordan is a handsome guy. Maybe even on Kade's level.

"OK. What's up?" I question.

"I was, um, hoping we could talk," he mumbles, his head bowing toward the ground.

I don't want to do anything to get in trouble with Ben. I can't afford a misstep with my secret looming over me. But I can't help but wonder why Hudson wants to talk to me, of all people.

He raises his eyes to meet mine.

He takes a deep breath as if he's mustering up the courage to speak again, and then he finally continues, "Max, I . . ." He pauses mid-sentence.

Oh, my gosh, spit it out. I'm dying to hear what he has to say.

Emmy appears next to me at the counter. His eyes dart toward her. He freezes for a brief second before spinning around and heading toward the exit. "Never mind, dude. I got to go. Bad idea," he shouts as he frantically rushes out of the building. "Bad idea. Just forget I was here."

Something has spooked him. Was it Emmy?

Hudson wanted to tell me something, but what could it have been? If it is club related, he has his brother to talk to, but perhaps he feels he can't trust his brother and he thought he could trust me for some reason?

Emmy and I stand facing the window and watch Hudson run down the street. He's not paying attention to where he's going and he's mumbling to himself. He slams right into a lady walking her dog. He appears to apologize, then takes off at a sprint, crossing the street and disappearing out of our sight.

"Max, what did that guy want? Strange fella."

I think on my feet. "He was asking if we had any first edition Pink Floyd albums. I guess he changed his mind. Probably too expensive."

"Oh." is all Emmy says before heading back to the stockroom.

* * *

It's been an eventful day, not including Hudson's unusual encounter. I've also been feeling the vibrations of my phone against my leg for the last hour, but I've been too busy to check. I'm dying to sneak away and see if any of them are Ivy.

"Hey, do you have any more of these in the back? I need two copies," a customer shouts from the aisle of new records.

"I'll go check," I say.

I already know that I don't have any more in the back, but I take the welcome chance to sneak away for a quick second. Emmy's ringing a line up at the register, so I know I need to hurry back. I step off the sales floor and into the stockroom. I first take a sip of my coffee and then pull out my phone. I have a few notifications from Socialite. Three of them are from Ivy Peterson.

Ivy: Hey, cute pic. Thanks for the add!

Ivy: Do I know you?

Ivy: You look familiar.

Ok. I'm in the game. Now I have a chance. I want to start typing back, but I'm not sure what to say. I've never done this before, but I need to keep her on the hook.

I can do this.

I respond to Ivy with a smiley-face emoji first, in response to the cute pic.

Then I continue my response with a lie.

Max: *Your profile popped up in my people*
I might know. I thought you looked familiar,
and if we don't know each other, I think you
are pretty, and I'd like to get to know you.

That sounds so corny, and immediately I look to see if it can be unsent, but three little green dots begin to flash on the screen. She's typing. It's too late.

Ivy: *Did you go to Green Lakes High School?*
Maybe that's why you look familiar.

Max: *Nope, that's not it.*

Ivy: *Have we met at one of Leah Murphy's parties?*

Max: *Shoot, I don't know her, so that's not it.*

Ivy: *Oh. . . .Well, maybe you just have*
one of those faces.

Max: *I've been told that before. Well either way,*
it's nice to meet you.

Ivy: *Nice to meet you too. So, Max, what are*
you into? Do we have anything in common
now that I've worked my way into your DMs?

Max: *Well, I'm obsessed with coffee and I'm
a huge movie buff.*

Ivy: *OMG me too. What's your go-to coffee
and your favorite movie?*

Max: *I love a tasty iced mocha, and—don't
laugh—I'm a sucker for anything Adam Sandler.*

Ivy: *OMG! Me too! I love 50 First Dates.
It's my favorite.*

Max: *That's a great one.*

Ivy: *Well, Max it was nice to meet you.*

Max: *Nice to meet you too, Ivy.
Have a good day.*

Ivy: *Hey, you too!*

I'm disgusted with how quickly the lies pour out of me. I need
to get back out on the sales floor; that customer is waiting and
Emmy isn't going to be happy I've completely abandoned her.

I slip my phone back into my pocket and can't help but feel like
I'm cheating on Jovie, the girl I would rather be messaging.

Ben told me to be patient. So, I'm going to obey and see what
happens. I'm just playing the game. I can't fuck up.

CHAPTER TWENTY-SEVEN

Hudson
Sunday, September 26, 11:15 a.m.

I panicked when I saw the girl. Her presence ruined my chance to speak to Max, but maybe it's for the best. I knew I shouldn't have sought him out outside the club. What was I thinking?

That girl, though. . .

I've seen her before. That round, chipmunk face and those wide brown eyes. I know her, but where from?

Think, Hudson, think. The bright red lipstick. I can feel the memory on the edge of my conscious, but it's evading me right now. I take a mental screenshot of her features in case it comes back to me later.

Whoever she is, she threw me for a loop, but maybe it's for the best. Ben has a way of finding things out, and I know that all too well. I shouldn't have taken that stupid chance today. If Jordan knew what I did, he would be so mad at me. He has no idea the torment he's caused me by dragging me into this club.

There is a chance that someone is watching my every move right now, and I could already be in trouble with Ben and not even know it yet. But somehow, I don't think Max will call me out. God, I sure hope not. What was I thinking? Kade could've been there, and I for sure would have been in trouble then. I must play it safe from this point on—no more missteps.

CHAPTER TWENTY-EIGHT

Max
Wednesday, September 29, 7:00 p.m.

"Hi, Max. It's good to see you. I'm really looking forward to our one-on-one tonight. I feel we have a lot to catch up on," Ben greets me warmly, not showing an ounce of the man who wrote that red envelope a few nights ago. The man that threatened me. I'm not sure how to play my hand tonight. Do I come in guns a blazing, or do I hang back and let him lead?

I give a dismissive grin and decide to let Ben carry the conversation. I have my guard up and am ready to pounce if necessary.

"Have you made any progress with your target?" Ben presses.

"Why don't you tell me? You always seem to be one step ahead, so I'm sure you already know." My response comes out snarkier than I intend.

Ben's eyes drop, appearing hurt by my accusation. His perfectly groomed face has genuine pain upon it. "Whoa, Max, I'm not your enemy here. I want to help you. I sincerely do. Why can't you see that? Everything we are doing is for your own good. Don't you want to talk to Jovie? Here is your chance to practice. You need the control back in your life, and I'm here to assist you with that."

"Sure, I guess, but why the game?" I ask, tossing my hands up in the air.

"Why not?" Ben responds smugly.

He doesn't like being questioned, and something tells me the other members don't question him much.

For some reason, I feel the need to push back—to prove that I'm not a coward. I wasn't always like this. Before Chrissy, I would like to remember that I was stronger and more assertive. She's the one that whittled away at my self-esteem until it vaporized. Around Ben, I feel some of my old self materializing. Perhaps his methods are working, weaving their way through my subconscious.

I don't respond. Instead, I sit back in my chair with my arms folded across my chest.

"Max, men are wired a certain way. We have a primal need to win—survival of the fittest. It dates back to Darwin's theory of evolution. What guy doesn't like a little competition? So, I ask again, why not?"

"Maybe I'm the odd guy out, because I don't think I'm wired that way. I'm lazy and have no desire to be first. It's as simple as that," I respond.

"That's where you are wrong. You tell yourself that; you put little effort into your appearance, your job, your dating life, and the list probably goes on. Why, though? I'll tell you. You would rather set low expectations, so you don't have to win. You tell yourself that it's OK to come in last place, so you don't feel bad when you do. Max, look at your life. You don't date because you are afraid to get rejected. You've set your own life up for failure."

"Wow, thanks for the psychoanalysis, Doc, but I'm fine with my life as it is," I lie. Of course, it would be nice to be a winner. But

I have my reasons for behaving the way I do, and those reasons are not for Ben Matthews to find out.

"If you truly believed that, then why are you coming here?"

"Because you're blackmailing me." The words slip out of my mouth.

"Well, that simply isn't true, Max. I'm just reminding you of your past and who you were." Ben says.

"You have a fucked up way of helping."

Ben ignores my response. "That should get you excited for the new you. That's all. Now, can you please just trust me and trust that the work we are doing will benefit you? You really have nothing to lose."

"Whatever."

"Max, we are going to drop this conversation and move on. I need to know how you're doing with your target."

"Fine," I say. I'm exhausted with this back-and-forth. I whip out my phone and pass it over to Ben. "I've been chatting with Ivy."

"Nice," Ben says as he scrolls through our messages. "It seems she's taken a liking to you. This is wonderful news."

"She's so superficial. It's easy to pretend because I don't have any feelings for this girl. I mean, how could I? She's everything that I hate about people of my generation."

Ben's familiar, smug grin spreads across his face, and he responds, "That's perfect, Max. The more detached, the better for part two. I'm so happy to hear you say that."

"What's the second task?" I ask, afraid to hear the answer.

"Patience—you will find out with everyone else on Saturday. Now, I want to talk more about your relationship with Chrissy. I know this is a sore subject for you, but we need to get to the bottom of things so you can heal and move on. It's all part of the process. *Coward* is your trigger word. Why?"

Are you kidding me? What is with this guy?

"I told you last time she wanted me to stand up for her more. Why are you asking me about this? You already know what happened." If Ben wants to push my buttons, I'll do the same to him, see if he will release any more information.

"I don't know the whole story, Max. I don't know *your* story. Plus, this isn't for me. This is for you to work out. I'm simply a vessel that is here to guide you on your healing journey. You need to say the words, and you need to work through the issues. Otherwise, you will never be able to move on."

I check the time on the large clock on the wall. "It looks like our time is up. Maybe we can crack this one open next time."

Ben appears drained. I've frustrated him and he knows I'm not going to give him any more tonight. He huffs out a quick breath. "OK, Max, but I need you to keep up your conversation with Ivy. Can you do that for me?"

"Yes, it should be easy."

"Good. I will see you on Saturday. You are good to go."

"Yep, Saturday," I respond, leaping off the stool, hoping I have time to catch Hudson in the parking lot. I want to confront him about his visit on Sunday.

I make a mad rush for the door, but I stop in my tracks when I hear Ben's hushed voice behind me. He's walking down the hallway, his phone pressed to his ear. "Hi, it's me. I need you to check on my pet tonight."

Strange. I don't peg Ben as someone who would have an animal. Definitely not something fluffy. Maybe a snake.

Once I'm out the door, I take off in a sprint until I'm in the parking lot. I spot Hudson sitting in his car, exactly where I hoped he'd be. I watch him cautiously, careful not to spook him. I slowly walk up to his passenger-side door and tug the handle. It opens, and I slide into his car.

"Fuck, Max! You scared me shitless!" Hudson screams.

"A lot of good that's going to do now." I give an uncomfortable laugh.

"Sorry, bud, I didn't mean to scare you. I didn't want to make a scene in case anyone is watching." I laugh.

Hudson nods.

"Why did you come by the store Sunday?"

Hudson shifts uncomfortably in his seat, tugging on his seatbelt a few times before releasing it. "I don't know."

"Yes, you do. It wasn't a social call, that's for sure. You went there for a reason. I need to know why."

Hudson doesn't respond. Instead, he plays with the controls on his dashboard.

"Why?" I ask again.

"I'm scared."

"Why, Hudson? You have about thirty seconds before you need to get inside. Quit fucking around. What is going on?"

"I'm sorry. I want to tell you, but I can't. You need to get out of my car. I've got to get inside. Please just go. Sorry I bothered you."

He turns to get out of the car. I reach for his arm, locking my hand around his wrist. "Hudson, what has you so scared?"

"Please, Max, just let it go. I'm going to be late. Please get out of my car."

If Hudson is ever going to share why he came to speak to me, it's not going to be now. I let go of my grip, and Hudson doesn't waste any time exiting the car. I get out, he locks it and swiftly walks toward the club entrance, leaving me standing in the gloom of the empty parking lot.

What are you afraid of, Hudson?

CHAPTER TWENTY-NINE

Kade
Wednesday, September 29, 10:00 p.m.

I should be playing it safe, but I can't. I have a demon that needs tending. Otherwise, I might erupt and that's a risk I can't take. The poor recipients of the other side of my fist on many nights long ago would agree.

But that was my past.

I'm better now, but without proper nursing, my urge could change form, and that's even worse.

Tension is constantly brewing and making its way throughout my body to the point where my fingertips tingle. I had to get out tonight. I had to get back into my routine. It's for my own good. With everything going on with this Evie situation, I feel the anger inside of me rising and I will explode if I don't get back into my routine. I can't stay home another night. Drinking alone. I need company.

Each day that my innocence hangs in the balance is a day that I can't let myself get out of control. The walls are closing in and

I know they're watching me. Each time I see a cop car, I know they're waiting for me to screw up so they can take me down. Good luck, fuckers.

I can't help myself, though. I'm at the Rose Tavern, back where it all started less than two weeks ago. People want me to react a certain way, but I'm not capable of that.

I take a seat near the end of the bar. Mark spots me immediately. He puts a finger in the air indicating just a second. He doesn't seem to be bothered by my presence, which is a good sign.

He takes his bar towel and tosses it behind the counter. He walks around the bar and makes his way over to my side. He comes up right next to me and places a hand on my shoulder. We are so close it's almost intimate. "The cops came sniffing around here. I just want you to know that I didn't say anything that could incriminate you." His look is sincere.

I nod to show my gratitude. "Well, I'm sure you heard by now, they brought me in and questioned me last week. Sure, Evie and I left here together, but I didn't kill her, Mark. Bitch was alive when I left her apartment. Someone else did it after I left."

"I know, buddy, I believe you. I knew you couldn't have harmed that girl, but someone placed her here, and then somehow, your name was involved. They asked me if I remembered you coming in that night. I couldn't lie because you paid your bar tab with your credit card—they would have found out that I lied and that would have been much worse for you in the long run. But I wasn't the one who said you left with her."

"Do you know who did?" I ask

"Nah, bro. I wish I knew," Mark says.

I believe him. Anyone of these townie regulars could have thrown me under the bus.

"Although they asked for camera footage from the nights of

the other murders, and thank God you were here or you might be rotting in a cell, guilty or not."

"Well, thank goodness for my drinking problem." I chuckle.

"Speaking of which, can I get you a drink? On the house," Mark offers.

"No, thanks. I don't think I should stay."

I'm not that dumb to drink here again like a sitting duck. They all have their eyes on me, waiting to call my ass into the cops.

The urge, my demon, is still there. I can't go home. I need to feed the dark side of me. The side I pushed away for so many years distilled into an acute rage. Ben taught me to channel my anger into my other cravings. Like sex. I felt terrible at first, but then I realized the girls were using me just as much as I was using them. For them, it was a self-confidence thing. For me, it was a valve that kept the kettle from blowing up.

I drive to the other side of town and pick a bar that I've never been to. Hopefully, no one recognizes me. I need a quiet night. I need to go undetected. I grab a baseball cap from the back seat and slide it on. I don't need anyone bringing any unwanted attention to me.

My phone vibrates as I take a seat at the bar. Ah, my target is finally playing along. Ben will be pleased.

I respond with a winky emoji and slip my phone back into my pocket. I will play with her later, but right now, I need someone that is real and more than just a screen.

I slide into an open seat near the middle of the bar. I don't like this place, but it will do. The walls are lined with hunting trophies. Once-wild animals stare back at me—judging me. This place gives me the creeps, but it's the best I have right now. I gaze around the bar, searching for someone who has all their teeth, unlike the lady sitting next to me. She hacks each time she takes a drink. She reeks of smoke with a tinge of body odor. Normally I would move seats, but the more I move, the more likely people are to recognize me. I've been on the news, and there is now a Socialite group called "Hang Kade." I'm not the most liked person in town. I guess I can't blame them, I suppose I'd hate me too.

I order a gin and tonic and continue perusing the bar. There is a redhead by the outdated jukebox. Perfect.

I keep my head down and walk up behind her. I peek at her viewing choices. "A5 is a must for this crowd."

She turns around and smiles. "You think this crowd can handle some 'Sweet Caroline' this early in the night?"

Perfect, she doesn't recognize me.

"It's never too early for some classic Neil Diamond," I say with a devilish grin.

She's all too eager to play along. "Well, A5 it is. So, what's your name, good-looking?"

"Would you believe it if I told you my name's Neil?"

"No way, you're too cute to be a Neil, and that's way too much of a coincidence." She giggles. She's already had one drink too many.

"Can I buy you another drink?" I ask, encouraging her to have one more.

"Yes, please. I'll take another one of these yummy, fruity things." She raises her glass as she stumbles toward me. She giggles again, linking her arm with mine as we strut to the bar.

I flag down the bartender. "The lady will have another one of these." The drunk girl raises her glass to remind the bartender of her drink.

He nods and comes back moments later with what appears to be a wine slushie.

We take up residence in a booth, and she slides in next to me. "Neil, don't you want to know my name?" she says as she moves in closer. Her vibrant red locks smell of vanilla.

"Sure, what's your name."

"It's Jessica."

"Hi, Jessica. It's nice to meet you. Are you alone here tonight?"

"Yes, my friends ditched me. They have to work early tomorrow." She pouts.

"Well, that wasn't very nice of them to leave you all alone in a place like this."

"It's OK. I do just fine on my own," Jessica says, seeming pretty proud of herself.

"Yes, my dear. It looks like you are doing just fine."

"Cheers!" she shouts and knocks her glass into mine—most of her wine slushie spills out and lands on the table in front of us.

She laughs again.

Six and a half, but she will do.

I lean in and whisper into her ear, "Hey, you want to get out of here?"

She grabs me by the hand and leads me out of the bar.

CHAPTER THIRTY

Mr. Anonymous: *Hi. You look familiar. Do we know each other?*

[?]: No, I don't think so. I must have one of those faces.

Mr. Anonymous: *You're very pretty.*

[?]: Aww. That's sweet of you to say. Thank you. You're not too bad looking yourself.

Mr. Anonymous: *Thanks. Now that we're chatting. Tell me about yourself. What are you into?*

[?]: Dang, you move fast, Mr. Anonymous. Also, pretty lame handle.

Mr. Anonymous: *No harm in chatting. Is there? And ouch!*

[?]: I suppose not. Well, I'm a Pisces.

Mr. Anonymous: *Is that all you're going to give me to work with here?*

[?]: Let's see what you come up with to that first.

Mr. Anonymous: *Then I guess it's a good thing I'm a Scorpio, so we are already compatible.*

[?]: Well played.

Mr. Anonymous: *I guess we can keep the conversation going now that we've established that.*

[?]: All right, Mr. Scorpio, you win. I'll keep playing along. Hey maybe that should be your handle, Mr. Scorpio. I like that better.

Mr. Anonymous: *Good one. I like it too.*

[?]: ;)

Mr. Scorpio: *I changed my handle. Are you happy?*

[?]: It's an improvement ;)

Mr. Scorpio: *Tell me more about yourself.*
[?]: Now that you've put me on the spot, it's going to be a generic response.

Mr. Scorpio: *That's OK. I can work with generic.*

*[?]: I love being outside. I enjoy a tasty
burger and fries, and I'm into craft beer.
I'm not your typical girly girl.*

Mr. Scorpio: *You sound like my kind of girl.*

[?]: Do I?

Mr. Scorpio: *Yes, this may be presumptuous
of me, but would you want to meet for a drink sometime?*

[?]: Maybe.

Mr. Scorpio: *Oh, you tease. Are you
going to make me beg?*

[?]: Yes.

Mr. Scorpio: *OK, fine. Pretty please.
You can even pick the place.*

[?]: I'll get back to you.

Mr. Scorpio: *So, it's a maybe?*

[?]: Maybe.

CHAPTER THIRTY-ONE

Max
Saturday, October 2, 9:45 p.m.

The full and bright moon illuminates the sky as I pull my car into the furthest parking spot from the building. I check the clock, and it's about a quarter to ten. I give a rapid swivel of my head, eagerly checking both sides of the parking lot. I'm the first one here, as planned. Now I must wait.

"Come on, Hudson, pull in now," I say to myself.

My prayers are answered after just a few minutes. Hudson's black clunker of a car swings into the lot and takes the spot closest to the strip mall. I exit my car and slam the door shut, perhaps a little too hard, and Hudson gives a swift and frightened look in my direction. He sees me approaching. He quickly gathers his belongings, and it appears he's trying to escape his car before I reach him, clearly trying to avoid me now. I pick up my pace, but my plans are annoyingly foiled when I see Kade, and two other vehicles pull into the lot. The other guys are fast, and before I know it, Hudson is already inside, and I'm now walking in with

Kade, Owen, and Mateo. Owen and Mateo are chatting, but I don't pay attention. Kade has been MIA all week and has hardly said two words to me since his questioning. We acknowledge each other's presence but don't say a word. I miss how Kade used to be before I joined the club and before Evie Simmons was killed. He feels like a stranger to me now.

Owen enters the code, and we all file into the club room. Ethan and Ezra are right on our heels, following us inside. Bobby, Decklan, and Hudson are posted up at the table, snacking on the food provided. Hudson shoves a mozzarella stick into his mouth and is conveniently tucked between the other two guys. He appears outwardly normal for someone who just tried to avoid me. I give him an irritated grimace and keep my eye on him from a distance. I want to know what's got him so spooked, but this isn't the place to pry. All eyes are watching, and Hudson won't spill the beans here.

"Fuck, Owen, you won't believe the girl I got hooked. Huge fucking titties," Decklan shouts while cupping his hands out in front of him and giving imaginary breasts a jiggle as he breaks away from the trio at the table.

Fucking animals. I'm repulsed by these guys.

"Hey, fuckheads, didn't Ben say not to talk about your girls?" Kade says, slapping Decklan in the back of the head as he passes by him.

"Ouch." Decklan winces in pain.

Good for you, Kade. Call them out on their wrongdoings.

The door opens again, and Jordan joins the group, and before he can jump in on the guy talk, Ben's voice fills the room. "That's right, Decklan. Listen to Kade. I told you all to keep quiet. We can't have anyone getting the upper hand here now, can we? This part is a hush-hush assignment. Keep your targets to yourself." Ben brings his pointer finger to his lips and gives the shushing sound.

"Sorry, Ben. It won't happen again," Decklan says, hanging his head low, like a little puppy who just got caught peeing on the carpet.

A smirk spreads along my face but I quickly catch myself and shift my expression to a flat smile.

Ben chimes in again with his righteous voice. "All right, men, it's been a productive week. I'm so proud of all of you! All of you showed a vast amount of confidence and have completed your tasks. You all have a target! Good job. For that, I will award each of you ten points." Ben already has our names listed on the blackboard. He writes ten all the way down the line and then stops on Hudson's name. He writes sixty. "Hudson, you get an extra fifty points," Ben says.

Everyone immediately turns their attention to Hudson, who clearly doesn't want their scrutiny or even the extra points, I imagine. His obvious discomfort says it all. He awkwardly crosses his arms and then quickly releases them, dangling them toward the ground. He shifts his eye contact to the far wall avoiding reciprocating any accidental contact.

We all stare back at Ben in confusion. Why does Hudson get more than the rest of us? What did he do that was so great? For some reason, I'm jealous of Hudson. I don't know what caused this feeling. Maybe Ben was right when he said all guys want to win. Crap. I'm drinking the Kool-Aid, and I think it's spiked. But now I'm actually thirsty and could really go for some sort of refreshment. My eyes wander to the table behind us, searching for something to drink. I catch Hudson's eyes in my wandering and can't help but consider if this is why he came to me. Did he want to tell me about his extra points?

"Why does Hudson get an extra fifty points?" Jordan shouts, bringing my attention back to the group. Sibling rivalry is rearing its annoying head.

"He completed his extra-credit task," Ben says matter-of-factly.

"But. . . I. . ." Jordan starts to spit out his rebuttal but Ben cuts him off with a glare.

"It's my game, I can switch it up at any time," Ben adds.

"Extra credit? Hell, can I have extra credit too?" Ezra asks. His boyish good looks make it hard to hate him. He has kind eyes and such a laid-back vibe about him that he probably gets everything handed to him. With Ezra asking a question, it takes the attention off Hudson. But Ben doesn't respond. He simply shakes his head.

I, however, keep my eyes glued on Hudson. I watch as he blows a quick puff of air out, like he's been holding his breath the entire time that all eyes were on him. Like if he didn't breathe, people wouldn't see him. Such an odd guy.

"That's bullshit. Not fair that he already has a leg up on the competition. What counts as extra credit, Ben?" Jordan says, now with spite in his voice.

"Now, Jordan, everyone will have a chance to get extra points when called upon. You just have to wait your turn and do what's asked of you," Ben reassures him.

What did Ben make Hudson do? Now I'm dying to know. This has to be why he came to see me. But why me?

"Whatever," Jordan says, giving up the fight that he knows he can't win.

"If you guys are done being babies, can we please move on now? I know many of you are dying to know what task number two is." Ben struts back to the chalkboard and proceeds to write.

*2. Get your target to trust you. Make her
believe you are the real deal. Start planting
seeds. Set a date by next Saturday.*

"OK, fellas. This is more than just landing a date. This is where the fun and games begin." A sinister sense of elation sparks through Ben's already piercing glare. "You all have a target now, and you're probably wondering what's next. You guys have no idea how much this will change your lives. Mateo, doesn't it feel good to talk to a real girl? You don't need porn to live out your fantasies. You don't need to feel bad about wanting what you want. Never apologize for who you are. Never say no to your true desires. It's OK to want. Doesn't this feel amazing?" Ben's enthusiasm is bumped up a notch with each statement he slings at us.

I hardly feel amazing. Ivy does nothing for me. I don't even like her, so I'm not sure what Ben is going on about. It's just a game. It's not real.

"It's time to have a little bit of fun. Do what you need to seal the deal. To get a date, simply let the lies fly. Say what you think they want to hear. It will be fun, I promise. Remember, we are practicing lying here, guys."

"What did these women do to deserve this?" Bobby asks.

Ben lets out an annoyed sigh. "Every single one of you have been hurt by a woman, even me. My own mother. Think of all the women who hurt you. The words they called you, the things they did to you. It's not about these specific women, it's about what they represent. It's about you all taking some power back."

"I don't know. It doesn't seem right lying to these girls," Ethan chimes in.

"Yes, you're lying but you're using them too, Ethan. You're already doing this when you sleep around. You don't tell every girl you sleep with your life story. You simply tell them what they need to hear to get them alone for the night. You use them and they use you. So why not turn it into a game?"

Ethan nods in agreement. "I guess I see your point."

"So as a reminder, don't give away too much about yourself. This is time for you to play around and keep it light. I'm giving you assholes permission to let loose and be someone else. Fake it until you become it, remember?"

I don't want to hurt anyone, but the idea is enticing. I have no attachment to Ivy, and this is all practice for Jovie. I'm being permitted not to be myself for once. I'm being told to give as little detail as possible about the real me. I've never had much luck with the truth when it came to girls, so maybe I will have a little bit of luck when I'm in control of my 'new truth.' Little pangs of excitement flush through my midsection. I can't help but think that maybe this could be fun. I will keep my guard up, but what's a little fun, added to my current situation, going to hurt? I may as well enjoy myself a little. No harm in that, right?

CHAPTER THIRTY-TWO

Max
Wednesday, October 6, 7:30 p.m.

I study Ben as he sits across from me. He's casual tonight in straight-leg jeans and loafers. His V-neck sweater with a grandad-collared shirt underneath is more laid-back than his usual attire; it's almost alarming how casual he is tonight. The remnants of a past fraternity boy, I suspect. I clear the lump in my throat.

"We need to finish our conversation from last week. This layer needs to be pulled back before you're ready for Jovie. You must trust the process, Max."

Ben's always prying about Chrissy. There is more to me than just her. I can't get him to bite on anything else for some reason. But I play along. I will give him something so we can finally move on. Every meeting he's brought her up and I'm getting tired of it. He hasn't hinted that he knows more about that night, so I'm starting to call his bluff.

"Fine. So, before Jovie occupied my thoughts, there was Chrissy, as you already know. I loved her. I really did. She was pretty, and smart, and I always wondered why she fell for me out of all the other guys. Chrissy and I didn't have a lot in common, which probably would've been the downfall of our relationship had it gotten past what happened. I put on a good show to fake a happy relationship for her; she needed that in her life. We eventually lived together, but you would never have known it looking at our place. My stuff belonged downstairs and out of sight. My records and books were not allowed in the main part of the house; my world was downstairs. Our upstairs life was just for show. Happy pictures of us framed in every room. It was all fake. My friends said I was whipped and called me a pussy. They saw through the bullshit of it all. They wanted me to be happy."

"Why didn't you resist? Why do you think that you couldn't stand up for yourself?"

"Well, I suppose I could have, but it wasn't worth the fight."

"Pardon me if I'm wrong, but why wasn't it worth the fight? You weren't living your true life. You were shunned to a basement and not allowed to be yourself. Why did you stay with her?"

"I stayed with her because she was the best I could do, and it turns out, I was right. I haven't been able to get a single girl—not one since—Chrissy."

"Max, that's what Chrissy wanted. She ruined you. She didn't want you, but she didn't want you to be happy without her either. So, Chrissy won. Dude, you're so lucky you're here now. We will unfuck you, and you will be in control. I promise your next relationship won't be like the one with Chrissy. When you hear her words, that's what she wanted when she started planting those seeds. That's why we are first working on your confidence with Ivy before jumping into pursuing Jovie."

"But I'm not being myself with Ivy, so how is that helping my confidence?"

"I keep saying this, Max, fake it until you become it. Once you've faked the confidence for so long, it will start to come naturally."

"Don't you think that I could get so lost in faking it that I forget who I am?"

"Well, isn't that what you want? I want you to be yourself, Max, but if you don't like who you are, right now is the time to change that. I'm giving you the tools to reinvent yourself."

I sit for a moment, taking in what Ben's just said. I know I've made mistakes and I can be a coward, but do I really hate myself?

"She's getting married. Did I tell you that?"

"No, Max, you didn't," Ben says, his hand cupping his chin. "Does that bother you?"

"Yes, of course it bothers me. I wasn't good enough for her, but this sap is? I feel like I've been punched in the gut over and over and over again. And all this talk about me not being happy with myself and bringing up the past has me feeling sad, mad, and pathetic. If she only knew what I did for her. . ."

He cocks his head and produces a sly grin. "And what is it that you did for her?" Ben eagerly bounces on my intended slip. I want to see if he will come out and spill the beans on what he knows about the night my life imploded. But he doesn't offer any hint.

I let a long pause loom between us. Ben raises his eyebrow, waiting for me to reveal my juicy secrets but I won't give him that satisfaction.

"Nothing," I simply respond.

Ben returns to his previous position, sitting with perfect posture on his stool. "Max, after what happened between the two of you, wouldn't you think it's best to move on from her and not let her have the power over you? I personally think you won because you got out from under her control."

"Sure," I respond.

Ben's eyes land sharply on mine, now cold and unwavering.

"Did you ever want to kill her?"

Whoa, did I just hear that right? Did Ben just ask me if I ever wanted to kill Chrissy? My stomach begins to twist into little knots, fiercely tugging in opposite directions. Is he insane?

"No, absolutely not. What kind of question is that?"

"I just have to know where your mind was, that's all."

"No, she pissed me off a lot, but I never had a thought like that. I'm not sick in the head."

"I'm not saying you're sick in the head. It's OK to have extreme feelings. We can move on. Like I said, I was just seeing where your mind was during that time of your life. It will help me assess the way we handle you moving forward."

That is such an odd question to ask a person. Does Ben ask the other members questions like that? Who would say yes?

"Did you know that your friends were staging a plan?" Ben asks, his face flat and expressionless.

I feel the wind being knocked out of me. This can't be happening. How could he know that little detail about what conspired that fateful night? Everything that led up to that moment. Now I know he's not bluffing. He knows more than I thought possible.

"How. . .?" is all I can manage to say. My body begins to shift in my seat, but I quickly pull focus and stop all fidgeting. He can't see how much he's rattled me.

"That's not something to worry yourself with," Ben says sternly.

Friend or enemy, Ben? I've kept this secret safe for two years. If it gets out, it could ruin me and the life I've built in Clear River. Even if it is a sad, pathetic life. I want to lean over and vomit, but I keep my composure.

"I don't want to talk about Chrissy anymore," I say abruptly.

Ben doesn't press me to continue. He knows his words have stung me and his venom has gotten under my skin.

"Can we talk about something else for once?" I ask, trying to calmly change the subject. The palms of my hands are sweating profusely. I wipe them on my jeans when Ben turns around to look at the clock.

"Sure, what would you like to talk about?"

"Jovie."

Ben pauses for a moment before answering. "It's not time for that conversation."

"Can I at least add her as a friend on Socialite? She used to come into the store every week and I haven't seen her for almost a month now. I'm starting to get worried."

"Max, why do you care so much about a girl you hardly know? What if she sucks, what if she's not who you think she is? I'm sure she's fine, but I don't want you to get your hopes up. You've built this girl up in your head. You've imagined her to be your dream girl, but what if she isn't?"

"I just know, OK. I feel it. I feel a connection."

"Don't you think that if you felt a connection to her, it would have been effortless to talk to her? You had so many chances and you blew them all."

"I thought that you said you would help me!" I shout.

"If Jovie is what you want, then I will help you, but I will also show you your shortcomings and, in turn, help you see the bigger picture. We need to work on your self-esteem first, and then you can have any girl you want. You're actually a pretty good-looking guy, Max Jennings. You have some work to do, but the right girl will find you attractive and want to be with you for who you're working to be. Look at Owen—he's not the most attractive guy, but he gets more girls than anyone in this club. Even more than Kade."

"How?" I question

"He's confident. I didn't have to teach him that; he came out of the womb that way. But he knows and takes what he wants. Wouldn't it be fun to be more like Owen for once in your life? To stop overthinking every decision and just take what you want because you can?"

"I guess that sounds nice."

"Of course, that sounds nice. You deserve everything you want in life. You should be able to take what you want and not feel bad. You should've been able to talk to Jovie back when you had the chance. She should be so lucky to have you in her life. Max, get over your shit so you can move on."

"Maybe you're right. I know I overthink everything."

"Just like you overthink coming here every time, am I right?

"Maybe."

"Just like you're overthinking the question I asked you earlier about your friends' plan," Ben says with a salacious grin. "It doesn't matter how I know. All I know now is that this club is just what you need. I guarantee you will see things differently when I'm done with you. That's a promise I know I can keep. You can trust me."

Ben's smile chills me to my core. I know it's all in my head, but I feel a numbing sensation starting in my toes and making its way through one appendage at a time—a new form of torture.

CHAPTER THIRTY-THREE

Hudson
Wednesday, October 6, 8:01 p.m.

I wonder if Ben can see the panic trying to claw its way out of my skin. When I'm around him, I shiver in his presence, as if the man is made of ice.

"Hudson, are you still here with me, buddy?" Ben asks.

"Um, yes, sorry. What was the question?" I ask.

"How are you coping with what you did for the club?"

He wants to talk about that night. The night that girl died. *How am I fucking coping, you asshole? Are you for real?* is what I want to say, but instead, I let my silence linger a little longer.

I made a mistake going to Max, and now he won't stop trying to press me for answers. I ignored him again as we crossed paths tonight on the stairs. He sees through me, like I'm sure Ben does. His face says it all right now. Ben's been waiting for me to respond, but he's learned to let me take my time. The girl from the record store—I still can't place her. Every night, I wake up in a panic with her big brown eyes staring at me. I know her; I must. Otherwise, why would her eyes haunt me so?

I try to compose myself, but I don't want to talk about it.

"How are you coping with what you did for the club?" Ben says for the third time.

"What I did? What you made me do? How do you think I'm coping?"

"You know we've gone over this—it's not your fault. You simply did what was asked of you. You can't blame yourself, Hudson."

Flashes of heat rip through my body, my ears ring, and a tight pain presses against my chest, like I might explode. The walls are closing in. I can't catch my breath.

"You didn't kill Evie," Ben says calmly, placing his hand on mine.

"Don't fucking touch me!" I shout, spittle flies from my mouth.

"Hudson, you need to calm down. Trust me, this is not your fault."

"Well, I *got her killed*." I leap up from my chair, standing directly in front of Ben. "Who did it? Tell me. I know you know who did it. Was it you? Was it Kade? Did he actually fucking kill her? The cops think so."

Ben laughs off the questions, like it is preposterous that I would even ask him such things.

"Well, someone killed her, and it was all my fault. I know in my heart that she would still be alive if it weren't for you!" I shout.

CHAPTER THIRTY-FOUR

Mr. Scorpio: *Hey! Remember me?*

[?]: *Ah, yes, it's been a hot minute.*

Mr. Scorpio: *You never got back to me.*

[?]: *I thought you'd take a hint. ;)*

Mr. Scorpio: *Aww, come on now.*
I think you'd like me if you gave me a chance.

[?]: *Oh, you do now? So why would I like you?*
I don't know a thing about you, and your
profile is. . . lacking.

Mr. Scorpio: *Oh, so you looked into me?*

[?]: *Well, duh. You asked me out after just*
a few seconds of chatting. I had to see what
kind of creeper I'm dealing with. ;)

Mr. Scorpio: *Ouch. Creeper. I'm a little offended.*

[?]: Well, if the shoe fits.

Mr. Scorpio: *I'm actually pretty normal.*

*[?]: No one normal proclaims to be normal.
Hello, red flag.*

Mr. Scorpio: *Ouch again. Fine then.
We don't have to meet just yet. Why don't we
take a second to get to know each other first?*

[?]: Sure.

Mr. Scorpio: *Well, to start I am seemingly
normal. I have a full-time job, never been
married. No kids. I enjoy good music too.
I love a good concert. I'm also into craft beer,
and I'm a good cook.*

[?]: Sounds pretty generic.

Mr. Scorpio: *Well, that's what you gave me.
Tell me more about you. The more you tell,
the more I'll tell.*

[?]: You're lucky I'm bored.

Mr. Scorpio: *You're right. Lucky me.*

CHAPTER THIRTY-FIVE

Hudson
Friday, October 8, 6:10 p.m.

Every day, I see Evie's face somewhere. Whether it's in the newspaper, online or on TV, she haunts me. When I close my eyes, she's there. Ben says it's not my fault, but I know it is.

"Oh, it's so nice having you boys home for dinner," my mother says, interrupting my thoughts. She's been asking Jordan and me over for dinner for ages and I keep avoiding it. I don't want to look her in the eye after what I've done. But she's persistent, and so now I'm here and so is Jordan.

I haven't had any one-on-one time with my brother since he dragged me into this mess. He's been avoiding me, and I suppose I've been avoiding him as well. I can't make any mistakes. If I slip up, both of us will pay.

"I can't remember the last time we sat down as a family," my mother continues with a giant smile, beaming from ear to ear.

Dad looks gruff and has already had one too many drinks. "I'll tell you what would be nice, Nancy, is if these two fuckheads could get their shit together."

Mom's smile is immediately stripped off her face.

"Dad, I don't know what you mean. I have a job, and I'm doing well," Jordan responds. I know better than to engage. Dad wants to rile us up, as usual.

"Ever since that cunt ex-wife of yours—"

Mom cuts him off. "I know we don't like her anymore because of what she did to Jordan, but no one uses such foul language under this roof, Hank. We don't speak her name in this house, but can you please come up with something less profane?"

Dad ignores Mom and proceeds to tear into Jordan's ex-wife. "Well, that *b-word* of a girl— Happy? Is that better, Nan?"

Mom frowns, pushes herself away from the dinner table and scurries into the kitchen away from Dad's offensive talk. She always runs off as soon as he starts acting this way, letting us fend for ourselves.

Dad doesn't skip a beat. "That girl took everything you worked so hard for. She took everything from you, and what did you do about it? Nothing. You sat back and took her abuse, you sad sack of shit."

"Dad, that was a long time ago," Jordan says softly.

"Yes, and it took your sorry ass a long time to get 'back on track.' But I hardly call what you're doing now *back on track*."

"Dad, I'm really trying," Jordan pleas.

"Dad, can you ease up on him?" I ask hesitantly, afraid my dad will smack me straight across the face for speaking out of line. I know better, but I can't watch my big brother take all the verbal abuse.

"Oh, fuck you, Hudson. You have no room to talk. You've been slumming it over at your rental and slacking off since you were out of high school. You boys are both a disappointment to your mom and me. You let us down more than you could ever imagine.

I expected great things for you two, but instead, you flushed your lives down the toilet," Dad says, taking a long swig of his beer.

"Dad, we are just doing the best we can with what we've been dealt."

"You can't blame the dealer when you're the dealer!" Dad shouts, pounding another gulp of beer down his throat and finishing off the can.

"And Mom wonders why we never come around. She hides in the kitchen while you tear us down. If it weren't for Mom, we would never come here. You're the sad and pathetic one, Dad," Jordan shouts.

"Well, at least I can say I put the effort in, and we've got all of this to show for my hard work and dedication to this family," Dad says, waving his hand toward the living room.

Jordan and I sit in silence, both at a loss for words. There is no point in arguing anymore.

Dad pushes himself away from the table. He mumbles and grunts as he heads to the kitchen. "Sometimes, I wish you were never born." His voice is filled with hate and resentment.

I don't know if my dad is talking about Jordan, me, or both of us, but either way, the pain stings. Just as it always does. I know Jordan heard him too. He gives me a frown, and I reciprocate.

"Let's give Dad some time to calm down. I wish he weren't like that, but hell, he's always been this way. We are fuck-ups, and he hates us," Jordan says.

He's my big brother, and he always protected me from him when we were younger. But now, by dragging me into the club, I have to wonder where my protection is now? He should have known better than to toss me into the wolves' den—The Liars' Club.

I can't help myself, but I decide now is as good as any time to ask him. "Jordan, do you trust Ben?"

Jordan freezes in his seat. His glare turns ice cold. "I'm only going to tell you this once, so listen up. Never, *ever* bring up the club outside of the club again."

"But you're my brother. You dragged me into this. You recruited me. Can't we please discuss it?"

"No, just drop it. We can't. Ben will know."

"How will he know? We are sitting in our parents' home. I highly doubt he knows what's going on in this fucked-up house."

"Trust me when I say this, Ben always knows. Now let it go and don't bring up the fucking club again. Not to me, not to anyone. You got it?"

"Whatever. I hardly know you anymore." I push away from the table, slamming my chair into the wall. "I'm leaving," I shout as I exit the room. Dinner is already ruined, and no one will miss me anyway.

***

I'm startled awake, soaked in sweat. My hair is pasted to my forehead, and my sheets are cold against my back. I dreamed of that girl again. The one with the big, brown eyes. It's like little snippets of my memory flooded back while I slept. This time, her wide-eyed stare is filled with tears. That's more than before, but I still don't remember where I've seen her.

Well, crap, I'm awake now—no use in trying to fall back asleep. I roll over to the other side of my twin-sized bed and reach for the remote on my nightstand. I may as well try to drown out my thoughts with some mindless TV. I press power, and my dark room is illuminated by the cold blue light. I rapidly flip through the stations—something catches my attention, but I accidentally flip past it. I click back and I have to rub the grit from my eyes, making sure they're not playing tricks on me.

Breaking news. . .

The banner along the bottom of the screen scrolls with the breaking headline: *Local girl found dead with identical injuries as Evie Simmons.*

Oh, no. This can't be happening again.

CHAPTER THIRTY-SIX

Kade
Saturday, October 9, 8:01 a.m.

A rattling from my nightstand wakes me from a restless night of sleep. The blue glow from my phone flashes off the wall. Who the hell is calling me this early? This better be important.

I groggily reach for the phone. "Hello." My voice is hoarse when I speak.

"Is this Mr. Kinzinger?" a husky voice asks.

"It is," I reply.

"This is Detective Henricks. Remember, we spoke a couple weeks ago about Evie Simmons?"

My hand begins to shake. No. I thought maybe they were done with me since I never heard from them again. What could they want with me now? I answered all their questions.

"Of course, I remember. How could I forget the day that ruined my life?" I reply.

"We're going to need you to come down to the station. We have a few questions for you. Do you need us to send a car?"

"Can you first tell me what this is about?" I press.

"We just have some more questions for you," Henricks says vaguely.

Fuck! "No, I can drive myself this time. I can be there in an hour or so."

I just want to get this over, but this time I'm not going without a lawyer.

"Thanks for your cooperation, Mr. Kinzinger. We will see you shortly."

I abruptly hang up and dial Ben. He answers on the first ring.

"I need you," I demand, before he can even say hello.

"Good morning, Kade," Ben responds, his voice alert like he's been up for hours. "I figured you'd be calling this morning," Ben responds.

"Wait, why would you say that?"

"Have you not turned on your TV or been on Socialite this morning?"

"No, Ben, tell me what's going on."

"They found another body last night. It's very similar to Evie Simmons's death."

My stomach drops. "I can't fucking believe this. And what, the cops, they think it's me? I swear to you, I came home after work and drank alone. I wasn't out last night at all."

"Can anyone vouch for you?" Ben asks.

"I was working with Emmy until nine, and then after that, I suppose not."

"Oh, shit, hold on, Kade. They're releasing the girl's name."

As I impatiently wait for Ben, the silence gets the better of me and unwanted thoughts begin to make their way to the surface. What if they found a clue that could send me to jail? No one will care about the facts. They just want someone to blame, and right now, it seems like I'm the only person they have.

Ben clears his throat. "Kade, do you know a Jessica Biles?"

My heart plummets. The girl last Wednesday night in the new bar, her name was Jessica. The girl with fire-red hair. This is too much of a coincidence, but that was over a week ago, not last night.

"I'm going to need your lawyer."

"OK. I'll have him pick you up."

"Thanks, bro. I really appreciate it."

***

Dennis Miller, Ben's lawyer, picks me up in his sleek black Cadillac. I slide into the front seat, and Dennis doesn't waste any time. "So, Kade, Ben filled me in on your situation. I'm sure the cops don't have much to hold you, otherwise, they would've shown up at your door this morning with handcuffs and a warrant. I think they're just calling you in to see how you react. To see if they can ruffle your feathers and scare you into a confession. Also, they want to see if there is a connection between you and Jessica Biles."

A large lump is making its way up my throat. I have to swallow several times before it finally goes down. "I didn't kill Evie or Jessica, but I do have to tell you that I think I know Jessica. I saw her picture on the news when I was waiting for you. I met her over a week ago, and I went back to her place."

Dennis nods. "Good, Kade, that's a great start. I have your back, but you need to be honest with me. It's the best way that I can help you. I need to know the truth, OK? Ben fronted a lot of money for me to help you, and this won't work unless we are honest with each other. Can I trust that you'll always give me the God's honest truth?"

"Yes. I have nothing to hide," I respond.

"OK, then tell me what happened."

"I fucked both of those girls, and now they are both dead. They were both alive when I left them—I swear! If Jessica died last night, then I wasn't with her. I only saw her the one time, and that was over a week ago."

"Well, Kade, this doesn't look good," Dennis says.

"Hell, I know this doesn't look good. I think someone is framing me. I was with her over a week ago, so either it's a fucked-up coincidence, or it's targeted and for some reason, they waited a week to dump the body."

"I agree with you there, it does sound staged, but right now, you look very guilty. We only have a short time to get our game plan worked out. OK? We don't know the time of death for Jessica, but as long as she wasn't killed on that Wednesday night or Thursday early morning, we shouldn't have any problems. But, Kade, if anyone saw you two together, and she was killed last week, it doesn't look good for you."

"I'm so fucked."

"Who saw you together?"

"A drunk barfly who I sat next to, but she was too drunk to notice who I was, and the bartender maybe. I wore a hat so people wouldn't recognize me. I paid cash. Jessica didn't even have a clue who I was."

"OK, that's good. So far, right now, there is no real connection between you and Jessica. Tell them you haven't seen the news yet. We will let them tell us as much as possible."

"Ok." I nod.

"When we get inside, don't go running your mouth. Ben said you can be a hothead from time to time. This is not the place nor the time. Let me do the talking. I don't want you to say anything they can use against you later."

"I'll keep my mouth shut," I respond.

"And do me a favor—keep your dick in your pants until they catch the killer."

***

When we arrive at the station, there are already camera crews ready to pounce on me. I toss my jacket hood over my head as Dennis and I make a run for the door.

"Kade, did you murder all those girls?" a reporter shouts, shoving a microphone in my face.

"Mr. Kinzinger, did you murder Evie Simmons?" another hollers.

I keep my head down and a group of officers rush out to cover me until I get inside. The hungry press pack disperses once I'm through the front doors. Detectives Henricks and Clemens are waiting for me, both men wearing the same attire as the day I met them.

"Kade, you know the drill. You're not under arrest but we have some questions for you. Will you two follow me?" Henricks says.

We follow them into the same room as before, but this time both of them stay.

"Kade, I have to ask, do you know a young woman named Jessica Biles?" They slide a photograph of the red-haired girl in front of me. I glance over to Dennis, he nods, giving me the OK to answer.

I think quickly. "No. I don't know that girl. Why? Who is she?" I lie. I think it's better this way. Chances are no one saw us together, so it's easier if I don't muddy the water. If it comes out later that I did know her, well then, I guess I'm screwed. . .

My foot begins to fidget under the table, but I quickly catch myself and stop.

"Are you sure?" Detective Clemens presses.

"My client already said he doesn't know this person," Dennis responds. I'm thankful Ben called him.

"Can you tell us where you were last night around nine p.m.?"

A flood of relief rushes over me; she was killed last night. I wasn't with her. I haven't seen her since last week. But the coincidence is still haunting me. I think someone is framing me, but why?

"I was leaving Epic Records. My employee, Emmy, was with me. I'm sure the cameras out back caught us leaving at that time, or the cameras in the parking garage."

"We will have someone check on that."

"Why are we here?" Dennis demands.

"That girl," Henricks says, pointing at her photo on the table, "was found with her throat slit, propped up against the same tree as Evie Simmons. She was killed last night."

"Well, it wasn't my client. He was working, then went home. If you don't have any evidence to hold him here, I think that is all the questions we have time for."

"OK, you guys are free to go. Thanks for coming in. Kade, once again, I trust you won't leave town. I'm sure we will have more questions for you."

CHAPTER THIRTY-SEVEN

Hudson
Saturday, October 9, 9:01 p.m.

I'm scanning Socialite and my feed is filled with videos of Kade running into the police station this morning. He was later let go, with reports saying he's been cooperating and there is no evidence to hold him. If they had any evidence, he'd be rotting in a jail cell right now.

The first three girls were dumped, not propped up with their throats slit like the last two girls. They think we now have two different killers, or one who's really switched up their MO, but Kade's alibis prove he wasn't involved with the first three and possibly the last one, but there is still doubt with Evie. I can't help but think he might be innocent, but somehow, I know this is connected to Ben. It's way too much of a coincidence for him not to be. I have to confront him, and I think I have to do it now. I feel sick; I don't have the full picture of that night, but I know half of the truth. I only have a small piece of the puzzle, but Ben has the rest of the pieces.

Before I have time to chicken out, I grab my keys and drive to the club. My nerves are shot, and my heart is pounding.

I rush into the club, nearly out of breath, panting as I shout, "Ben, are you here? Ben! We need to talk now!"

The club room is empty, but I know he's here. "Ben!"

Ben casually walks out from his office and down the narrow hallway. "Oh, Hudson. Good to see you, but the meeting doesn't start for another fifty minutes. You're early. Why don't you go grab some dinner and come back?"

I'm shaking in my shoes, ready to jump down Ben's throat, and yet he's so casual. Doesn't he understand that I'm here to do some damage? I'm here to ruin him. I'm here to get him to confess.

"Ben, I need to talk. Now!"

"Can you save it for your session? I'm preparing for task three. It's a big one, and I don't want to miss any detail. How are things progressing with your target?"

"No, this can't fucking wait. I need to talk to you now. Quit sweeping me under the rug."

"Calm down, Hudson," Ben says, patronizing me.

"I'm not going to calm down until you tell me what's going on. Did you have something to do with the murder of Jessica Biles?"

Ben takes a slow step in my direction, his golden eyes locking on mine. "I'm getting really sick of this, Hudson. If you want, I can just call Jordan and we can tell him your secret now."

"Fuck you, Ben. Do what you want. I'm going to the police."

"And tell them what, exactly? You will sound insane."

"I don't fucking care at this point. People are dead."

"Trust me, you will care. Plus, if you think what you've done is bad, I have worse things on your brother. He's been with me for over a year now. I know everything about him. If you go to the police, I will release everything I have on Jordan. Oh, and your dad's business that he's worked so hard for, isn't quite on the up and up, if you know what I'm saying. I've done my homework, not to hurt you but to protect you from hurting yourself. Your mom would be so broken if some of these things got out. It's such a shame." Ben's words ruthlessly slice through me.

"You're sick, Ben."

"No, I'm smart. It's called insurance."

"So, if you're warning me against going to the police, then you must be guilty of something."

"No, Hudson. I'm not, but we don't need the attention on us and what we're doing here. You must trust me. I can forget this little betrayal if you promise to be a good club member and loyal brother to the others. It's not just about you. We all have a purpose. We need to move past this moment so we can heal and move on. You've got your instincts all wrong."

I shakily let my legs guide me down to the recliner behind me. I'm at a loss. I don't know what to do now. I'm not a fighter, what did I think I could accomplish with Ben, the master manipulator?

I let my head hang as the night of my extra-credit task plays on repeat in my mind. I'm sick to my stomach. I know Ben had something to do with Evie's death. I just know. I'm dizzy, I'm shaking. How do I get out of this mess? That night when I came back to the club—that night when my entire world changed. . .

Oh my fucking God. That's when I saw her. That's where I know that girl from. Oh my God.

Goosebumps quilt my body.

The girl with the big, brown eyes. She was in her car outside the club.

Her big, brown eyes filled with tears, just like my dream.

I want to lean over and vomit on the floor, but I need to keep my cool. There is something bigger going on here and everything is connected, I know it. I don't trust Ben. I don't trust this club.

But what I do know is that I need to get to the bottom of this. I need to stay under Ben's radar because there is too much at stake.

"Hudson, do we have an understanding?" Ben asks.

"Well, since you're blackmailing me, I fucking guess so."

CHAPTER THIRTY-EIGHT

Max
Saturday, October 9, 9:15 p.m.

I have to play the game. Ben knows too much. But with that worry hanging over me like a dark cloud, I nearly forgot tonight is my deadline to set a date with Ivy. The things Ben could possibly know about me would ruin me—destroy me. I don't even know how he could know those things, about Chrissy, about how my friends had a plan, but somehow, he does, and his threat is real. It feels as if he's just waiting to let the bombs drop.

Right now, though, I need to play the game.

Max: *Hey girl. Wanted to reach out and
say hi. Hope you've been well. I enjoyed
our brief chat the other day.*

I feel so fake. I don't talk like this.
Three little green dots flash on the screen. Ivy's typing. Good.

Ivy: *Hey. Life has been pretty hectic. I don't have much time for chatting these days.*

Max: *I'm sorry to hear that. I know you just said you've been busy, but I was hoping that maybe we could get together sometime and meet in person. I'd love to take you out for a drink. You seem like a nice girl.*

Ivy: *Oh, I don't know, Max. We just started chatting.*

Max: *Sorry, you're right. That was rude of me to ask.*

Ivy: *No, it's not rude. I'm just so busy right now.*

Max: *Busy doing what, if you don't mind me asking?*

Ivy: *Oh, it's just some family stuff.*

Max: *I hope everything is OK.*

Ivy: *That's nice of you. It will be OK. I hope.*

Ivy: *Hey, you know what? Maybe I could use a distraction. I could squeeze you in for a quick drink and a bite to eat.*

Max: *That would be nice. I can make any time work. You pick the day and time.*

Ivy: *Monday night is the only time I have a free moment. Not a traditional date night, but if you're willing to make that work, I*

*can meet you at seven. I have to make it an
early night, though.*
Max: *Seven on Monday works for me.
We could meet downtown somewhere.*

Ivy: *Sounds good. What about the Rose
Tavern? Does that work? They have good
food and a good vibe.*

Max: *Yes. Perfect. Looking forward to it.*

***

The club is quiet tonight. I suppose Kade is on everyone's mind. After I'd finished my chat with Ivy, I couldn't help but see everyone posting about Kade.

Sales at Epic Records are suffering because reporters are standing outside our store. Customers don't want to come in. People don't want to support a murderer and be caught on TV doing so. Kade hasn't been implicated in the murders of Jessica and Evie, but he's already been charged in the court of public opinion. Until the police have new leads, the focus remains on Kade. I don't know if I should feel bad for him, or fear him. I want to believe he's innocent.

"Where's Kade?" Owen demands as soon as Ben enters the room. No hollers or claps this time. Everyone is serious.

"Kade is innocent and spent the entire day proving that to the police," Ben says. "This will all blow over soon. Kade didn't even know the second victim."

"Her name is Jessica. She's a person. Use her name," Hudson says, emerging from the rear of the crowd. His hand is balled tightly into a fist. This is the first time I've seen any guts from the guy. He's definitely not one to be ballsy or give any pushback.

"Um, yes. Jessica. Her name is Jessica, but either way, Kade says he doesn't know her, so he has nothing to worry about."

"Well then, where is he?" Owen presses

"He thought it would be best for the club if he kept a low profile and stayed home tonight. I will see him for a special session later this evening. He didn't want the news crews following him here, and we didn't want you guys to be seen on camera and questioned on what your connection to a 'murderer' is."

"No, I guess that makes sense, but doesn't it make him look guilty?" Owen asks.

"Not to us. We know Kade and this horrible crime is not something he's capable of," Ben responds.

"How can you be so sure?" Owen keeps pressing.

"Don't you trust me, Owen?"

"Yes, but—"

"No *buts*—trust me."

Owen skulks back into the group.

"It's becoming clear that we have a bit of a trust issue growing in this club. We must kill this disease before it takes over," Bens says.

"I'll trust you when you show me who got the extra credit this week," Hudson fires off another quarrelsome remark toward Ben.

"Since Kade's not here this week, I will keep the points reveal under wraps," Ben responds, giving Hudson a cold glare.

"That's bullshit!" Hudson shouts. His brother pulls him back by the shoulder.

"Hudson, remember what we talked about less than an hour ago? Or have you already forgotten?" Ben says in a grave voice.

Ben's eyes shoot from Hudson to Jordan and then back to Hudson.

"If we have no further interruptions, I'd like to get back to our meeting."

Most of the members appear unnerved by what just unfolded. Ezra, Ethan, and Mateo are fidgeting like little squirrels, and it seems like the air has been sucked out of the room.

"What is the worst thing you've ever done?" Ben asks.

Everyone freezes stone-dead in their place. The mere movement of their flickering eyes gives away their fear. I bet everyone in this room has a secret, and I suspect Ben knows what it is. I'm not the only one.

Ben lets a long pause hang in the room.

"What is the one thing you hope no one ever finds out?" he says.

The room is so quiet you could hear a pin drop.

"I want you to pair up and share that secret with your partner. This is my version of a trust fall. Instead of trusting your partner will catch you, you are trusting they won't spill your secret."

Is he for real? Does he really want me to tell someone in this room the worst thing I've ever done? I can't. No way.

"You can't be paired with the person who brought you here. I want you to pick your own partner. The person without a partner will be paired with Kade by default. You will be allowed to set up one meeting with each other outside of the club. Think about your pairing throughout the meeting and we will pick our partners before we leave here.

"If your secret gets leaked, then we know we have a rat, and it will be easy to figure out. Everything we do in this club is built on trust; I have to trust you and your brothers have to trust you. You must not judge your brother for you are just as guilty."

This is most definitely an interesting turn of events. What good is going to come from this bizarre exercise? All I know is that Hudson has to partner with me. This is my chance to get him alone.

"OK, so moving on to task number three. Since we're not discussing points this week, if you didn't complete your second task, you get a second chance to redeem yourself. So now the real fun and games can begin, just like I promised."

Ben flips the board again and reveals the third task.

THE LIARS' CLUB
RULES TO THE GAME

1. Create a fake profile (liars) on Socialite.
(Use your real name and photo but that is it.)
Everything else is a lie. Get the attention of
your target. Strike up a conversation.
2. Get your target to trust you. Make her believe
you are the real deal. Start planting seeds.
Set a date by next Saturday.
3. Get your target to tell you a secret.

"Keeping with the theme of tonight's meeting, I want you to get a secret out of your target. Lay the groundwork for her to trust you during your date. Oh, you'd be surprised how many people are willing to spill the awful things they've done to mere strangers as a means of redemption."

Ben's eyes eerily wander back to Hudson and stay pinned on him for a few moments before returning his gaze back out to the crowd.

"The test isn't just getting her secret, but it's also about how well you lied to gain her trust. You will report back to me once you have her secret, and I will decide how to proceed," Ben says.

"What if my girl is a good girl and has no secrets?" Owen asks.

Ben laughs darkly. "Everyone has a secret. There is a darkness in all of us."

"That can't be true. What if mine is a church-going goody-two-shoes?" he responds.

"Ha!" Ben barks. "I suspect your girl is not that. A girl like that wouldn't have put her blind trust into someone she just met on the internet. Am I wrong? Plus, I know who your girls are. Remember? Trust me, she is no angel. Pulling their secrets out of them is the fun part, Owen. I thought you'd love this task."

"OK, I got it. I was just wondering. Sorry," Owen responds, quickly backing down.

Ben is slowly losing his composure, a sense of unease is creeping in. Perhaps it's the pushback he's gotten tonight. Things are clearly not going the way he wants.

"Sorry, one more question." Ethan says shyly. "What if your girl doesn't freely give up her secrets? Then what?"

"Well, then you lose the game. And trust me, you don't want to lose. Just get creative. I don't care how you do it—just fucking do it!" Ben shouts.

Ben sucks in a deep breath and then rubs his hands down the front of his collared shirt, pressing it out down to the bottom. He readjusts his collar and then speaks again, more controlled this time.

"OK, it's partner-picking time. Choose wisely—picking the wrong partner could come back to haunt you later." Ben storms off to his office.

Is he not going to watch? That's when I realize that he doesn't need to be out here, because there are new devices in each corner of the room. The fucker installed cameras. He's always watching.

I need to pick Hudson but I'm also afraid to. Do I play it safe and let someone pick me? The clock is ticking, and Owen has already grabbed Ezra. Ethan's making his way over to Mateo. Think, Max. Think.

What should I do?

CHAPTER THIRTY-NINE

Hudson
Saturday, October 9, 10:28 p.m.

I need Max to pick me. I can't choose him. Ben is testing me. He wants to see what I will do. His newly installed cameras ensure he can see everything. That sneaky bastard. Did he think we wouldn't notice? The flashing green light isn't exactly incognito.

But then that's the point. He wants me to know he's watching.

Ben's waiting to see if I will spill the wrong secret and toss him under the bus, or will I play along and spill my secret about Nadia. The one that seems so minuscule now on the grander scale of my life choices since joining the club.

Come on, Max. I need you to pick me. You've been wanting me alone since my initial slip-up when I came into the record store.

As everyone scurries around the room, pairing off, I start getting anxious. But Max is still unspoken for.

I stay still. I don't move, and worst-case scenario, I get paired with Kade because no one picks me. I just don't know if I can trust Kade, and for all I know, he may have murdered those girls and Ben is helping him cover it up. Those poor beautiful girls. They had their entire lives ahead of them and now they're simply a sad memory.

Mateo grabs Ethan.

Owen takes Ezra.

I wonder if they have their reasons for picking their partners. Do they know things about each other too? I watch my brother Jordan circle around the room, assessing each of the remaining members before landing on Bobby.

Only Max, Decklan, Kade, and I are left. Decklan must choose Kade for this to work.

"It's not fair for Kade to be the default last pick, so I choose him." Decklan responds.

Oh, yes, perfect. Decklan picked for us. He put us together. There is nothing Ben can say about that. Neither Max nor I had anything to do with our pairing. Thank you, Deck.

Max shuffles his way over to me. I keep my head down. I don't know how good Ben's recently installed cameras are, so I speak down toward my feet, and I suspect Max understands why. "Sunday, seven at the Blue Heron."

Max nods.

I walk away, and a few others follow behind me.

This couldn't have gone any better. In fact, it's perfect.

CHAPTER FORTY

Max
Sunday, October 10, 10:45 a.m.

Emmy's moping around the store this morning as we prepare for opening. She's not her usual chipper self and I suppose the weight of the recent developments is taking its toll on her.

"Emmy, are you sure you're doing OK?"

"I'm fine, Max. You need to stop worrying about me."

"I can't help it," I respond.

Emmy gives a grateful smile.

"Hey, it's cool you're working today. I know you haven't had much time off lately. Thank you," I say.

With the help of Jake and Jed, the two of us have been keeping the store afloat in Kade's absence. We are a good team here. Most people would've jumped ship. Kade is lucky to have us, even if he doesn't seem to acknowledge it.

"The extra cash is nice, although the store isn't making much money these days. It would be nice if these reporters would leave our sidewalk so we could do some dang business. If I were Kade,

I would just close up shop until this blows over. He's paying us more than he's making. I think I'm going to go out there and give them a piece of my mind."

"I bet Kade thinks if we close, then they've won, and he's guilty of something. They want to get to him, and Kade's not like that. It would be nice if the reporters got the hint that he's not coming in, though."

"That's it. I'm going to tell them." Sweet but sassy, five-foot-two Emmy takes off for the front door. Before I have time to respond, she whips the door open. "Kade's not coming in today, so would you please leave us alone? We have a business to run. I will call the cops and report you. This is harassment and we've done nothing to deserve this. Please let us do our job."

I'm shocked but also thrilled that Emmy spoke up. It's about time someone wasn't a coward and did something about the reporters, but right now I wish I was the hero. I let Emmy handle something I should have done days ago.

"Max, did you happen to see that interview Teddy gave yesterday?" Emmy says when she comes back to the counter.

"Oh, no. What did Teddy say?"

Emmy bites her bottom lip. She opens her phone and shoves it in front of me. A local-news clip is playing. A reporter has their mic shoved in Teddy's face outside his store. "I was the one who told Kade about Evie's death, and when I said her name, he dropped his keys and froze before rudely excusing himself. That moment hasn't sat right with me since. I don't know how the cops don't have any evidence to convict him. I think he did it. I don't know about the other murders, but we have a suspect, and we need justice for Evie."

I'm sick to my stomach. I know I was there, and that's how it happened, but how has Teddy so freely thrown Kade under the bus without any real evidence? Everyone who lives and works downtown knows Teddy. Even though he works in a men's clothing store, he makes his rounds and gossips with everyone, especially at the café and bookstore. What Teddy said to that reporter is definitely hurting Kade and the store. "This is not good. No matter the outcome, Kade's reputation will forever be tarnished by this," I say, handing Emmy back her phone.

"Are you starting to doubt him?" Emmy asks softly.

"I truly don't know what to believe anymore. Kade would be in a jail cell if they had even the slightest shred of evidence or anything linking him to those girls, but nothing's come up yet. But that doesn't mean it won't either. He admitted to knowing Evie, but so far, he's standing his ground that he doesn't know Jessica. Plus, he's already been cleared of the first three murders, so as sick as it sounds, I hope whoever killed the first girls killed Evie and Jessica, and then Kade would be innocent."

"I think I know what you mean."

"Em, I am honestly surprised that you stayed. It says a lot about your character."

"If the only female at his store quits, what does that say about him?" Emmy touts.

Hopefully, Kade will remember that loyalty when this is all over. "You're a good friend," I say.

Suddenly, Emmy's demeanor changes, and her body hangs limp, like maybe she's regretting her decision.

"Let's talk about something else," she says. "So, what have you been up to these days?"

"Not much. Just holding my shit together." I respond.

"Do you know that you've been pretty closed off lately?" Emmy asks.

"Oh, sorry, I don't mean to be like that. I've just had a lot on my mind with Kade and other things."

A long pause draws out between us before Emmy blows out a short breath. "Is that because of Ben Matthews?"

My heart drops to the pit of my stomach. I don't know what to tell her. I've been skating around this, hoping it wouldn't get brought back up.

"Max, when the police came for him, why did Kade tell you to call that guy?"

Why does it matter so much to her?

I followed my boss, and I accidentally joined a club that may or may not be blackmailing me into attending and playing a game of lies. Of course, I can't say any of that.

Instead, I opt for a simple, "What do you mean?"

"Max, we didn't think that guy was good for Kade, and now look where Kade is. So, you should play it safe." Emmy reaches out and grabs my hand. She gives it a thoughtful squeeze.

From her perspective, me knowing Ben shouldn't be a big deal. So why is she asking me to play it safe?

"I'm being safe." I'm lying, of course. I'm in a whirlwind of brewing trouble. I'm in a club that has dire consequences if I don't participate. The club members don't trust each other, and to top it off, tonight, I'm going to meet Hudson and demand he tell me what he knows. And I think I'm supposed to torture Ivy Peterson into telling me her secrets. I've been avoiding thinking about our date on Monday. I have to create a plan and come prepared, as this could be my only opportunity to get her to open up to me. What could the poser girl be hiding besides using her friends to look like the pretty one on Socialite? That's all I can think of, and it's all too inconsequential to matter. Then again, does any of this really matter?

I walk away, wanting to avoid further conversation about Ben, but Emmy follows me, hitting me with a shocker.

"Hey, that girl you like hasn't popped by in weeks. I hope she's OK."

My stomach turns itself inside out and I feel all the color leaving my face.

How does she know about Jovie? I never told Emmy about my dream girl.

"Just be careful, Max."

CHAPTER FORTY-ONE

Max
Sunday, October 10, 6:50 p.m.

I arrive early at the Blue Heron restaurant. I pick a seat at the far end of the bar, away from the other customers; I can't risk anyone overhearing us tonight. We have a lot of sensitive matters to discuss.

I've never been to Blue Heron before. It's a nice place—a little too nice for us. I'm surprised Hudson recommended it, although I suppose it's a restaurant where no one would know us since we both don't fit in with the regular patronage. I'm underdressed, and knowing Hudson, he will be even more so, but that's the least of our problems. I summon over the bartender. He's not as nice or quick on his feet as Mark, but that's a good thing tonight. I order a beer and continue to wait for Hudson.

Once my drink arrives, I take slow sips, checking out my surroundings. The bar has about twenty barstools around its horseshoe shape. The bar top is a reddish mahogany wood. It's very nice, but I prefer the unique look of the Rose Tavern.

I glance down at my phone. It's 7:05. He's late.

What if he chickened out or never planned on actually meeting me? It wouldn't surprise me; his behavior is very erratic at the best of times.

That's when I notice him outside. He's pacing near his car and appears to be talking to himself. Is the poor guy losing his mind, or has he always been this way? Can I trust him?

His eyes meet mine and he quickly composes himself.

A minute later, he is standing next to me at the bar, staring awkwardly.

I shift in my seat. His discomfort makes me uncomfortable.

I open my mouth to greet him, but the words don't have time to vacate my mouth because Hudson already chimes in with a list of questions.

"Do you think anyone followed us here? Do you think anyone here knows we're part of the Liars' Club? Do you think we should go somewhere else?" Hudson is sweating, and his ears are as red as lava.

"Whoa, Hudson, calm down. You're starting to sound like a conspiracy theorist," I respond, and follow it up with an uncomfortable laugh.

Hudson pulls the barstool out to sit down. He wipes his hair away from his perspiring forehead. "Did you see the cameras last night at the club? They weren't there on Wednesday, Max."

"Yes, I noticed, and I know Ben has eyes watching, but I think we're safe here. You should order something."

I flag down the bartender for him.

"What can I get you, sir?"

"Jack and Coke," Hudson responds.

Hudson's eyes race across the entire bar, back and forth like a Ping-Pong ball. I already had time to assess the room, and it is mostly older men in golf attire, even though it's no longer golf season. But hey, I'm not here to judge.

"I don't think we have much to worry about, Hudson. I don't think Ben has anyone here in his pockets. Plus, Ben wanted us to meet and talk," I say, reassuring Hudson. 'So, we're just doing as he asked.'

The bartender returns with Hudson's drink, and I watch as he takes a long sip before continuing with his paranoid rant. "Ben doesn't want us to really spill our secrets," he says, "because if we do, it will hurt him. He's testing me."

There is a certainty in his voice that intrigues me.

"OK," I respond, leaning in closer, "I knew you wanted to tell me something, but you're acting more fidgety than usual. What's going on, Hudson?"

"I want to tell you, but it's a test."

"Well, we are here and I'm not going to tattle on you, so are you going to tell me what you wanted that day?"

"Yes, but first, I have something I need to ask you. How well do you know that girl you work with?"

"Who, Emmy?" I question. This is not where I thought this conversation was going.

"Yeah, probably. I don't know her name."

"Why?" I question.

"Please answer me. How well do you know her?"

"Pretty well, I think. We've worked together for eight months."

"She's working with Ben." Hudson spits out.

"No, that can't be true. Have you lost your mind? Why would you say that?" My head is spinning at his words. Why would he say such a thing?

"Listen. . ." Hudson leans in even closer and whispers in my ear. "I saw her at the club the night of our first meeting. The night Evie Simmons died. She was in her car. It was around one in the morning."

"Why the hell would Emmy have been at the club at one a.m.? That doesn't make sense."

"I don't know, but I saw her. She had tears in her eyes like she was crying."

"How do we even know Ben was there at that time? And why were *you* there so late?"

"Has Ben ever given you another little red envelope, just like the one he gave us with our target on it?"

"No."

"Are you sure?"

"I think I would remember that. Why? Did you get another one? Is that how you got your extra-credit assignment?" I ask.

"Yes," Hudson says, hanging his head so far down that his hair sweeps the bar top.

"What did your envelope say?" I press.

Hudson slowly turns his head, and his eyes are filled with sadness. "I don't know if I have the guts to spit it out."

Hudson picks up his mopey head and surveys the room again.

"I think we're safe here," I respond

"Max, I'm so scared."

"I can help you. You can trust me, but you have to tell me first what was in your envelope."

"Everything is at stake. My relationship with my brother, my family's future, and even my own freedom."

"OK, let's talk through this together. We will figure things out. I promise. I have your back," I say, reassuring Hudson. I need to know what Ben made him do. Something tells me it's not good and how is Emmy involved? Hudson has a lot of information that I need right now to make sense of it all.

"OK, let's talk about Emmy first. We can ease into it. Ben doesn't know you saw her. Is that correct?"

"Not that I'm aware. Max, why do you think Emmy would have been at the club that night?"

"Maybe she followed Kade and me, just as I followed Kade that night," I respond.

"You followed Kade? He didn't recruit you?"

"Shit, I shouldn't have said that. I can't get Kade in trouble. Em and I were worried about Kade, and I followed him. Remember the entrance I made the first night? Well, it wasn't planned. I met Ben once when he was looking for Kade and he left his business card at the store, and there was a code on the back. It was all a coincidence. I used the code, and magically the door opened. I saved Kade's ass by pure dumb luck and good timing."

"I wouldn't call it luck. You're fucked now, and so am I," Hudson says.

"Well, now you know one of my secrets," I say to Hudson, hoping to give him some comfort. Although, that's really Kade's secret that I just leaked.

"OK, so if Emmy followed Kade just like you did, then why would she still have been at the club hours later?"

Hudson makes a good point. This isn't adding up.

"Hey, come to think of it, this morning at work, Emmy did say something to me that caught me off guard. It was personal. She knew something that I had never told her. Only Kade and Ben knew that specific information about me. I mean, Kade could've said something, but I highly doubt it. He's been too busy, and he's not a gossip. Although I would prefer that over the assumption that Emmy could be working with Ben. But then, she also warned me to be careful."

"Maybe she's being blackmailed by him too. He loves to use secrets against people to get what he wants. You heard him last night."

"I hope Emmy's not in over her head with Ben. I will be cautious around her, but what if she needs my help?"

"Keep an eye on her, but I don't think you should let on that you know anything. What if she is loyal to him?"

I didn't even think of that. I thought I knew her.

"Let's get back to the red envelope," I say, pushing the thought from my mind.

"So, Ben called me after I left the club. He asked me to come back as he had a favor that he needed my help with."

"And that's when he gave you the envelope?"

"Yes."

"What did it say?"

Hudson slips his right hand into his back pocket and produces the little red envelope. He passes it to me from under the table. I take it and carefully open it under the bar top. I find myself paranoid now too, checking for any new faces that may have entered the restaurant.

In small print, the note reads:

Follow Kade. Keep an eye on him all night.
Then report your findings to me. This is
important. I know you won't disappoint me
like your brother would be disappointed
if I told him about Nadia.

"Follow Kade? Who is Nadia?" I say, confused. None of this makes any sense.

Hudson awkwardly swivels in his chair. He lets out a long puff of breath and swallows hard. "First, Nadia is my brother's ex-wife. I'm the reason she left him. I fucked up, Max. And Ben's holding that over my head."

"OK, so that would destroy your relationship with Jordan. I get that, and by you following a simple task, you get to avoid that. But why did Ben want you to follow Kade?"

"That's the night Evie died," Hudson whispers in my ear. "I followed him to the Rose Tavern that night, Max."

A new customer walks into the restaurant, and Hudson stops talking. The man circles the bar. The suspense is killing me. Just hurry up and pick a damn seat so Hudson can continue. Once the customer carefully chooses his barstool, thankfully at the other end of the bar, I have to coax him into resuming his story.

"Hudson, it's OK. Keep going," I say.

"I followed Kade and Evie back to Evie's apartment. I left Evie's around quarter to one. I didn't know how long I was supposed to wait for him. I figured he would spend the night at her place, and I was free of my duty. When I came back to the club to report my findings, that's when I saw Emmy.

"When I saw Evie's face plastered all over the news. That beautiful girl that Kade was with, I started to question why, and I assumed it was all my fault. Either Ben was worried that Kade would do something like this, and that's why he was being followed, or worse, that someone was framing Kade. Ben knew Kade was with Evie, and if Kade was telling the truth and really did leave at one thirty, and Evie was alive, then someone else came in to finish the deed. Someone killed her."

"Why didn't you go to the police?"

"At first, I was scared. She was dead because of my information. Second, Ben threatened me with my secrets. Plus, I would be implicating myself if I were right. So, I had to choose. But trust me when I tell you that I've been absolutely sick about all of it. But Ben knows too much. About me, my brother, and my entire family. It would ruin us all."

"Were you asked to follow him again? The night Jessica was killed?"

"No, it wasn't me. I hoped he would release who got the extra credit because then I would know who it was. The other members would have no idea, but I would."

"But Kade says he doesn't know Jessica," I respond.

"What if he's lying? Either Kade is killing these women, or someone in the club is, and I suspect it is Ben himself. After I gave him that information, he could've snuck out and gone to Evie's apartment and waited for Kade to leave."

"Well, fuck. This is not what I expected to hear from you tonight."

"I feel relieved to tell someone, but I'm also more scared that Ben will find out. What should we do, Max?"

"To be honest, I had a little bit of hope at first that Ben would help me and fix me as he promised. A little part of me hoped he was everything he said he was, but a huge part of me knew something wasn't right. Now I see that's not his endgame—everything we tell him is just blackmail material to force us to carry out his plan. We need to stop him."

"We need to find what he has on Kade," Hudson says.

"Kade's using Ben's lawyer. He is deeply indebted to Ben. This is not good for him," I respond.

"So, what we need to know is: Did Kade kill those girls? If yes, which ones? If not, who did and why? What's Emmy's involvement? Why the game? And what is his next plan?" Hudson adds.

"I agree."

"Now, what about the game? If we don't keep playing, Ben will suspect something is up. I don't want to hurt my girl, Max. She is really nice, and I really don't care to find out her secret," Hudson says.

"My girl is nice too. A little superficial but doesn't deserve the wrath of Ben Matthews and whatever he has planned next." I respond, feeling myself relaxing a little more. I'm not in this alone anymore.

"When's your date?" Hudson asks

"Tomorrow. When's yours?"

"Thursday."

"Perfect. We will go along with Ben's game as best we can. I think we have to until we know more. We could always lie about what we find out. I mean after all he's the one teaching us to lie."

"Do you think he will know if we're making something up?"

"I hope not. I guess it's a read-the-room, think-on-your-feet, use-your-best-judgment kind of scenario."

"So, what should we tell him about our meeting tonight?" Hudson asks.

"Well, you said you hurt your brother. I hate to ask this, but I will need to know more about your betrayal. Ben will want details. I'm sure of it. I'm sorry, I know it's hard to talk about, but if he's really testing us, we need to play this part smart."

"OK, I think that's a good idea, as much as I don't want to." Hudson says. He takes a long pause, "I've never told anyone this, and somehow Ben found out. I have no idea how he knew."

"It's OK. I won't judge you. You can trust me."

Hudson looks down at his drink, he swirls it around a few times. He takes a deep breath before he begins.

"I had an affair with Nadia, Jordan's wife. She was so beautiful, and she wasn't happy. I was there for her when Jordan was off doing whatever it was that Jordan does. I knew it was wrong, but I've never had a girl like that give me any attention—ever. It felt good, and I enjoyed spending time with her. She was sweet and kind, but I knew it wouldn't last forever. Eventually she broke it off, because it was wrong, and she thanked me for helping her see that Jordan wasn't the right man for her. She asked for a divorce shortly after she ended our affair. It's all my fault that Jordan's life is ruined. I wasn't thinking when I got involved with her. Now, saying this all out loud, I can't help but feel it's my fault that Jordan found the club. If he were still married to Nadia, he wouldn't have found or needed Ben."

Oh Hudson, your secret is bad, but mine is so much worse.

"Don't beat yourself up about that. Yes, it's a huge mistake, but you said Nadia was sad. If it had not been you, it would have been another guy. Jordan finding Ben is not your fault."

"OK, what about you? I need to know the worst thing you've ever done."

"It's a long story. Maybe we should order another round of drinks."

CHAPTER FORTY-TWO

Max
Sunday, October 10, 7:39 p.m.

"This is hard for me to say. I don't even know how to verbalize it. I've kept this part of me hidden for two years. I'm sure Ben knows most of it—he's hinted as much—but he hasn't come out and said it. Since he knows yours, chances are he's not bluffing. So, this is the first time that I've ever spoken about this since it happened."

I pull in a deep breath. I'm reluctant to give away my secret but I'm wedged between a rock and a hard place.

"Trust me when I say this: I don't want to know your secret, Max."

"I know, Hudson. But it is what it is, and we are both wrapped up in this web together now. Ben will know if I don't tell you and would punish me somehow, most likely using it against me. So, I may as well pull off the very large Band-Aid."

I take a long gulp of my beer, gaining some liquid courage and buying myself another moment.

"My ex-girlfriend," I begin, "she was beautiful and smart but manipulative. Of course, I see the latter now in hindsight—I have had a *lot* of time to reflect on our time together. I had no say in our relationship. My friends all saw it, and they gave me crap for it. She whittled my self-esteem down to practically nothing. It was lower than it ever was. She called me a coward for not sticking up for her when people talked about her—to be fair, primarily true things, so it was hard to defend her when it was the truth.

"She wanted me to be a normal guy—the doting boy toy. I was not what she wanted, but she tried to mold me into her perfect boyfriend. The more I resisted, the more vicious she got."

"Why didn't you leave her if she was so awful?"

"Hindsight is twenty-twenty, I suppose. I knew it was bad, but I didn't realize how much I was hurting until later."

Hudson nods.

"I don't know. . . I guess after someone whittles you down for so long, you start to believe that no one else will love you, so you might as well stay. I guess that's why I'm the way I am now. I know I'm judgmental and cynical, but I lived with a superficial person for so long. An addiction to showcasing a perfect life for social media, eats at a person, you know."

"I imagine that would be hard."

"I know that's why I hate all this Socialite, social media bullshit. I saw how it changed a person. She cared more about her likes than her real happiness. Everything she did was for show. Nothing was real. All of it was staged. It was exhausting.

"So, my 'friends'—I use that term loosely in this retelling—came up with a plan, unbeknownst to me. They wanted her out of my life so I could finally be 'happy Max' again. But what they don't remember about the *Max* before I met her: I was even more sad and lonely. I was just better at hiding it. At least now I had someone, even if she was terrible. They all had their charm to get dates and propel them from one night to the next. Sure,

I was excelling in other areas of my life but not in the dating department. I didn't have what they had, but they never cared to ask how I felt in all this. Sorry, this is a long story, but it's kinda therapeutic to finally talk about it."

"I understand. What happened next? What was their plan?"

"My 'friend' Cal thought it would be fun to test her loyalty to me. If she passed, then they would drop it. At least, that's what Cal told them.

"Every year, my ex would throw an epic New Year's Eve extravaganza. We lived in her parents' old house. It was a gorgeous estate: five thousand square feet and more bedrooms than I can even remember. Everyone but me came from money. Mostly trust-fund kids. Well, her dad passed away before we met, and her mother died when she was younger, so everything was left to her. Anyway, this big, grand, exquisitely furnished house made for the perfect party setting. That year's theme was the Roaring Twenties—a rehash of a party she threw the year before she met me. She had the perfect outfit—a vintage flapper girl dress complete with fringe headwear and shoes. She did look stunning, but none of that mattered to me. I would've preferred a quiet evening alone, but I knew that wasn't ever going to be an option. I was also coming down with a cold, and I begged her to cancel, but she wouldn't. She said I was being a baby and would feel better once the guests arrived. She told me to man up and said I had to put on a good show as she threw my costume in my face—the one she insisted I wear. I dutifully did as I was told."

I pause, not sure if I can go on. It's too painful.

"Max, if you don't want to continue, it's OK."

"I don't want to, but I don't have a choice."

Hudson gives a sympathetic nod.

"After a few hours," I say, "I was sick of the small talk and gave up trying. I took some night-time cold medicine and snuck down to my basement—the one place I could be myself. Little did I know that my friends were scheming upstairs. They took my absence as the perfect opportunity to put their plan into motion. Cal was my one single friend. He was the best looking of all of us too—he kind of reminds me of your brother as far as looks go. No one said no to Cal. So, he was the perfect one to try to get her to cheat on me.

"Hours later, the party was still roaring, and feeling a little better after a nap, I decide to sneak back upstairs and rejoin the land of the living. My ex was nowhere to be found. I thought perhaps she got too drunk and wandered off to bed, but that wasn't like her. She always said goodbye to all her guests.

"I thought I'd check upstairs anyway, and I pushed the door open to our bedroom. . ."

"And?"

"And, and there was Cal—" I choke on air as my breath catches. "There was Cal—on top of her, fucking her. I didn't know what I was seeing. I—"

My throat is closing, and my vision begins to blur from the tears welling in my eyes. I drop my head to avoid attention from the people around us. I grab the napkin from under my beer and use it to inconspicuously dab my eyes.

"I hate myself for everything that I'm about to tell you. I was disoriented, and I didn't know how to react. In that moment, I just stood there. Emotionless.

"When Cal noticed me in the doorway, he pushed her down into the bed, reclaimed his clothing and shoved me into the wall as he passed me.

"She laid there in bed, naked, covered only by a thin sheet."

"'Are you going to fight for me?' she hollered. There were no tears in her eyes, just anger toward me.

"Everything from that point on was a haze. Maybe it was the cold medicine or the trauma of the event. I stumbled down the stairs back to the party where only a few people were left. One of my friends said, it wasn't meant to go that far, vaguely filling me in on the events that led to the incident. 'I didn't think he'd really go through with it,' one of them said. I was so confused. Did he rape her, or did she willingly have sex with him? The confusion shifted to anger as both thoughts zipped through my mind.

"Then I heard a loud thud, she was throwing my stuff off the balcony and onto the lawn. 'You're a coward, Max Jennings,' she yelled.

"And in that moment, I couldn't argue with her. I didn't fight for her, I simply gathered what I could, tossed my stuff in my car, and let the anger course through my veins; I was heated. I was upset. I was confused. Everything I knew was falling apart."

I pause, patting my eyes again.

"Hudson, I honestly don't know what came over me, but a foggy idea crept into my head—If she wanted me to fight for her, I was going to fucking do it.

"I went back inside, and by this time, the final few stragglers had taken our fight as a cue to leave. I marched downstairs to where her dad's collection of guns was, and I grabbed a rifle from the cabinet. My ex's dad used to hunt, and his gun collection was his most prized possession. I didn't know how to use a gun, which was another thing she hated about me. 'You live in America, you should know how to use a gun,' she'd say. I didn't know how to check if it was loaded or not. I assumed it wouldn't be. I mean, why would the guns be stored fully loaded?

"Everything from that moment on was a blur, but I know I drove to Cal's house, blind with rage. I think I just wanted to scare him and show her how I stood up for her, for us." Tears stream down my cheeks. "I-I fired into the room. . ."

"Max, then what happened?"

"I honestly don't know. I shot at him, but I don't know if he's alive, dead, or injured. I don't even know if I even hit him. I just ran. I skipped town that very night.

"She wanted me to stand up for her, not to be a coward, and well, that's what I did. I fought for her and then I ran out of the room like the coward she says I am. If she only knew that I tried. I was late, but I tried, and I fucked up."

"So, you've been on the run ever since?"

"Pretty much."

"Did you ever look into what happened to Cal?"

"I always had one eye over my shoulder, expecting someone to find or arrest me. After crossing state lines, I stumbled upon Clear River and found an apartment and a job with Kade. No one came looking for me, so I stayed. After the first year, I eased up a bit. I assumed—and hoped—Cal was OK, and if he was dead, then someone would have surely come for me."

I take a swig of my drink, taking a second to reprocess the past I've been trying so hard to leave behind.

"Maybe my ex didn't even notice the missing rifle. She had a fleet of them, so one absent might not have been easy to spot. I did protect her, after all. I mean, perhaps what she thinks is that she broke up with me, and I disappeared, and Cal was 'shot' by an intruder. I know it's a stretch, but I can only hope that's what they think. I honestly don't know what happened. I don't know what I would do if I ever saw Chrissy Parker again."

Hudson's face paled. "Your ex is Chrissy Parker?"

CHAPTER FORTY-THREE

Max
Sunday, October 10, 8:09 p.m.

I'm paralyzed in my seat. I'm terrified by Hudson's question. I slowly open my mouth, but the words don't come.

"Chrissy Parker? She's your ex-girlfriend? The one from your story?" Hudson says slowly. His small, beady eyes are locked on mine.

I gulp, swallowing hard, several times buying myself another moment. "Yes," I cautiously reply.

Hudson's face is as white as a ghost.

"That's. . . That's my target's name. . ."

His words hit me hard, like a sucker punch to the stomach. All the air whooshes out of me. The room begins to spin. I want to hurl up my drink. My world is crashing down around me.

Immediately, I jump into defense mode. It's the only thing that makes sense; get defensive.

"That, that can't be right. Are you fucking with me? After everything I just told you. That's messed up, bro. Plus, she doesn't live anywhere near here, and she's engaged. You're lying."

A couple sitting near the end of the bar shoot me a nasty glare. I'm causing a scene, but I can't help myself.

Hudson fidgets in his seat, concern spreads across his face. He shoves his hand into his pocket and pulls out his phone. I sit in silence, waiting for a response. Instead, he slides his phone across the bar top. My jaw drops open.

"Is this your Chrissy Parker?"

I turn my head to the side and vomit.

CHAPTER FORTY-FOUR

Max
Monday, October 11, 6:48 p.m.

Last night's revelations were a massive gut punch but also frighteningly eye-opening. After the bartender kicked us out for my unplanned upchuck, we sat in my car, devising a plan to move forward.

"We must keep playing the game. If we go rogue and abandon the club, Ben will hunt us down, our secrets will come out and our targets could get hurt," Hudson stated in the most rational tone he'd had all night.

So, here I am at the Rose Tavern, waiting for my "target." That sounds so fucking twisted. I'm almost shocked that I'm here, given my history. This is the part where I usually take off running—skip town. Oh, that doesn't mean I haven't thought about it—I even started packing a getaway bag when I got home last night—but in the middle of tossing in my T-shirts, I stopped and thought about the situation. I can't run forever, at least not from Ben, and he needs to be taken down. Plus, deep down, I know Ben would find me, eventually. I mean, he found out about

Chrissy, Jovie, and only God knows who else. He apparently has eyes and ears everywhere, so I may as well stay and fight. What on earth have I got myself into?

"Hey, buddy, you're back. Good to see you. Boneyard's Hop Venom again?" Mark the bartender says, disrupting my unruly thoughts.

"Yes, please. Thanks for remembering."

Mark nods his head and then begins to pour my beer. I'm impressed he remembered me from the single time I was here, and he even recalled my drink order.

I can't help but wonder if Kade's been back since Evie.

I nestle myself onto one of the cozy handcrafted barstools. I allowed myself extra time before Ivy is due to arrive to gather my thoughts and take in a little liquid courage before the shit show of my life continues. I didn't have time to prepare a list of questions to seek out Ivy's secrets—I have more significant problems on my mind—I will simply have to wing it tonight.

Mark slides my beer over to me. I give him a friendly smile before returning to my maddening thoughts. I've been digesting the information from yesterday, and one thing is crystal clear: Ben is playing us as pawns in his sick and twisted game. That's all we are to him. A game piece, like the tiny thimble in Monopoly, moving us around the board. Some players have even been to jail, and Ben is the only one with the get-out-of-jail-free card. And then there is Emmy. Is she a pawn too? Is she a player in this game?

Today at work, I could barely think. Luckily, Emmy had the day off, so I had time to figure out what to do with her. I replayed the past few weeks in my head over and over until I wasn't sure what was real anymore and what I'd fabricated. Everything seems so unreal that nothing makes sense. The lies, deceit, and games have woven themselves into a web that I'm stuck in. Ben is the spider, and we are all the little bugs wrapped tight, connected in fear while stuck in the nearly invisible fibers of Ben's twisted mind.

I would never have pegged Emmy as a pawn, well, that is until her little slip-up about Jovie yesterday. I would've had no reason to suspect Emmy of working with Ben, and Hudson's revelation could have simply been written off as a fucked-up coincidence. But now I know there is no limit to how twisted this game is.

Hudson and I decided I would feel her out, and if it comes to it, just ask her point-blank. That wasn't the initial plan, but after much deliberation, we realized we need to pull the Band-Aid off fast and see what's under it. If she's stuck like us, then she's likely to be eager and happy to help us out. But if it's the other way and she's voluntarily working for him. . . Well, we will cross that bridge when we get there, but I can't see the latter being true. God, I hope not. I trusted her.

Then I have the Chrissy situation. I mean, holy hell, what a bombshell. Hudson gathered from Chrissy that she has just moved to the adjoining town, but she didn't say anything to Hudson about being in a relationship or having a fucking fiancé, for that matter.

Ben gave Hudson Chrissy for a reason. Ben knows Chrissy is my weakness, and he found all of this out in a matter of a few weeks. Things are not adding up.

I take a long gulp of my beer and grab a handful of communal pretzels from a bowl near me. I chomp angrily on the salty snack.

Hudson is a lot like me, whether I want to admit it or not. We are both insecure but have good qualities that we overlook. He could be easily manipulated by Chrissy, and Chrissy enjoys toying with weak men; it's a self-confidence booster for her.

But what is bothering me is, what happened to her fiancé and why and when did she move? Knowing Chrissy, she would have posted every aspect of her engagement on her socials, right down to the very last detail, because that's who she is. But the only thing I saw on Socialite was a simple announcement. Nothing else. No wedding-dress shopping photos. No champagne toasts with her girls. Nothing. Unless Chrissy has changed her ways, which I highly doubt. Also, there is the fact that Chrissy would never give up her parents' house. Not just for sentimental reasons but status.

Maybe there is a simple reason they broke off the engagement— it happens— but if that is what happened, and she needed a change of scenery, why Clear River? Does she know where I am? Is she looking for me? No, that's silly, it's been two years, and if she wanted to find me, she probably could have by now. Look how easily Ben found out my secrets. I clearly wasn't hiding as well as I thought.

When I told Hudson she was engaged, he said there was no mention of that on her feed now or when he did his recon work. It's simply gone. Chrissy never mentioned it to him. He said their conversation was cutesy and nothing too flirty, but she did agree to meet him easily. He didn't have to twist her arm, or anything and he was shocked by this. It was almost a little too easy.

I need to know why Ben chose her for Hudson. What's his endgame with all of this? I told Hudson I was going to watch his date from afar. I'm curious about Chrissy. I need to see her without her seeing me. But that's Thursday's problem. Today is Ivy. Tomorrow is Emmy. Wednesday is Ben. This is a vicious cycle. Life was simpler just a few short weeks ago. No club. No dead girls. No game.

"Max, is that you?" an airy voice asks from behind me. A chill runs down my spine.

I give myself a mental pep talk. OK, Max, you got this. Yes, it's part of the game, but it's also a chance to be someone different and practice for the real thing. That is if I ever get the opportunity to have a real date. As long as Ben and this game don't completely implode my life.

I get up from my chair like a gentleman and extend my hand to shake hers. She reaches in for mine, but I can tell I've caught her off guard. She's not used to this proper behavior. Everything is casual nowadays. I know that I'm the odd one. Everyone is doing the same thing, but me. I'm drowning in this new world.

Be confident Max. You got this.

"You must be Ivy. It's so nice to meet you. Gosh, you're more beautiful in person," I find myself saying without premeditative thought. It was a true statement; the girl was very pretty but still not my type.

"Oh, stop, you've got me blushing," Ivy gushes as she flips her beachy waves behind her shoulder.

"Should we get a table?" I ask.

"Yes, absolutely," she says with a bright white smile.

After we get our table, we order Ivy her first drink and me my second. I realize that I don't know what to say to her. We really didn't have anything in common, but then I remember this is a game, and everything I say is all a lie. I feel bad lying to Ivy, but I have to play along. I doubt Ivy will have any real feelings for me, so it won't hurt her.

Then a horrid thought hits me right in the gut. If Chrissy was chosen for Hudson because of me, then who does Ivy belong to? She must be here because of another member. We are all pawns, even our targets. Maybe I can ask questions to get her to tell me about her previous boyfriend? I don't waste time, and I dive right in.

"How is a girl like you single?" I ask flirtatiously.

"I guess I haven't found the right guy," she replies, letting out an uncomfortable laugh.

"Oh, so when was your last serious relationship?" I press. After all, this is more of a fact-finding mission for me than a date.

"What is this? An interview? That's a little too forward for a first date, don't cha think?" she says with a smile and takes a drink of her IPA that the waiter had brought over.

"How about you start by telling me more about yourself? After all, you were pretty vague. I'm here because I'm intrigued and want to know more about you," Ivy says, quickly turning the table on me.

This is not going as planned, but I have to go along with it to keep her interested and find out why she was chosen for me and who she belongs to.

Time to play the game, Max. I'm surprised at how quickly I select my lies.

"I graduated with a degree in history from Oregon State a few years back. I didn't do anything with it, though. Then I kind of bummed around Portland and enjoyed the art and music scene for a year before settling in Clear River."

"Why history?" she asks. If I were her, I would have asked about my time in Portland. That sounds much more interesting, but whatever. It's all a lie, anyway.

"The past is fascinating. The future is what's scary," I respond.

She wrinkles her flawlessly tanned nose. I suspect she doesn't like my response. So, I elaborate to see if that changes anything.

"We can learn from the past. To avoid making the same mistakes, but the ignorance of most people leads to a frightening future."

She bites her lip and takes another sip of her drink. Completely disregarding my statement. She doesn't even try to banter or even disagree.

I can't even lie myself into being a confident man. It's no wonder I can't get a real girl. I'm drowning. This is supposed to be my chance to try and I'm failing.

Ivy gives me a blank stare, as if she's looking straight through me. Ignoring everything, she jumps in, "So, I went to UCLA for marketing. I mostly do social media marketing for startups," she says while running her fingers through her long, wavy blonde hair. "I work for myself," she continues, "and I love it, and I'm quite good at it."

Is that what she calls getting to know me? OK, whatever, but I'm not surprised by her response. Of course, that's her job. I can't help but roll my eyes. Luckily, she has already diverted her attention and has her head turned down toward her phone. Can't miss any precious notifications. I haven't checked mine all night, and the world hasn't ended. Ivy keeps her head buried in her phone and barely looks back up at me.

When the waiter comes over to take our food order, he actually has to wait for her to finish typing on her device before she even acknowledges his presence. We both order the Rose Tavern signature burger with steak fries. At least we really do have that in common.

As the server walks away, it's clear that Ivy's lost interest in our conversation. How does Ben think I'm going to pry a secret from this girl? She's hardly said two sentences to me.

"The building is on fire. Should we toast some marshmallows?" I say jokingly in an attempt to catch her attention.

"Yeah, sure. Sounds good," she mutters back, clearly not listening to a word I'm saying.

Is this a normal date nowadays? I haven't been on one in years. Do people still talk to each other? I glance around the restaurant and see several couples placed around us—all ages. At least one person is on their phone at each table.

"I've got two signature burgers. Can I get either of you any ketchup or anything else?" the waiter says when he returns a few minutes later. The service is definitely speedy.

"No, I'm good. Thanks," I respond.

Both of us look at Ivy, and she doesn't say a word. I find it rude that she doesn't even thank the waiter for bringing the food.

"Great burger," I say after the first bite.

"Yep," she responds and then glances back at her phone.

I know Ben will make me pay for my mistake. This shit show of a date is going to cost me.

CHAPTER FORTY-FIVE

Mr. Scorpio: *Let's meet for real. I'm dying to get to know you better. Come on, let's meet up. Burgers and beer on me!*

[?]: *I don't know. I have a lot going on. I don't know if I'd be good company.*

Mr. Scorpio: *You pick the place. Out in public. Tell your friends where you will be and that you will check in. I'm dying to meet you.*

[?]: *You don't give up, do you?*

Mr. Scorpio: *Nope.*

Mr. Scorpio: *I sense a real connection with you. If I'm not your type, then what do you have to lose? An hour of your time,* but the free food and beer should at least make up for that.

[?]: Fine. You've twisted my arm. Let's meet at Clear River Brewing Company tomorrow. Wear something warm because I want to eat outside so I can run if you're a creeper. Just being honest.

Mr. Scorpio: *It's a date. Meet you at seven.*

[?]: OK. See you then.

CHAPTER FORTY-SIX

Emmy
Tuesday, October 12, 10:35 a.m.

"We need to talk," Max demands the second I walk through the front door of Epic Records.

"Can't a girl take off her coat first? Dang. What's the rush, Max?" I playfully respond, although my entire body is throwing up red-flag alerts. My heart begins to race, and my temples start to pulsate. Max's tone is cold. Could this be the moment I've been fearing? I attempt to control my breathing. I don't dare meet his eyes as I hurry past him.

"Now!" Max shouts.

I anxiously bite my bottom lip with my two front teeth, but quickly catch my nervous giveaway.

"Hold your horses, bucko. Just give me a second. Traffic was crazy out there. I've barely had a moment to think. Just let me take off my coat and get settled first. It's not like I'm late or anything, and there is hardly a soul in here this morning," I shout back toward Max, keeping up my usual banter.

"It's important, Emmy," Max scoffs as I round the corner to the backroom.

My heart plummets. I swear it's crashing into the pit of my tummy and nestling itself into my breakfast of eggs and toast. He was never supposed to find out. Maybe I'm in my head. Maybe he doesn't know. Perhaps he wants to yell at me for forgetting to flip the open sign to closed again. Yes, that's probably it; I have been a bit all over the place these past few days.

I take a deep breath and hope for a slap on the wrist for announcing to the world we're open when clearly a dark-lit store suggests otherwise. I keep my cool and jump back into our usual back-and-forth. "Dang, Max, what's got your panties all in a bunch on this beautiful Tuesday morning?" I tease. "Have you heard from Kade lately?" A pathetic attempt to divert the conversation.

"No, I haven't."

"We need to talk, Emmy."

"OK, what's going on, Max? I've never seen you like this."

"I'm just going to ask you. I know I shouldn't, and you're probably going to tattle on me, but fuck it. Are you working with Ben Matthews? I just need to know. Give it to me straight, Emmy."

"What do you mean 'am I working with Ben Matthews?' Are you kidding me right now, Max?"

My heart is swirling around now, mixing with my breakfast and slowly making its way up my esophagus.

"I'm not working with Ben. That's insane," I say, tossing my hands in the air. I pick up a stack of records and slam them back down on the counter. "I should be the one asking you what's going on with Ben and Kade and every other weird thing that's been going on here since you started asking about Ben," I shout with so much drama that I would consider my performance Oscar-worthy.

I watch as Max stumbles for his words. He knows I'm right, and my theatrics have caught him off guard. This is not normal behavior for either of us. We don't fight; we play. It's our thing.

"Em, I thought I could trust you. I want to trust you," Max says. His eyes wallow up with sadness, and I want to throw my arms around him and tell him everything. But I can't.

"Why were you at the club the night Evie Simmons died?" he asks.

"Whoa, are you saying I had something do with Evie Simmons's death? Now I know you've lost your mind."

"I don't know. I just know someone saw you leaving the place where Ben Matthews was that night. It just so happened to be the night Evie died, I'm simply using it as a reference. But Emmy, if you know something—something that could help Kade. . ."

Fuck, shit, damn it, and every other cuss word I can't think of right now. I bite my lip, and immediately the copper taste of blood hits my tongue. I'm so anxious I hurt myself without realizing it. I instantly suck on my bottom lip to stop the bleeding before Max notices that I'm a full-blown nervous wreck.

"That's absurd," I tout back, stomping my right foot into the ground.

"Is it?"

"Yes."

"Just tell me what Ben has on you, and I will help you. Emmy, I know everything—well not everything, but I know stuff," Max says, losing some of his confidence.

I take a deep breath before the words automatically come out. "Max, I told you to be careful. You need to watch what you say and do next." I can't help myself. I care for Max. He knows something, and I don't think he will give up.

"Emmy!"

"Max!" I reciprocate.

Our eyes lock into an intense stare-down. My eyes erupt with tears, and Max's eyes flood with an emotional mixture of pain and sadness. Tears rush down his cheeks at the same pace that I can feel my own as if they're in a race against each other. We're hurting each other so much; I can't stand it. The hairs on my arm stand straight up, and I fear for everything in this very moment.

The world is spinning, and I burst. I can't take it anymore. The lies. The secrets. The sneaking around.

"Ben's blackmailing me," I whisper into our empty store. I have to repeat myself in case it wasn't real the first time. "Ben's fucking blackmailing me, Max."

CHAPTER FORTY-SEVEN

Max
Tuesday, October 12, 10:45 a.m.

My feet give way and I crumble to the ground. Emmy is the one person I thought that I could trust, and it turns out Ben has her on a leash too. She must have a good reason for getting mixed up with this vile creature. I mean, I *hope* she does. I don't want to see anything other than remorse from her from this point on. I understand the kind of hold Ben can have on a person, and I can forgive her if her story is that of Ben being a lying-ass monster.

"OK, I need you to tell me everything. How long have you been working with him? When did Ben get to you, and why and how?"

Emmy kneels next to me on the ground. She bats her eyes a few times, attempting to clear away the tears and pats her sweater against her cheeks. She avoids looking me in the eye. "First, tell me how you found out?" she asks.

"Someone saw you."

"Well. . ." Emmy says, looking down to her hands fidgeting in her lap. "He found me on campus, sitting in on classes that I didn't pay for."

I quickly interject. "What on earth was Ben doing on a college campus?"

Emmy looks up, giving me an annoyed glare, her face still splotchy. "Anyway, it's been a while since I was in school, and it's my dream to go back to grad school. But I can't afford it. I'm stupid-ass broke. But then, I don't know, something got the better of me one day, and I just started sitting in on lectures and no one noticed. That is, until Ben did."

I nod for her to keep going.

"Ben was nice when he told me he knew about my little secret, and I begged him not to tell anyone, and I promised that I would quit coming to the classes. He laughed and said he didn't care about that, and I remember feeling relieved but then also a little scared. So why did this guy care then? At that point, I didn't know if he was a student or a TA, but he seemed too old to be either of them, but who am I to judge? He then proceeded to tell me that he wanted to fund my grad-school tuition, but he wouldn't do it until the following year. He had a few simple tasks that he needed me to complete for him. I told him he was out of his mind. I thought he was talking about sexual favors, but he assured me that it wasn't that, but I still didn't care. I walked away, and I didn't step foot back on campus."

"So, where is this going?" I say impatiently.

"Well, you see, I wasn't going to do what he asked, but then I got these little notes at my house. The bastard knew where I lived. He tracked me down. His first task was laid out inside an envelope shoved in the mailbox, along with a massive stack of cash. The more I did, the more money he would give me, it said. I'd done the math many times, and I knew I would never be able to afford grad school on my own; the grants I could apply for wouldn't cover what I needed, and my parents make too much money but they would never give any of it to me, so there goes any aid I could get. I used everything I had to get into college in the first place. I'm broke, and I have so much student-loan debt that I can barely stay afloat. So, I broke down, and agreed to help Ben. The first thing was to get a job here. That seemed simple. Plus, I could use the cash from working here, anyway."

"Are you serious? You've been working with Ben that long? Emmy, you're one of Ben's spies. How do I know that I can trust—?"

At that moment, the door flings open and we quickly stand, alert.

I almost forgot the store is open. We both go quiet, and I observe the guy, making sure it's not one of Ben's cronies but then again, how would I know that? He's probably handing envelopes of cash and to-do lists out all over this town. We wait until the guy walks to the end of the aisle, and then Emmy continues.

"Max, I'm laying it all out there. I'm telling you my whole truth. You can trust me. I promise," she says, placing her hand on top of mine.

I yank my hand from under hers. "Keep going."

She frowns. "At first, it was easy. I took the job with Kade, but Ben didn't come around. I got antsy—I wanted to see more of the money he promised. I didn't understand why he wanted me to work here. I called him, and he was pissed that I was greedy. He didn't speak to me for two whole weeks. I was about to quit and give up, but then another envelope showed up at my house with cash and a second task to keep an eye on Kade and report back to him. I did that for months."

"I can't believe you kept tabs on Kade."

"I know, and it got harder the more I got to know him. I really like Kade, and I do worry about him. All my feelings and emotions about him are real. I love working here. I really do. I just hate the premise of why I'm here. When Ben's not asking me questions, I can forget for just a minute and enjoy my job with the boys. I even like Jake and Jed."

"So, when did I become part of this?"

"Max, please don't hate me. Ben was curious about you for some reason. I don't know if Kade talked about you, or if Ben saw you in here, but he was intrigued by you. I think he was hoping Kade would bring you around, but it didn't happen. So, he asked me to leave you hints. Things that would get you asking questions and lead you to him. But I couldn't. Plus, you're judgmental about shit like that and people like Ben. Nothing I would do would work with you anyway. I lied to Ben, and I suspect Ben caught on to my ruse.

"The day you first asked me about him, I was shocked that he came in on his own. I had to think quick and pretend. I couldn't warn you, but I did tell you he gave me bad vibes. Then he came back in later that night and yelled at Kade. I couldn't help but think Kade might be in serious trouble with Ben and mixed up in a bad way. I didn't know what Ben was capable of, I just knew he was a sneaky son of a bitch. I didn't realize all my comments about Kade would send you off on a hunt for answers. If that's what happened, I'm sorry, Max. I never thought someone like you would ever seek out someone like Ben on your own, so imagine my surprise when Kade asked you to call Ben that day he was led out of here by the detectives. I had no idea that you actually were in contact with him. He didn't tell me, Max. I was so mad at you. I honestly thought you wouldn't bite at whatever he was dangling. I'm so sorry, I, I, I had to play along."

"Does Kade know any of this, Emmy?"

"Oh, God no."

"Do you think Ben could be dangerous?"

"Maybe?" Emmy says with hesitation.

"Why maybe?" I demand.

"Well, that night that you said someone saw me—the night of Evie's murder—I was there at the club, or whatever Ben calls it. He asked me to come, and he's never done that before. It's usually phone calls and notes. He was wild with anger for some reason. I think he was mad at Kade. He told me Kade had messed up."

"But he didn't tell you that I joined the club?" I ask.

"Like I said, no."

"He must have known that Kade didn't recruit me and that I came on my own. He was probably pissed at Kade and me for lying to him."

"He wanted more information on Kade that night. He wanted to know where he would be and what he's been doing. I didn't have any more dirt than I usually do. Ben was furious and told me to leave. I sat in my car crying."

"That's when my friend saw you," I say.

"Then suddenly Kade is a wanted man? I'm truly worried that Ben has something to do with those girls, Max. I'm afraid of Ben and what he could be capable of. That's why I've been acting the way I have lately."

Knowing what I know about Hudson following Kade, do I tell this to Emmy? Hudson, Emmy, or I didn't kill those women. I doubt more and more that Kade did, but someone killed them, and the list is getting shorter of who could be the killer.

"Emmy, you promise on our real friendship that I can trust you?"

"Yes, Max. How many times do I have to say you can trust me? I'm sorry for what I did. I'm sorry I went through your phone when you left it out. I spied but I had to play along with Ben's wishes."

Whoa, that's a new revelation, but that explains how Ben knew so many things. Emmy interrupts my thoughts.

"I'm pretty sure he has a hacker, anyway, to get the information he needed. So don't use your phone or computer. He tracked me down, remember?" Emmy adds.

"This explains a lot. I need to tell you I'm working with someone—another member," I say.

"Can he be trusted?" Emmy asks.

"Yes, we both have dirt on each other—things I have to trust him with. He's a little awkward, but my gut instinct says he's one of us."

"Oh my gosh, it's the weird guy that was in here a few weeks ago, isn't it? I thought he looked familiar. He's the one who saw me, isn't he?"

"Yes, that's him. Emmy, you need to carry on like normal until we can figure out what to do. Can you do that? And do you realize that this will mean giving up your chance at going back to college? Well, at least right now. I promise I will help you figure out how to pay for it once this is all over."

"Yes. I know, but I didn't realize what I was getting myself into, and I'm ready to be out. It's too dangerous, and I feel so much better now that you know everything."

"I'm glad we're working together too."

"Do we clue Kade in?"

"I'm not sure yet."

"He probably needs to be warned, but we don't know for sure if we can trust him. He's been with Ben a long time. Even if Ben is trying to implicate him, Kade owes him a lot, so we can't be too careful. Plus, he needs Ben's lawyer right now. We can't fuck that up for him."

"What if Ben's lawyer is working against Kade?"

"I sure hope that's not the case. We will play that by ear then. We will try to do what's best for Kade, regardless of Ben's orders."

"Let's take the son of a bitch down."

CHAPTER FORTY-EIGHT

Mr. Scorpio: *Good morning, beautiful.*
I had a great time with you.

[?]: I have to admit that I had fun too.
Maybe we can meet up again on Saturday?
I thought you were witty. I like that.

Mr. Scorpio: *Oh, shoot. I have plans on*
Saturday. How about Friday afternoon?

[?]: What, you got another girl already?
What do you have going on that you can't meet up?

Mr. Scorpio: *It's a thing with my buddies.*
Sorry, babe.

[?]: Babe? We are already using pet names?

Mr. Scorpio: *So, Friday?*

[?]: Fine. Clear River Brewing Company OK

with you again? Maybe we can sit inside this time.

Mr. Scorpio: Perfect. See you at one?

[?]: OK.

Mr. Scorpio: I'm dying in anticipation. ;)

CHAPTER FORTY-NINE

Max
Wednesday, October 13, 7:00 p.m.

I'm playing the game—*my* game—tonight. I have the upper hand. I know things Ben has no idea that I know. I just need to play it cool and not give wind to the fact we're on to him.

"I'm sorry, Max. I've got to fit in the original five tonight, so, it will be just a short fifteen-minute session. Let's dive right in, shall we?" Ben says with haste. "I want to know about your date. Did you get her secret? What is Ivy Peterson hiding?" Ben presses.

"I've told you before, Ivy and I don't have much in common." Which is true, but now I need to keep my blonde target safe from Ben, so even if she had spilled any secrets, I wouldn't tell him.

Ben furrows his brow and curls his lip in disgust. "Max, you know I don't fucking tolerate excuses. Grow up and act like a man and do what is asked of you, for fuck's sake. I'm sick of all your pushback and lazy attitude. You need to do the work, or you will never be able to move on and be the man you were meant to be."

I rock back in my seat. Ben's temperament has done a one-eighty. Ben leaps off his chair, letting it bang against the bar top. I've been the one with an outburst during our one-on-one time; never Ben. He's usually well composed and has a level head, even when I pushback.

I'm getting under his skin.

Or maybe he knows Hudson and I have teamed up.

Well, game on, Ben. Game on.

Ben walks back to me, and before taking his seat, he recomposes himself. He readjusts the collar on his shirt and continually presses it down as if it's an ingrained behavior that recenters him.

"Well, you're not playing the game right, Max. You were told to fake it and become what you need to win: to get her secrets. So, did you get anything out of that fake bitch?"

"No, I didn't. I know I failed, but she was so tied up on her phone the whole night, I could hardly get her to talk."

"Could you see what she was doing on her phone?"

"No, I didn't think to look."

"Max, you have to be open to all possibilities. Most people's secrets are hidden right there on their phones. Some people show their secrets in plain sight when they think no one is watching. Pay better attention."

"OK."

"And maybe that's the way to get to Ivy. In-person dates might not be her thing. Maybe she'd open up more in messages—less-personal, less-real kind of thing. Max, I trust you will get what you need by Saturday. I can't have you dropping out of the game so soon. I'd hoped to see you in the finale—don't disappoint me."

"Finale?"

"Of course! Every game must have a finale. And trust me when I say you won't want to miss this."

What the hell is Ben planning?

"So, tell me about your time with Hudson," Ben continues, a bit calmer now.

"He told me about Nadia. I'm sure you already know the whole story."

Ben gives me a frustrated scowl. "Yes, I do. That's the only thing he told you?"

"He feels responsible for their divorce, and it's a huge burden on him. It really messed him up. He feels awful, and it would kill him if Jordan ever found out."

"OK, good. But that's it?"

"Yes, why is there more to the story?" I ask innocently.

He's testing the waters to see if Hudson slipped up and told me about his extra-credit task. I'm not faltering; I'm stone and I'm enjoying watching him squirm. Oh, yes, Ben, we see you now. We see who you really are. We have our own game to play, and you, sir, are my pawn now.

"Um, no. I was just curious if he said anything else," Ben says, his uncertainty very thinly veiled.

I'm surprised he doesn't ask me what I told Hudson, but I don't dare bring it up. I can't chance making any mistakes. It's all up to Hudson now.

CHAPTER FIFTY

Hudson
Wednesday, October 13, 7:30 p.m.

"I'm glad to see you've calmed down since our last time together, Hudson," Ben says, smugger than usual. Is he one step ahead of us? We are all fucked if he is, but we were careful. Right?

"We have a lot to discuss since the last time you were here," Ben continues. "I hope you've moved on from the Kade thing, and you've realized that it's not your fault that Evie died."

"Yes." I lie. "I don't think Kade did it, and if that's true, then I didn't have anything to do with the murder of Evie Simmons."

All lies. I still feel guilty, and I'm leaning more toward Kade being set up, but I still need proof. No matter what, I was a part of this, and nothing will make me feel better. But I must put on a show.

"I'm so happy to hear that you've come to terms with that. Now you're ready to do some real work."

"How did you know all those things about me? About Nadia?"

"You can find out anything you want to about a person if you know where to look," Ben says matter-of-factly.

"What the hell does that mean?"

It's clear Ben isn't going to give up his secrets.

"When is your date?" he asks.

"Tomorrow."

"Good."

"So, I'm dying to know how the secret trade went with Max. Did you guys put it all out there like I told you to?"

"I only told him about Nadia, if that's what you're asking."

"Well, that secret was a huge burden of weight on you. I hope you feel lighter now."

"I suppose I do," I respond.

Ben is silent, expecting me to continue. I'd rather not talk about this, but if I don't, I'm afraid he will pick at me until I tell him what Max and I know; the web of Ben's game that we are unpicking together.

"I guess it felt good to talk about it, but the memories stung. I hurt Jordan, but it was easy to do back then when he was being an ass to me and everyone else, including Nadia. He neglected her and she was unhappy. I was a shoulder for her to lean on, and then things went too far. I was too nice, and she needed that. I feel bad, but Jordan didn't deserve a girl like her, and I never had a girl like her. So, things happened."

"Why do you think Jordan was being an ass back then?"

"I don't really know. I didn't see him much and when I did, he was moody, but he was successful, so I always chalked it up to the stress of that."

"That's not your fault. It's Nadia's. She was the whore who strayed."

I'm unnerved by how freely he tosses that word around. I want to defend Nadia because she's not a whore, but Ben doesn't want to hear that. She's a good person who was stuck in an unhappy marriage. I used Nadia as much as she used me, but she's not a bad person.

"I trust you're telling me the truth when you say that's all you spilled," Ben continues.

Panic ripples under my skin. "Yes. That's it." I respond, hoping my elevated voice doesn't give me away.

"So, what about Max? Did he tell you the worst thing he's ever done?" Ben looks eager to hear, and I'm relieved that he didn't pick up on my tells.

I have to play it cool. I can't say anything that will link my target to Max's ex. I suspect that's something Ben wanted us to connect for some sick and twisted reason.

"He told me about his ex. She really messed him up. She emasculated him. Called him names like *coward*. It was emotionally hard on him. His friends saw it, and they didn't like the girl, and something awful happened. Max fucked up, and he might have hurt his friend."

"Did you say who his ex was or who the friend was?" Ben asks. The exhilaration in his voice is undeniable.

"No, he didn't use names. He was pretty vague."

"Oh," Ben says, almost disappointed. "Well, the practice worked. You both have something on each other, so that should bond you in trust."

"OK, Hudson, we're cutting the session short tonight. I'm seeing the original five in between sessions, so it appears that's all the time I have tonight. Do me proud tomorrow."

On my way out of the club, I catch a glimpse of Kade. He's gruff-looking and walking in haste. He doesn't look happy to be here. I thought he was lying low. I don't acknowledge him when we pass by each other. I suspect Kade would prefer it that way too.

CHAPTER FIFTY-ONE

Kade
Wednesday, October 13, 7:45 p.m.

Ben requested the old members come in for a one-on-one session. I haven't been to one of these since the new recruits were brought in. I didn't want to go in, especially with what the police are doing, but Ben didn't really give us a choice.

Thankfully, the reporters have let up a bit since nothing new has been released. But I'm still freaking out. There is no evidence that ties me to the murders, but I'm connected—somehow.

I pass Hudson on my way into the building. That guy, Jordan's brother, always looks sad and scared, yet when I catch his eyes, I see pity for me in them. Hudson pities me! No one ever used to pity me.

"Hi, Kade. No one followed you over here, did they? No reporters or police?" Ben says as I walk into the club. He's paranoid and on edge; a side of him I'm not used to seeing.

"No, I was careful. I haven't seen anyone in a couple of days. Don't worry—I'm not stupid," I respond.

I need Ben's full attention because I need help.

"Ben, someone is trying to make it look like I killed those women. Don't you see the connection?

"I don't know what to do. Dennis said to sit tight, but I'm getting nervous. I told the police that I didn't know Jessica, but I do know her. I slept with her a week before they found her body. The cops didn't tie us together, so I lied. Someone is out to get me, but why?"

Ben takes a seat and stares into my eyes. His energy has shifted to one of utter concentration. He doesn't answer right away, but lets the stillness linger before responding.

"Did you kill them?" Ben asks with a straight face.

"What the hell, Ben? Are you really asking me this?" But his tone and expression doesn't suggest he's kidding around. He's told me over and over again that he believes me. I'm using his goddamn lawyer, for Christ's sake.

"Well, it's a valid question. You don't respect women, and you already discard them like trash when you're done with them," Ben responds coldly.

"Yes, that's because you taught me to do that." I throw my response back in his face. It's his fault, and he's acting like he's had nothing to do with the man I've become.

"No, I taught you to give up feeling bad about it. It's who you are, and you should embrace that. Be true to yourself. That's what I taught you."

"Are you kidding me right now? You pushed me to be this way. You coaxed me into feeding my urges with sex and drinking."

"It's better than the alternative—feeding your urges with violence. Kade, you have a dark side—demons that were eating you alive when we met. If I didn't help you the best way I knew how, you'd probably be in jail for hurting someone—or worse—by now."

"Well, a fat lot of good that's done, because the police want me for two murders no matter if I did it or not. I guess the cosmic joke is on me. I tried to behave, and it didn't matter."

"So, you didn't kill them?" Ben asks with almost a laugh in his voice.

"No, I didn't fucking kill Evie or Jessica. If you're messing around with me, I need you to knock it off." I raise my hand toward Ben's face. I'm not going to hit him, but I'd like for him to think I just might. What I wouldn't give to punch him in his righteous, smug face.

"Come on, Kade, you know you're not going to hurt me. That would be the worst thing you could do for yourself. You could say bye-bye to your lawyer, your store, and um. . . One more thing. . . What is it? It's on the tip of my tongue. Um, yes, that's right, your freedom. You make one wrong move, and it's behind bars for you, my friend."

Ben is right; I can't screw this up. He is the one thing that is standing between me and a guy named Earl who wants to make me his bitch. Let's face it, a pretty face like mine wouldn't last long in prison. And Ben will ensure I end up there, guilty or not.

"Ben, let's quit this game. I didn't kill those women, and I get it, you will always have a hold of me. Now can we move on and figure out what to do about all this shit?"

"If that's what you want. After all, this is your session. But first, can you tell me how you rated Evie and Jessica?"

"Ben, do we have to do this?"

"Yes, it's important."

"Fine, Evie was an eight and a half, and Jessica, a six and a half."

Really, Evie was a nine, or at least I thought she was or could be. I didn't get a chance to confirm it. If a girl is nine or higher, then, of course, she is more fuckable, but if I meet a nine or higher, then I need to stop and treat her better. Maybe she could be the one I date or at least try for a second night. But she was just an eight and a half. A slut who had a purpose. I thought maybe I'd met my match, but I was wrong. She really did just want to be spanked and left, never to be seen again.

"So, Jessica, only a six and a half, and you still took her home. You haven't gone below a seven in a while.

"She was pretty enough, but that's all she had going for her."

"Did you want to hurt her?"

"No, I wanted to use her to feed my malfunction. I didn't hurt either of them."

"And Evie, an eight and a half, is one of the closest you've had in a while to your goal. Did you want her to be a nine?"

"Maybe for a minute, but in the end, she was like all the rest."

"And your target?"

"It's fine. I have my date Friday night."

"I hope you have a good time. Don't disappoint me."

CHAPTER FIFTY-TWO

Hudson
Thursday, October 14, 7:00 p.m.

Chrissy picked one of the nicest places in town to meet. I really can't afford to spend money on a place this fancy, but more importantly, I can't afford to make a misstep in the game. Max fronted what little cash he had so I could play the part. The thousand dollars my brother bribed me with already went to bills.

Max is curious about Chrissy. I know he's in here somewhere. Staying out of sight, but he's here. I get it. Dude has a past, and he needs to see Chrissy. It's so messed up that Ben chose her for me.

We need to keep playing. Not to hurt these women, as Ben wants, but to protect them. Chrissy might have done some horrible things to Max in the past, but she doesn't deserve to be a pawn in Ben's game.

I check my phone; Chrissy is late.

I bet Max is getting anxious. I let my eyes wander, trying to locate him, but I can't. He's done an excellent job staying out of sight.

The host keeps asking me if my date has arrived and if I want to be seated, but I keep telling him I'm going to wait. He looks annoyed.

I keep checking my phone. No messages from Chrissy, and the time is fleeting. Have I been stood up, or is this really a trap to see if Max and I put together Ben's puzzle?

Fuck.

Fuck.

We are so fucked.

What if Ben releases my secrets and ruins my family? I need to stay in the game. I need to keep fighting for the Evies and Jessicas that have no voice. I need to keep my secret safe to avoid hurting Jordan. I don't know what my dad would do if it all came out. The man already has a temper and a drinking problem. My poor mom would be crushed. I don't know what Ben has on Jordan, but it couldn't be good. He has devastating information on all the people in this club.

I glance at my phone again. She's now thirty minutes late.

I'm a sucker.

Chrissy is a no-show.

As I walk out of the restaurant, Max runs by me, but catches on my coat, slipping something into my pocket. I don't make eye contact with him in case someone is watching. For all I know the host is working with Ben. My paranoia is reaching new heights.

I wait a few moments and let Max exit the building, and I follow suit. Once I'm safely in my car, I pull the item from my pocket.

It's a burner phone. I open it and find a text message alert.

Unknown: *403 S Locust Drive*
Unknown: *Now!*

CHAPTER FIFTY-THREE

Max
Thursday, October 14, 8:00 p.m.

I watch from my apartment window. Hudson's black car pulls up, and he quickly crosses the street and enters my building. A few moments later, Emmy does the same. I left a burner phone for her at work before heading to the restaurant. I texted her as soon as I saw Chrissy was a no-show, which is highly unlike her. If she sets out to do something, she follows through.

I greet them both in the lobby. None of us say a word until we are in my apartment.

"Max, have you lost your mind?" Emmy says the second the door latches behind us.

"I know we're taking a chance, but it's about time we all got together. Ben still has all the control and after what just happened at the restaurant, he's still playing us much better than we're playing him. I fear he is onto us. We're in over our heads with a guy like Ben Matthews."

Hudson nods, and Emmy gives us both a puzzled look. I don't want to say too much about the Chrissy situation because I'm not ready for Emmy to know who I really am. I can't have her hate me yet.

"Em, I will fill you in on things, but we need to lay everything we know about Ben out on the table. Hudson, meet Emmy. Emmy, meet Hudson. Now let's get to work."

They give each other an uncomfortable smile.

"Are you sure your apartment is safe?" Hudson asks.

"No. But it's a chance we have to take. Both of you turn your phones off, and no one gets on my computer. We assume he has a hacker, and who knows if he's tracking our cellphones. We might be overreacting, but we can't take that chance."

Both of them turn their phones off and leave them on my entryway table.

"I know this is serious, you guys, but we need to shake off the bad energy before it consumes us. Ben wants to ruin us and he's getting his wish. Look at us, living in fear," Emmy says as her eyes light up, catching a glimpse of my bong. She picks it up, and heads into the living room.

"Make yourself at home, why don't you?" I joke, trying to take her advice.

"Dude, we've been working together for going on a year, and I've never been inside your place. It's exactly how I pictured it."

Emmy sets the bong down on the table and walks over to my albums. She grabs Crosby, Stills & Nash's eponymous album and puts it on the record player.

Hudson and I both stare at her.

"What? If we're going to do this, we need a good playlist." She picks up the bong again. "And I might need this later," she says, carrying it over to the kitchen table, taking a seat next to us.

She retakes a look at the Rasta-themed bong and says, "I shall call you *Bong Marley*."

"No way. That's what I call it."

"Max, you're just jealous because I came up with that first. You're just saying that."

"No, for real. That's its name. Look on the bottom."

Emmy carefully tips the bong upside down to read underneath, where I have a piece of masking tape with the words *Bong Marley* written.

"Dang, Max. You're clever," she says, laughing, and then takes a hit with the leftovers from my last session.

She passes it to Hudson.

"No thanks," he says. "Normally I'd say yes, but I need a clear head to get through this night."

"I don't think I could handle this with a clear head," Emmy replies. "Trust me, guys. I'm better with this."

She passes it over to me. "Max?"

"I think I'm with Hudson on this. Maybe later," I respond while taking the bong from Emmy and placing it farther from her reach. I don't know how much she can function on weed, and I don't need her crashing on us.

"So back to business. Hudson, why don't you fill Emmy in on what we know about Kade?"

"Are you sure?"

"Yes, we can trust her. Even if she's high as a kite."

Emmy gives me one of her classic sassy grins.

I listen as Hudson rehashes the story about the little red envelope, which leads to Emmy's blackmail story and how she came to work for Ben. We also fill Emmy in on the game and our targets. I tell her about Ivy, and how I failed. Then Hudson tells Emmy about his target and how she didn't show tonight.

"There's one more thing," I reluctantly say. I don't want to say too much, but I know I will need to fill Emmy in, so she has the whole story, and three heads are better than two. I will leave out the part about Cal, of course. "Hudson's target is my ex, Chrissy."

"Whoa. Mind blown," Emmy says while extending her hands on opposite sides of her head and letting out a catastrophic whoosh sound. "Ben sure knows how to create a puzzle, doesn't he?"

"A puzzle. That's exactly what it is," I say, ignoring her theatrics.

"We are missing a bunch of the pieces, though," Hudson says.

"For example: Is Ivy someone's ex? I didn't get any information out of her, so we don't know."

"Hudson, do you have a girl that wronged you?" Emmy asks.

"Good thinking," I respond. "Maybe we need to look at every girl who's wronged a member."

"No, just Nadia, but she wronged my brother more than me."

"Who is Nadia?" Emmy asks.

"Oh, yeah, I forgot you don't know that story yet. I will keep it simple. But no one besides Ben and Max know this. So, keep this to yourself. Got it?"

Emmy nods in agreement.

"This is the dirt Ben has on me besides the Kade thing. I slept with my brother's ex-wife before they got divorced. My brother is in the club, but he doesn't know any of that."

"Another bombshell," Emmy says, "Why isn't your brother here? Can we not trust him?"

"No, he is ride-or-die on Ben's side. I tried to talk to him at our parents' house, but he shot me down right away. I'm never to talk about Ben or the club to him. We've never been super close and the past few years, we've both moved further apart," Hudson says with sadness in his eyes.

"Well, shit, this story just keeps getting more twisted. You guys are stuck in a web so sticky that we might never get out of it."

"Well, that's encouraging," I respond sarcastically.

"When do you guys see Ben next?"

"Saturday," Hudson and I respond in unison.

"And you both failed at your task?" Emmy asks.

"Yep, but we have until then to complete it, technically."

"OK. At least that buys you some time, but not much," Emmy says, twirling her copper curls around her finger. "My theory is. . ." Emmy pauses and looks up at the ceiling, gathering her thoughts—or is too high that she forgot what she was saying. "Chrissy isn't real. I mean, like Chrissy is a real person, but not real to Hudson. Does that make sense? Like Hudson got catfished by someone in the club, maybe Ben, or maybe that's someone's extra credit."

Emmy could be right. I think carefully before responding. "And Ben is using this to see if we talked. To see if we put the pieces together. If that's true, then Ben could have had someone watching the restaurant tonight, and if that's true, then we are all screwed," I say, walking over to the window. I look out, but I don't see anyone watching the building or any suspicious cars, but that doesn't mean anything.

"Another theory—just hear me out—what if Ivy doesn't belong to anyone and Ben wants you to fail the game? What if Ivy doesn't have a secret, and Ben wants to see you fail?" Emmy suggests.

"Why did Ben want me to join the club in the first place, if he wants me to fail?" I ask.

"I don't know. I'm just pulling at strings." Emmy says.

"Why did Ben want any of us to join the club? What is Ben's endgame?" Hudson asks.

"He's awfully curious about what happened to me and Chrissy. We talk about her at every session. I tell him I want to talk about Jovie, but he won't give it any time. He keeps pushing it off. He won't even let me add her on Socialite."

"Ben wanted to know if you had a girlfriend or anyone you fancied when he first started sniffing around your business. I didn't know anyone, so I asked Kade, and he said he thought you had a crush on one of our customers. I gave that info to Ben, but I didn't think he'd do anything with it," Emmy says.

"Well, he hunted her down, he found out who she was. I didn't even know her name, and he managed to figure it out. Emmy, I wish you had come to me before this situation got out of control, but it is what it is now. You know I haven't seen Jovie in weeks. She came in every Friday, and now she's gone," I respond.

Everyone pauses for a moment.

"Fuck. You don't think Ben did something to her?" I whisper, as if saying it any louder would make it real.

"I don't know, but with what happened to Evie and Jessica, anything is possible. Maybe Jovie is someone else's target?" Hudson adds.

I feel sick that something could have happened to my dream girl because I had the audacity to have a crush on her. A simple crush, and now she could be part of a game. I can't believe the thought didn't cross my mind earlier. If something terrible happens to her, I would never be able to forgive myself. My funky record-store girl. . .

"Max, we will find her. We will figure this puzzle out. Maybe Jovie just left town. You don't know a thing about her. Maybe she never even lived here to begin with and she was on a long vacation. We just don't know, but we will find her and make sure she's OK," Emmy says, stroking my arm to comfort me. Then she reaches behind me and passes me the bong.

I take a hit. I need it. I can't take the pain inching its way throughout my body.

"So, what about Kade?" Hudson asks, redirecting the

conversation. "If Kade didn't kill Evie and Jessica, then who did? Ben? Another member? And why?"

"So, who are the other members, and who recruited whom?" Emmy asks.

"Owen recruited Ethan. Decklan recruited Ezra, and then Bobby brought Mateo. My brother Jordan brought me, and, of course, Kade and Max," Hudson recalls.

"Does anyone look like a killer?" Emmy asks. "I know anyone can be a murderer. People didn't think Ted Bundy was a killer until it was too late, but like any creeper vibes or anything off with any of them?"

"Honestly, Owen kind of gives me killer vibes," Hudson responds.

"I agree with Hudson. That guy is intense."

"OK, boys, so anyone else or just Owen? And what else do we know about him?"

"Nothing. I don't know much about any of our so-called brothers. Ben likes to keep it that way. We all have a fucked-up past, but we don't get to talk about it much, and I'd prefer to keep my secrets hidden, and I suspect the others feel the same way," Hudson says.

"I think the other new recruits—Mateo, Ez, and Ethan—are just in it for fun. Decklan, Bobby, and my brother, I, I really don't know what to think. They're loyal to Ben, that's for sure, but why?" Hudson says.

"We're not getting anywhere," I say, feeling defeated.

The record on the player ends and Emmy gets up. She turns off the turntable and flips on the TV.

"You guys, you've got to see this," Emmy says, her eyes glued to the television set.

Emmy turns the volume up as Hudson and I join her.

Local Girl Missing flashes along the bottom of the screen.

A young woman appears with the news reporter.

"Max, is that your Ivy?" Emmy questions.

"*When did you suspect your sister was missing?*" the reporter asks.

My head is spinning. I'm going to be sick. It's her. It's Ivy. If her sister was missing, it would explain why she was so distracted on our date.

"*My sister can be flaky, so I didn't think much of it,*" Ivy says, emotion causing her voice to falter. "*She takes off all the time. Weekends at the coast, last-minute concert trips, and festivals, but she eventually checks in. I haven't heard from her in weeks. I am always checking my phone to see if it's her.*

"*With a killer still on the loose, I can't help but think my sister might be in trouble this time. If anyone knows anything or has seen my sister, please contact the police. She's twenty-seven. A hundred and fifteen pounds. Blonde hair, blue eyes. Five foot three.*"

An image appears on the screen. A funky, blonde girl with messy curls, bright blue eyes, and a tiny little nose, wearing a black leather jacket and a Ramones T-shirt.

And the bottom falls out of my world.

"That's her," I say. "That's Jovie."

CHAPTER FIFTY-FOUR

Emmy
Thursday, October 14, 8:35 p.m.

"Max, I need you to take a deep breath. Max, can you hear me?"

I try to remain calm and hold my composure. I know darn well this is not good. Trying to get Max's attention, I snap my fingers, but he doesn't respond. His eyes stay glued on the TV. With each passing second, his breathing becomes more labored.

"I think Max is in shock," I say as I turn my head to Hudson, but Hudson doesn't move either. His eyes are pinned to the TV too.

"Hudson!" I shout, attempting to break his trance. "Help me!"

With the help of Hudson, we lower Max to the couch. Max is unfazed by the movement.

"Max, buddy, I need you to listen to me. We don't know anything for sure. I need you to focus on me. This is not your fault." I snap my fingers in front of Max's face again. Max's eyes slowly divert from the screen and lock on mine. Huge tears well up in his bloodshot eyes.

"She might just be on a getaway like her sister said. This is normal behavior for her to up and leave without telling anyone. There is a chance she is OK," I say the words to my friend, but I don't believe them. I know Ben has something to do with this, but right now, Max needs to have some hope to hang on to.

This is not Max's fault. This is my fault. I'm the one who told Ben about her in the first place. I'm the guilty one. I need to save this girl.

"Do you think someone took her? Someone in the club? Could she be. . .?" Max asks.

"Shh, Max." I silence him before he can say the word—*dead*.

"We have to go to the police now," Hudson interjects.

"Yes. Hudson is right. We have to report what we know," Max says. His voice cracks like a prepubescent boy.

The clip of Ivy pleading to the public about her sister's whereabouts comes on the screen again. I pick up the remote and flip the TV off. The scent of fear mixed with remnants of marijuana masks the stale air in Max's apartment. I'm sick to my stomach, but I have to keep it together.

"Guys, you're not thinking straight. We have to play our next move carefully. If we do anything rash, we could get Jovie killed. I'm going to assume she's alive because Jessica and Evie were found almost immediately. Jovie has been missing for weeks. No body yet. This is part of Ben's game. It has to be. If we want to find Jovie, you guys have to keep playing. If we go to the police, she dies. We don't have anything but hunches to go on. The police won't know what to do with this information."

Max ignores my statement; he's too upset to think. "Poor Ivy. Thinking her sister could be the next victim. That's why she was so preoccupied the other night. I bet she was messaging people about her sister. She didn't want to assume the worst, but I bet it was eating at her. I thought she was a bitch, but she was simply distracted."

"So, Emmy, what do you propose we do? We need to do something," Hudson asks.

"You two must go to the meeting on Saturday. You have to keep playing Ben's game, and that means Ben will be expecting an outburst from you, so give it to him."

CHAPTER FIFTY-FIVE

Max
Friday, October 15, 1:40 p.m.

Hudson and Emmy stayed at my place until dawn. We went over every detail again and again until nothing made sense. The one thing we did figure out is that Hudson and I must keep up appearances for Ben. It's our only option.

It's now been nearly twenty-four hours since Ivy reported her sister missing. Someone would know if she were on a trip or at a festival. Someone would have connected with her to tell her to phone home. The only good news is that no body has been found—yet. We still have time. But if Jovie went missing when the game started, that was over a month ago. I hate to imagine—

"Max, get out of your head," Emmys says, tossing a pencil in my direction, dislodging my thoughts. I have to remember that I'm at work now and must put on a show in case Ben is watching.

"I know. I know. I can't stop thinking that we could be doing something to find her."

"Max, we have to stick to the plan. We have to go on like normal. We both couldn't call in sick to work. Ben would know something was up."

"I know we need to stop talking about it, but I'm so mad at myself that I didn't see the connection sooner. I can't believe there was no photo of Ivy and Jovie together on Ivy's social media."

"Maybe they're not close. I mean, how close could they be if she jets off all the time without a word. It took her sister being gone for weeks before she reported her missing. So, you can't blame yourself for not catching that detail."

"You're probably right. You know, I see the resemblance now, but they're nothing alike. I had no reason to think they'd be related. I think Ben wanted me to make the connection sooner."

"Max, for real, we need to stop talking here."

Emmy is probably right, but I feel the damage is done, and we've already set the wheels in motion. Ben is going to figure us out sooner or later. I just hope we find Jovie before shit hits the fan.

I go back to checking in new inventory and let Emmy handle the customers today.

Kade still isn't coming into work, and we don't know when he plans to return, so we have to keep the business running.

My mind keeps replaying every event over and over since Ben came into my life. I'm beginning to think Emmy's theory is correct. Chrissy isn't the real Chrissy. Ben wanted to get under my skin and watch me squirm. He knew that if Hudson and I got together, we'd connect the dots, and we'd lie to him.

We played the game exactly as Ben had hoped.

CHAPTER FIFTY-SIX

Kade
Friday, October 15th, 5:40 p.m.

No one's been waiting to arrest me or take me in for questioning in the disappearance of Jovie Peterson. It's been a whole day since she was reported missing. That's a good sign for me and my fight to prove my innocence.

I want to believe that Ben has my best interests in mind; he saved my business and my sanity a long time ago, and I owe him for that. Now, I owe him for his lawyer, Dennis Miller. He has to be costing Ben a pretty penny, and I can't afford to pay him back and maybe never will. The thought of ultimately signing over the business to him seems likely at this point, as long as I don't get dragged back into the Jessica and Evie situation. The cops should have some new leads by now, you'd think. Whoever has Jovie probably killed both of them too.

It's not safe for me to meet my target tonight. It'd be irresponsible for me to see her. If my suspicions are correct about Evie, Jessica, and Jovie's connection to the club, Ben or someone else is behind all of this. I can't risk another girl's life just to play a game. Even if that means I'm going down in flames in the process.

Ben can disown me, take away my lawyer, sue me for the money I owe him, and let my secrets out of the bag. But, for once, I need to do the right thing. Ben's stupid game has to end.

I open the Socialite app on my phone, and I click on the chat with my target.

K: Hey, I'm so sorry to do this, but something came up, and I have to cancel our date tonight.

N: Seriously? Are you kidding? I'm all ready to meet you.

K: Yes, I'm sorry.

N: I knew you were like all the other guys.

K: No, it's not like that. I promise.

N: What, am I not pretty enough? Not intelligent enough? What is it? Did you find someone better to take out tonight instead?

K: No, I swear. You're gorgeous. Just trust me, it's for your own good.

N: You're just like my ex. Always coming up with excuses.

K: I'm sorry. Really. It's nothing to do with you.

N: My ex, Jordan, used to say that to me too. Men always have something 'that comes up.' I knew I shouldn't have trusted you. I should have gone with my gut instinct about you. I knew you were too good to be true.

Wow, she's just tossing her past out so freely. Would she chat about her ex the entire date? Is this woman crazy? I think I dodged a bullet with this one. At least she never put two and two together and figured out I'm the most hated guy in town.

K: *Seriously, I need to go but I'm truly sorry.*
Something really did come up. I will make
it up to you. I promise.

Of course, I'm lying. I need to keep this girl safe, even if she's psychotic.

N: *Screw you, Kade. All men are the same.*
You've just confirmed my assumption.

But, wait. Jordan. . . Her ex, Jordan. This could be an insane coincidence, but it can't be the Jordan from the club. Could it? He had an ex-wife that took everything. Would Ben have assigned me a club member's ex? I mean, why would he? No. I'm paranoid. But what if I'm not? There has been one too many things going on these past few weeks that haven't been adding up. This girl already hates me, so I may as well just ask.

K: *This is going to sound really random, but*
does your ex have a brother?

N: *How do you know about Hudson? Is this*
some kind of sick joke? Who put you up to this? Y
ou sicko.

Holy hell. This is Jordan's ex-wife. The one who left him. The unease in my gut grows.

It's no coincidence that she is my target,
is it? Ben is up to something.

K: *Nadia, I swear to you. It's not a joke.
This is going to sound crazy, but stay
safe and don't trust anyone.*

N: *You're crazy. Go fuck yourself.*

CHAPTER FIFTY-SEVEN

Max
Saturday, October 16, 9:49 p.m.

I arrive early, anticipating Ben being primed for a fight. It's what he expects from me. I push through the coded door, hopefully for the last time. I need to get everything from Ben tonight—I never want to step foot in this room again.

Ben is waiting for me. He doesn't give me a chance to speak.

"Max, I'm so sorry to hear that Jovie is missing. Such a shame that you didn't get a chance with her. I hope it's not too late." The son of a bitch sounds perfectly sincere, but I'm not falling for his lies anymore.

"Are you kidding me right now? Ben, what did you do to her?"

"What on earth are you talking about? I didn't do anything to that poor girl."

"Ben, you had to know she was my target's sister. Strange coincidence, wouldn't you say?"

"I understand how this must look, but I honestly didn't have anything to do with her disappearance. It merely is a sad coincidence."

"Really? Just a bunch of sad coincidences? She's Ivy's fucking sister, Ben. The girl that you knew I had a crush on is Ivy's sister. What is your game here, man? If you hurt her. . ."

"Max, calm down. There is nothing to worry about. I am sure she is fine. Everything always has a way of correcting itself in the world."

"What the hell does that mean?"

"Just wait and see, my eager boy."

"I'm done playing games, Ben. Just tell me where she is," I demand.

"Max, you need to remember who is in charge here. I think it would be wise of you to settle down and wait for the meeting to start. Soon, you will have what you need. I promise."

The door opens, and other members start filing into the room, including Hudson and Kade. Hudson's eyes lock on mine but not for more than a second. I do as I'm told. I need to find Jovie, and Ben isn't going to hand her over.

The room is quiet. No one is bantering or remarking on their tasks. The atmosphere is eerie. Things have changed, and I suspect other members are feeling the wrath of Ben too. It's not just us. It's all of them.

Ben turns to face the wall when he begins speaking.

"I am genuinely annoyed with most of you. I don't even want to look at you. This was an easy and fun game, and you guys are ruining it. How hard is it to follow simple instructions?" Ben slams his fist hard into the wall. He doesn't flinch from the self-inflicted pain.

Now turning around to face us, his eyes are wild. He runs his hands through his hair.

"I had high hopes for this club and the new recruits, but you've all disappointed me. Some more than others. But this weekend, it is game time. It's Liar's Weekend—the finale."

"But we only are on task three," Owen asks, trepidation in his voice.

"Well, since some of you are still stuck on task two, and because you can't follow instructions, I've decided to lay the rest of the rules out there. If you complete your set of five by morning on Monday, you are still in the game. Got it?" Ben snarls.

We all stay silent. I know what that means. I have tonight and tomorrow to find Jovie, or it's game over.

"I'm getting increasingly irritated with all of you. After everything, I've done for you. All I ever wanted was for you to see your true selves. And this is how you repay me? You're such ungrateful little bitches."

"Well, some of us are on track," Jordan says, looking as if he wants a pat on the back. "I'm doing everything you've asked of me."

Disappointment is written across Hudson's face as his brother attempts to redeem himself.

"Me too," Owen adds.

Ben ignores Jordan and Owen.

"So, what happens on Monday?" Ezra asks.

"If you don't complete your five tasks by then, everything that I have on you will be released into the world. I mean everything."

"This is not what we signed up for, Ben," Ezra says, his voice flickering with fear.

No one is safe. Ben knows too much. He must be taken down.

"I don't want to go to extremes, but you guys give me no choice. So, without further ado, let me unveil the final two."

Ben walks over to the chalkboard and flips it around for all five of the rules to be seen.

THE LIARS' CLUB
RULES TO THE GAME

*1. Create a fake profile (liars) on Socialite.
(Use your real name and photo but that is it.)
Everything else is a lie. Get the attention of
your target. Strike up a conversation.
2. Get your target to trust you. Make her
believe you are the real deal. Start planting
seeds. Set a date by next Saturday.
3. Get your target to tell you a secret.
4. Use their secret against them.
5. The mindfuck!*

Ben clears his throat. "If you didn't lay the groundwork, then I suspect you will be scrambling around trying to get your target's secret in order to move on to the next task. I expect you will do everything you can imagine to pull it from them. You will then move on to number four, where you will use it against them to get something you want. Then finally task five. This one is my favorite: the mindfuck."

Ben's jaw tightens, and his lips curl into an evil grin.

"See what we are doing here?" he continues. "We are making sure your target will never hurt another person again. They all have a secret, and they've all hurt someone. This is your chance to rip the carpet out from under them. Make them think they're going crazy. They trusted you, and you hurt them. See the twist? The more creative you are, the more points you will be rewarded. And that, my friends is the mindfuck.

"Oh, and a few of you still have to complete your extra credit. Dang, some of you have a lot to do. I suggest clearing tomorrow's schedule."

Ben reaches into his back pocket and pulls out the remaining red envelopes. I know one of them belongs to me, but who do the others belong to?

I watch as Ben hands out his poison letters. Kade, Owen, and I all get one. That means Ezra, Ethan, Bobby, Jordan, or Mateo know what happened to Jessica, and one of them probably catfished Hudson. What have the others been asked to do?

Kade is the first one to rush out of the building. He doesn't even wait for Ben to excuse us. We all follow suit and run outside.

Some, I suspect, are still playing the game in hopes of keeping their secrets hidden; some may be fleeing town.

Once in my car, I tear the envelope open and read:

Forest Road 40537—Drive to the end of the track.
You will know when to stop.
Sunday, 8 p.m.
Don't bring your friends.

CHAPTER FIFTY-EIGHT

Mr. Scorpio: I have a confession.

[?]: Yeah, what is your confession?

Mr. Scorpio: I like to play games.

[?]: That's not a confession. That's
a statement, silly.

Mr. Scorpio: Do you like to play games?

[?]: Sure, who doesn't? You're being
weird tonight. When are you taking
me on our next date? I hope it's soon!
I could use a distraction.

Mr. Scorpio: Does tomorrow work for you?
Please say it does.

[?]: Yes.

Mr. Scorpio: I have the perfect spot. Let's meet at the edge of town. Park in the lot heading up toward the mountain. You know the one where the skier's park to carpool up to the resort? I have the perfect surprise for you!

[?]: I love surprises.

Mr. Scorpio: I'm sure you will just die when you see what I have planned.

[?]: I can't wait!

Mr. Scorpio: See you at 7:30.

CHAPTER FIFTY-NINE

Emmy
Saturday, October 16, 10:35 p.m.

Max sent a text to my burner phone asking me to meet him at his apartment. So, I'm waiting for him to arrive. My windows are fogging up, and I feel like a sitting target. Hurry, Max.

My real phone vibrates in the center console, nearly startling me to death. I slowly glance down, afraid to see who it's from.

Ben: *Emmy, I need you to meet me tomorrow night. We have a lot to discuss. Don't disappoint me. 7:30 at the club.*

I quickly switch my phone off. Knowing Ben, he probably already knows where I am. But screw it—I need to know what happened tonight at the guys' meeting. I don't have much to lose if I disobey Ben. The second I started working with Max and Hudson, I knew that I would have to kiss my tuition money goodbye.

I shouldn't have sold my soul to the devil—Ben Matthews. The money was nice, but the price was too high. I'll have to live with what I did to the people I care about for the rest of my life. I think Max already forgives me, but I don't know how Kade will handle what I did. I'm dreading the moment I have to be honest with him. As long as he's innocent. If he really killed Jessica and Evie, then he can fuck himself.

The one thing I'm sure of is that we can't let anything happen to Jovie Peterson. I need to make things right and make sure she's safe, then everything else will be dealt with later. If anything happens to her, I won't be able to live with myself. I hate seeing Max hurting so much. I still don't understand his infatuation with a girl he doesn't know, but that is another problem for the back burner. Right now, we must put the puzzle together so that everyone can stay safe. That's our first priority.

Max pulls up first. I wait for him to exit his car, but he doesn't get out right away. Come on, Max. Hurry the fuck up.

In my rearview mirror, headlights flicker from a block or so down the road, slowly inching their way closer. I can't help but slink down in my seat. I turn my engine off and slowly turn my head around to see the car rolling up behind mine. The headlights flip off and the engine stops.

I let out a sigh of relief when I see it's Hudson.

All three of us exit our cars at the same time without acknowledging the other. We wait until we are inside Max's apartment before we speak.

"What the hell was that?" Max says to Hudson when we're safe inside.

"I knew Ben was crazy, but I didn't think he'd throw all that in our face tonight," Max says. His words spew out fast and shaky.

"What happened?" I demand.

"Emmy, we have to complete all five tasks before Monday morning, or all our secrets will be leaked," Max responds.

"What does that mean?" I ask.

"We have to get our girls' secret, use it against them, and then mindfuck them. Whatever the hell that means. I can only assume Ben wants us to wreck their lives, but we didn't stick around to ask questions," Hudson says. "Both of us are going to fail. My girl isn't real, and Max's girl has a missing sister she's dealing with, so we both know we aren't going to win this game. Max could message Ivy but that's just mean at this point. He can't. I'm coming to terms with the fact that my brother will know what I did. I just feel sick if my family's secrets come out. It will destroy them. My poor mom."

"Well, didn't Jordan say he's doing what's asked of him?" I ask.

"Maybe, he wouldn't punish Jordan and your family if he wins. That would be cruel to do to the winner," Max says.

"Do you think Ben cares? Anyway, for Jordan to win, that means he has to do some real harm to another person. I know my brother and I aren't close, but I don't think he's capable of that," Hudson responds.

"I think Ben has such a strong hold on him, anything is possible. I'm sorry, Hudson. I hope I'm wrong," Max responds.

"What did you guys find out about Jovie? Did he mention her tonight?"

"Not during the meeting," Hudson says.

We both look at Max.

"I asked him about her before everyone arrived. I just know he wants me to keep playing the game, but he knows I can't win with Ivy, so I don't get it. Plus, there is this."

Max produces his little red envelope.

We read it.

"Fuck. He knows we are working together. He probably knows we are all here conspiring against him. What do we do? If we go with you, it could blow everything up. If we don't, you could be walking into a trap—" Hudson says with fear in his voice.

"Ben wants to meet me tomorrow night at seven thirty!" I say before we get too far into the plans.

"Not alone, you're not," Max sternly responds.

"Max, you can't be in two places at once. I will be fine," I say.

"Ok. So, Hudson, you follow Emmy. Make sure she's OK, then both of you come and check on me at the address Ben gave me. If any of us gets into trouble, then call the police," Max instructs us.

"Max, you can't go by yourself," Hudson demands.

"It's our only option," Max says. "As I said, you follow Emmy. Make sure she's safe, and then the two of you come later. My note said to go alone, so I must show up by myself. If I get into trouble, you guys will be there later to save me or call for help. I just know that address is where he's holding Jovie. It has to be."

I can tell Hudson doesn't want to agree to Max's plan, but he nods his head, and then so do I.

"But for now, I think it's best we stick together. You guys are welcome to stay here. Safety in numbers," Max says.

"Emmy, you can take the couch, and I will take the floor," Hudson offers.

"I'll go grab some blankets and pillows."

CHAPTER SIXTY

Max
Saturday, October 16, 11:20 p.m.

I've been drifting in and out of sleep for what feels like hours. Each time I feel myself falling into a deeper state of unconsciousness, I'm jostled awake from nightmares of failed attempts to save Jovie and defeat Ben.

There's a soft knock at my bedroom door, putting a pause on my restless night.

"Yes?" my ruffled voice manages to say.

"Hey, Max, it's Em. Can I come in?" she says softly.

I quickly tug my blankets up to cover my naked torso.

"Sure. Come in."

Emmy enters the room and tiptoes closer to my bed. "Hudson is snoring. Would it be weird if I asked to join you?"

"I suppose that would be all right," I respond. I try to free a second blanket, so we don't have to share, but Emmy is already sliding into bed and tugging on my group of blankets. I immediately feel self-conscious. I'm only wearing boxer shorts.

Emmy doesn't seem phased by my lack of clothing. Instead, she slides closer to me. That coconut smell.

Her feet accidentally rub up against my bare leg as she tussles around in the bed, pulling half of my blankets closer to her.

"Your apartment is cold, Max. You should really keep it warmer in here. You're going to freeze to death one of these days."

"Well, it would be a gentler death than Ben killing me, I suppose."

We both let out a nervous laugh, but it's not a joke.

The October wind bangs against the window, startling both of us and causing me to move an inch closer to Emmy.

"Max, I feel like this is all just a bad dream, and soon if we don't wake up, it will turn into a nightmare," Emmy says, scooting her body closer into mine. She claims she is cold, but the heat from her body is radiating in the space between us.

"Me too, Emmy. When I close my eyes, I wish I could wake up at a different time. A different day. Before Ben Matthews was a part of our lives."

"I wish I never met him," Emmy says with pure sadness.

Emmy turns her head on the pillow and faces me directly. The muted light from the streetlamp outside my bedroom window leaks into the room. The light accentuates Emmy's big, brown eyes. They twinkle with each movement. I want to reach out and tuck her hair behind her ears so I can see more of her face, but I catch myself.

"I feel safer in here with you," she says.

I smile. I'm unsure what to say.

We both let a moment of silence seep in between us.

"Why her, Max?"

Her question catches me off guard.

"What is it about, Jovie that makes her so special?" she softly asks.

"I don't know. I just feel a connection to her. She seems different from all the other girls. Plus, she has stellar taste in music. I can't ignore that."

"You don't even know her."

"Maybe I have built her up to be the girl I hoped she would be, but it's at least something to hang on to. It's better to have a glimmer of hope than to be wrong and not have anyone or anything to dream about."

Emmy turns her body around to face the door. Her voice is hushed now, "You never see what's right in front of you, Max Jennings."

CHAPTER SIXTY-ONE

Hudson
Sunday, October 17, 8:00 a.m.

Max and Emmy both emerge from Max's bedroom at the same time. I had wondered where she snuck off to in the middle of the night when I woke up and saw the couch empty.

They both take a seat at the kitchen table. Neither of them saying a word. If I had to guess, they slept together, but I could be wrong. Max is oblivious to her adoration of him because he's a fool in love with a girl that doesn't even know he exists. He's too blind to see that Emmy is perfect for him.

I sense an absence of the usual lightness between them. The playfulness is gone. I tackle the awkwardness in the room.

"What's going on with you two this morning?"

They both shrug their shoulders.

"Well, we've got a shitty day ahead of us and nothing is going to change that, but we can't do it on an empty stomach. We need to fuel ourselves, so I'm going to make you guys the 'Hudson Special.' Max, do you mind?" I ask, before tugging his refrigerator door open."

"Nah, have at it."

I scan the barren shelves and hope for something to work with. I rummage through the refrigerator and spot some wilted broccoli, eggs, mozzarella cheese that's a week past its sell-by date, half of a sprouting onion, mushrooms that have gone from cross-your-fingers to a quick prayer, and a bottle of hot sauce called Helly's Hellfire Habanero Sauce. I check the cheese for mold, pull the eggs, onion, and hot sauce. It looks like I'm making a toned-down version of the 'Hudson Special'—a basic omelet.

"Coffee first," Emmy moans.

"Are we not using *please* and *thank-yous* this morning?" I taunt.

"No. Coffee," Emmy repeats, sticking her tongue out at me.

"Yes, coffee first," Max chimes in.

Perfect for each other. Both are rude in the morning before they get their caffeine fix.

"Coffees in that cabinet, man," Max says, barely picking up his hand to point to the cabinet next to the stove.

"I guess I'm making coffee and the food then," I tease.

"Not fast enough," Emmy orders, and she lays her head down on the table.

I know we're hunting a killer and trying to find a missing person, but I'm enjoying my time with Emmy and Max. In some fucked-up way, I could see us being friends if we live through the next twenty-four hours.

"Are you guys going to work today? I guess we didn't discuss that last night."

"Oh, right. Work," Emmy says.

"If Kade doesn't care to check in, or go into work these days, maybe we just close the store?" Emmy suggests.

"Ben did say for us to clear our schedules so we can work on our target. Maybe Max should take the day off. But if Emmy doesn't show up and the store is closed, don't you think Ben will find out and know we are really up to something?" I say.

"I think my red envelope suggests that Ben already knows we are working together. Does it even matter anymore? Shit is going to hit the fan tonight," Max says.

"We don't know for sure that Ben knows Emmy is working with us. He could simply think it's you and me," I respond.

"Hudson might be right. Emmy, we have to keep you safe," Max chimes in.

"Don't you guys have any other employees?" I ask.

Emmy laughs. "Right? You'd think it was just the two of us. I will go open the store and see if Jake or Jed can come in. Hudson, you should follow me to work and stay close if anything happens. You should still pretend to work your target too. If you are being catfished, then Ben will know if you're not trying. Max, I don't think it would be appropriate to message Ivy. Given the fact, your date didn't go well, and she's in the middle of the search for her missing sister."

"What the hell does Ben expect from us?" I ask.

"He's driving us crazy, and I think that's part of his plan," Max responds.

"Fine, I will continue to play along. I wonder which guy he has messing with me. I'm sure whoever it is, is getting a kick out of it," I say.

Hudson: *Hey Chrissy, you didn't show for our date on Thursday. I hope everything is OK.*

Hudson: *Let me know if we can reschedule sometime.*

"OK, done. I kept it simple," I say.
"Perfect. If 'Chrissy' replies, keep the chat going," Max says.

"I think we have a plan. I will keep an eye out for things at Epic Records and then follow Emmy to the club at seven thirty," I say.

"I will play dumb with Ben," Emmy adds.

"And if Emmy is in the club too long, do what you can to keep her safe. Then try to meet up with me, but keep a low profile for now," Max says. "OK. Stay safe, guys."

"But first, some coffee and the Hudson Special!"

CHAPTER SIXTY-TWO

Hudson
Sunday, October 17, 7:00 p.m.

My heart pounds with every glimpse of movement on the street as I anxiously wait in my car and watch for Emmy to close up shop. Are we doing the right thing? Are we walking into a trap? Is Max safe without us? Time is dwindling down and gears are in motion. This train must keep going, or we will fail—at everything. We have to at least try.

My phone vibrates several times, one directly after another.

Is it Max? Does he need us now? My is heart racing.

No, the string of texts is from Jordan.

Jordan: *I fucked up.*

Jordan: *I need you, bro.*

Jordan: *I'm desperate.*

Jordan: *Please come. I will text you the
address when you tell me you're on your way.*

A knock on the passenger-side window startles me. It's Emmy motioning for me to unlock the door. "I didn't mean to scare you. Can you give me a ride to my car? It's in the parking garage."

I say nothing. Instead, I shift my car into drive and slip Emmy my phone.

Emmy takes her time reading the messages as I round the corner to the garage. "Hudson, you have to go to your brother. He needs you. Ben probably fucked him over too. You need to see what this is all about."

"But I promised Max I'd go with you. You can't go see Ben alone."

"I've been handling Ben longer than both of you. I got this. Trust me, it will all be OK."

For someone so small she sure knows how to stand her ground, perhaps she will be fine.

"Are you sure?"

"Yes, and that's me right there," Emmy says, pointing to a little red Toyota.

"Call me if you get into any trouble," I respond as Emmy exits the car. "Seriously, stay safe, be cautious."

"Same to you."

"Let's try to meet back up before we head up to Max's location. Use the burner phones."

"Hudson, we got this. We are going to take him down."

I nod and then wait for her to pull away before messaging my brother.

Hudson: *On my way*

What could Jordan possibly need from me? What did Ben make him do? My stomach lurches as I wait for my instructions.

Jordan: _Forest Road 40537—End of the road._

Panic rushes over me. Did I read that right? That's the address Max is supposed to go to tonight. Was Jordan sent there too?

I pick up the burner phone and call Max's burner, but he doesn't answer.

This can't be good.

CHAPTER SIXTY-THREE

Mr. Scorpio
Sunday, October 17th, 7:24 p.m.

I've never felt more alive than I do at this very moment—the intoxicating feeling of having all the control. I'm drunk on it. My mind is filling up with excitement and is madly fluttering in anticipation. My puppet master is no longer pulling the strings and guiding me through my malfunction. He cut the cord, and this Pinocchio is ready to be in charge of his own destiny.

I pat my pocket to ensure I have the string. Yep, It's here. I can't help but laugh. Pinocchio needing string after he's been free of it. The far ends of my lip curl at the irony. The tingly sensation that pulsates through my blood is what I look forward to most. I would compare it to what marathon runners call 'runners high'; that moment when they're free of pain and they're in such a euphoric state that they keep going. That moment when their endorphins kick into high gear; that is what this feeling is like for me.

My darkness, it's been inside of me for as long as I can remember. I could feel it, but I didn't know what it was. My brother, he picked at my layers of armor until he uncovered it. I knew there was something buried in the depths of my inner being, but I never knew what it was until my world imploded around me. He fixed me, layer by layer. He knew I was hurting, and he helped me release my demons. It was amazing to have such enlightenment. The gravity of my darkness was always pulling me in, but I resisted, and it drained me. With my brother's help, he taught me to use it and control it. He fixes people. He has a gift for finding broken souls and mending them by bringing out the very thing they hide from everyone, even themselves. He's a master of reading people. I was dead inside and broken like shattered glass. He has a way of restructuring the pieces to make something better than before, something maybe even beautiful.

At first, I acted out in haste, and it nearly got me caught, and it didn't calm the beast inside of me the way we hoped. So, we changed our method. My brother knew we needed to make it more satisfying. To make it count for something other than to briefly curb the urge.

We started with street girls first. Only the ones on drugs, so that it would be easier. Society had already discarded these women as trash, so no one would care. But soon I realized that it wasn't about the kill; it was about the game—the chase. I loved luring women into comfort and then pulling the veil from their eyes. The moment of my betrayal was everything to me. A prickly sensation rushes up my spine as I remember my first real girls. Not the homeless crack addicts, but the pretty ones who had a bright future but a tainted past. This time, instead of picking desperate women, he picked women with a layered history of secrets. They needed to pay for what they'd done. We were careful and covered our tracks. I can't believe no one has found them yet.

My brother is well connected, you see. He is good at getting info to hold as leverage over people—another one of his specialties.

Then there were the other girls. Evie Simmons and Jessica Biles. They weren't as satisfying as my brother promised. They were quick and easy—no chase. They were handed to me.

But now I'm here, and I'm ready to be on my own. I get to pick a target. This time mine wasn't listed for me. This time, when I opened my task, it read.

*You've been good. I've chosen three girls
for you, and it's your choice which one you
pick for the game.*

Then three names were listed. I got to decide for once. Oh, it was fun researching all three of them. Each girl had a reason for being on the list. Each a little tarnished and all with a huge secret. I knew it would be fun.

I was almost angry while I was making my choice. I wanted all three. I actually went back to my brother and told him I wanted all the women, but he told me I couldn't be selfish; I had to save some for the others.

I was a little greedy. I went back for seconds.

***

I pull up next to her car. She doesn't see me right away. I continue to watch her as she pulls down her mirror and fixes her lipstick. She smooshes her pouty, red lips together and blots the excess. She messes with her hair, and I'm annoyed with her vanity, so I stop the madness by honking my horn. I give a friendly wave, and she eagerly waves back. I sit and wait as she gathers all of her belongings. Then I get out of my vehicle and walk over to meet her, opening her car door for her.

"Hey, babe. You look great. I can't wait for you to see what I have planned for tonight." I've always been good at faking it. I flash a devilish smile.

"Hi. Brrrr. It's freezing cold out here tonight," she says as she shivers.

Duh, look how you're dressed, you stupid bitch.

She rounds my car, heading for the passenger side.

Game on.

"Where do you think you're going?" I ask, quickly diverting my tone.

"I'm getting into the passenger seat. Duh," she says with a bit of uncertainty in her voice. It cracks a little.

A euphoric sensation evades my body. The high takes over, and I say with a straight face, "I think you should ride in the trunk."

Her eyes go wide, questioning if I'm joking or kidding. I laugh to ease her mind.

She continues to walk toward the front of the car. I lean down and pick up a rock, and before she can even reach the door handle, I shout, "Bitch, I said you're riding in the trunk!"

She spins around, her survival skills kick in. She reaches out to claw at my face but she's not fast enough. I kick her feet out from under her, and she crashes to the ground, face first in the dirt. I hover over her with the rock in my hand. As I bend down, I use all of my momentum and I crack her over the back of her head with the rock.

It doesn't entirely knock her out as I hoped. I turn her around. Her frightened, doe-eyed stare gives me tingles in all the right places. This is what I love. The moment when they realize they trusted the wrong person. The moment they know, they might die. A little preview of the mindfuck to come.

I smack the rock again into the side of her head, and this time it does the trick. Her eyes roll back into her head, and she's unconscious. Perfect. I take the rope out of my pocket and wrap it around her tiny wrists. I pick her body up and toss it into the trunk. I grab the duct tape from my back seat and put a piece over her mouth.

"Sleep tight, my sweetie," I say softly to her as I close the trunk.

CHAPTER SIXTY-FOUR

Max
Sunday, October 17, 7:23 p.m.

I shouldn't have come early, but I couldn't help myself. I couldn't wait around and do nothing. Jovie needs me.

The unmaintained forest road is bumpy and littered with potholes. One wrong turn, and I could fuck up my car, and then how would I help her? I can't take that chance, so I have to go slow, even though I am conscious that every second Jovie is in more danger. I have to get to her if she is here.

I take each rut in the lane with caution. This road is much higher in elevation, and it's already had snow and has been recently traveled, leaving muddy stains in the already dissipating slush.

I drive for miles, continuing at snail's pace but with a heart rate that feels like it's going to leap out of my chest. Snowcapped peaks from the mountain range pop in and out of view. My stomach is uneasy with the possibility that Ben sent me on a wild goose chase to the middle of nowhere, to get me out of the way. Where is this road going?

Finally, in the distance, I catch a glimpse of smoke puffing out of a chimney, and I know I've arrived. I don't want Ben to know I'm here yet, so I backtrack to the last service road that I remember seeing about a quarter of a mile back. I drive my car down, so it's not visible to other vehicles on the road.

I pull my gloves on and zip my coat up to my chin. Then I begin the short hike. Thankfully, I left my Birkenstocks home and chose tennis shoes for this mission. The chilly air blasts my face and feels like sandpaper against my skin. I don't care about my discomfort. All I care about is ending this game and saving Jovie.

The snow is coming down hard, covering my tracks. That's good. As I emerge from the trees, a small cabin comes into view, illuminated by the full moon. Smoke is still billowing from the chimney, making the cabin look cozy. The rustic building is nestled in an array of pine trees, looking like a postcard. A small red canoe is turned upside down and rests to the right of the cabin. Nothing seems amiss from first glance, but someone must be there to stoke the fire. I quickly scan the outside. No cars, no Ben, and no club members so far.

I cautiously walk up to the side window and press my face against it. I scan the room inside, and it appears empty. My eyes catch no movement except the fire spitting and crackling in the fireplace.

That's when I see the light of the fire catch on something tucked into the corner of the room. A chair and something on it. I wipe the window with my coat to get a better look.

It's a person. A girl slumped over in a chair. Her curls, raggedy and dirty, cascaded down onto her lap. Jovie? I can't tell. This person is about fifteen pounds lighter, which makes sense if she's been here a while. Even if it's not her, I can't leave her there.

I rush over to the front door, tossing all reasoning to the wind, but of course, it's locked.

I sneak around the backside of the cabin, and I locate a back door. I wiggle the handle, hoping and praying for a miracle that it's unlocked. But it doesn't budge.

I check for a key under all the doormats. No luck. I run my hand above the doorframe, and my finger runs across a little bump. I stop and grab the small item, and sure enough, it's a key.

I'm shaking. I'm being a hero. I'm saving someone. Take that, Chrissy. Who's the coward now?

I reach for my phone to message Hudson and Em that I've found someone and to hurry, but I have no service. I must be too far out of town. I didn't think about that when we made our plans.

Oh crap. I can't waste any more time. I have to save her. Now.

A rattling sound rumbles in the distance. My stomach drops. Am I too late? I pause for a moment to listen. It's a car making its way down the bumpy road. Shit.

The noise stops.

I need to get inside. Now. I unlock the door and sneak my body inside before hearing the car door slam shut. They are coming.

I rush down a short hallway and into the first room on the right, leaving the door ajar so I can see what I'm dealing with. Thank goodness the hallway is short enough to hide me but not too long that I can't see the room with the girl. My heart is pounding.

The front door opens, and a heavy thud echoes off the walls.

I take a deep breath and peek with one eye through the door opening. The girl slumped in the chair hasn't moved despite the loud intrusion. I can't tell if she's even alive. Her arms are tied behind her back, and her ankles are strapped to the chair legs.

The loud thud I heard appears to be another body as another lifeless girl lies in the middle of the floor with a rope around her wrists. All I can see is her back. Long hair runs alongside her and spreads out on the hardwood floor.

The person who brought them here hasn't stepped into my eyesight yet. I can't do anything until I know who I'm dealing with first. If that person catches me, I'm no good to either of these girls.

I look at my phones again, praying for service, but both show no bars. Ben told me to come here. If he's planning on meeting me, is this part of the game?

Soon a voice fills the air. It's familiar, but I can't place it.

"Good, you're awake. I knew you'd be surprised."

Goosebumps line my arms as I watch the body on the floor squirm around. Her long hair is zigzagging along the hardwood floor as she tries to wiggle herself free.

I want to rush into the room and take him down. Be the hero, but Chrissy's words are right there, front and center. *You're a fucking coward, Max Jennings. Did you really think you could save Jovie? Did you think you could be the hero in this situation? This is where you run, because you can't stand up to anyone. You're a fucking joke.*

Get out of my head, Chrissy. I'm thinking, plotting, and waiting for the right moment. I can't rush the situation. I shake my head to get Chrissy's words dislodged from my thoughts. But Chrissy is right. I know that I'm no hero. I'm a coward. I can't bring myself to burst in there and save the day. All my pathetic ass can do is watch and hope no one gets killed.

The man's voice fills the room again. "Oh, sweetie, you want an explanation. Well, good thing we've got a little bit of time to kill." He's almost giddy. He's getting a sick kick out of this. Like it's a game—Ben's game.

Come on, Max. You know this voice. I press my ear harder against the door in between peeking out. I can't get caught. If I do, I'm going to end up like these girls—tied up and fearing for my life.

"Don't give me that look—that you-are-sick-in-the-head kind of look. That's not very nice of you." His cruel voice filling the cabin again. "Aww, sweetie, you shouldn't judge me until you hear everything. Once I lay it all out, then you're free to judge me all you want. I mean, it's not like it will matter much anyway, but hell, I probably owe it to you."

I cautiously peer around the door, finally getting a glimpse of a tall man dressed all in black. He's now pacing behind the girl on the floor. He has his hood pulled over his head, and I still can't catch a glimpse of his face.

"If looks could kill. . ." the man says in a light tone. The sick fuck is finding this funny. The girl is wiggling fiercely on the ground. I can't imagine the state of fear she is in right now. I need to do something fast.

The girl on the chair still hasn't moved. I don't think the girls have noticed each other yet.

"OK, OK, I know I said I would tell you the whole story, so I better get on with it. I can tell you're *dying* to hear how it all started." the man says. He moves to straddle her body. One leg on each side of the girl. He's just standing above her, staring down at her. What the hell is he going to do to her?

Come on, Max, just fucking get out there. Save those girls. My palms are sweating, and my heart is racing. I don't know what to do. Think Max. Think.

All I brought with me was a pocketknife. I quickly scan the room, searching for a gun, knife, or ax. Nothing jumps out at me. I can't rummage through the drawers or closet without being heard. Maybe the guy will get bored and leave again. After all, he left the one girl tied to the chair here all alone.

I check my watch; it's almost eight. That's when I was supposed to arrive. Is this what Ben wanted me to see?

"Anyway, let me get back to my story. So, sweetie, when I saw your face for the first time, I knew it had to be you. I couldn't stop thinking about you and that photo. You must have known what you were doing when you posted that specific one. That tiny circle they give you to showcase yourself. You have to be choosey and pick just the right image. How does one choose what picture goes in that itty-bitty circle?"

The body on the ground is wiggling, trying to free herself once again as the man has moved from his awkward stance above her. I know she needs help now. But how? The man begins to pace the room. I could run in and attack him from behind. I could catch him off guard. He doesn't know I'm here. But then what? I don't have a real weapon.

"Social media is the biggest tease of us all, but we have to play the game. We must choose to put our best foot forward. So, what did you choose? Let me remind you."

The man yanks his phone from his pocket and shoves it into the girl's face. "This photo! Who do you think you are? Virtually begging for someone to treat you like this?"

This can't be happening. I need to do something. Now.

"See, sweetie, you made me do this. You made me choose you for the game. Oh, sorry, you don't know about the game, that's right. Let me fill you in. So, it's this little game I'm playing, and you, my sweetie, were my pawn. And guess what, babe? I believe I won the game, but that means. . . Well, my dear, that means you lost."

Holy fuck. It *is* a club member. He's completing the game.

"But first, I have to feed our pet."

Pet? I heard Ben on the phone asking someone to look after his pet after one of my sessions. I don't see an animal anywhere.

Oh my God. Is he talking about the other girl?

I want to vomit. My hairs stand erect on my arms, and my stomach turns to knots.

The man struts over to the girl in the corner. He gathers her hair in his large hand, pulls it tight, and yanks her head up. The girl on the ground lets out a loud, muffled screech. The pain from her noise cuts through my soul.

The guy steps aside, and I can see the girl in the chair better. The dirty hair that was once messy curls. The adorable face that used to beam with that scrunched-up expression. Record Store Girl—Jovie. It's her. I cover my mouth to avoid the shriek that's tunneling up my throat. I buckle over and wince in pain. This is all my fault.

She looks deathly pale and painted with grime. She's so skinny. Her eyes are hollowed and sickly. Jovie's eyes flutter. But she's alive! It's all I have to hold on to at this point.

Both the girls lock eyes, and tears flood Jovie's face, mixing with the filth, streaking brown lines down her face. Jovie's body jerks repeatedly, and her eyes flutter faster. She's using all her energy to shake and rattle her chair.

The body on the ground thrashes hastily, and in doing so I see a flash of her face.

It's her sister! It's Ivy that Jovie is seeing lying on the floor. The two sisters.

I turn my head to face the room that I so cowardly ran into and slump down the length of the door. I have to do something, but all my body allows me to do is sulk. I have to act, but I can't. I'm paralyzed with fear. Ivy and Jovie are here. I'm failing them. Both of them.

A creak from the other room draws me back to the terror-filled room, and the mystery man says, "Just in time for the fun to begin." I can't even get up to see what's caused his reaction.

Then a familiar voice responds, "Oh my God, what did you do?"

CHAPTER SIXTY-FIVE

Emmy
Sunday, October 17, 7:29 p.m.

"Ben, it's Emmy. Let me in," I shout at the coded door. Ben has never given me the code. I'm not privy to such things or the ongoings of business behind this secure entry. He makes me wait. I've only been allowed here once before. The night everything changed.

"Ben. Seriously. Open the fucking door!" I shout as I pound my fist against it.

Where is he? Did I get the time wrong? The light is on. I can see it through the window. Someone must be here.

I pull out my phone to text Ben when a swift breeze wafts through the stairwell. I pivot, but not quickly enough. I feel a tiny prick against my skin.

I raise my hand to my neck. "Ouch!" I shout.

My visions starts to blur and my legs give way beneath me. I fall backward, but rather than hitting the floor, I'm caught by someone's arms.

No. This can't be happening. I try to turn my head, but it's heavy. My eyes fall shut on their own. I can't pry them open as hard as I will them to. Everything is dark and unfocused.

I want to scream, but the words don't come either.

I'm drifting into blackness.

CHAPTER SIXTY-SIX

Kade
Sunday, October 17, 7:29 p.m.

I'm waiting for Ben at the club. I know what he's doing. Nadia is my target. Jordan's ex-wife. The reason Jordan's life fell apart. I suspect Ben wants revenge on Nadia to help heal Jordan. But I'm not going to let that happen. I can't believe I'm thinking about someone else for once. Maybe I'm not as broken as Ben makes me out to be.

I crack the lock on Ben's office door. It was easier than I thought it would be. I'm sure his new cameras alerted him to my intrusion and he'll be here soon. I'm counting on it.

I start rifling through Ben's desk, pushing and moving papers, when I see a list of names and pictures.

Nadia Dressler
Chrissy Parker
Ivy Peterson
Sasha Brody

Tanya Beatty
Marisa Lopez
Laura Voss
Kelsey Sinclair
Whitney Jones
Helena Fitz

I run my finger down the list, and it lands on Whitney Jones. No information is safe with Ben. She was my first and only love. She is everything a nine and above should be. But she saw the real me and didn't like it. She broke up with me years ago, and I've never been in a relationship since.

She hurt me, but she doesn't deserve to be on this list.

Ben must only be targeting women who've injured members in the past in some way. Why? So, we can move on? That seems far too selfless for Ben. There is always something in it for him.

Speaking of which, where is he? Ben has a lot of explaining to do. He should be here any minute. He wouldn't let me rummage around his office and then miss the opportunity to hold me accountable.

An obnoxious pounding alerts me back to the main room.

"Ben, it's Emmy. Let me in."

Did I hear that correctly? I walk out into the open area and step closer to the door.

"Ben. Seriously. Open the fucking door."

Yep, that is Emmy and her little attitude.

Wait, how and why is she visiting Ben?

How could she possibly be connected to him? What the hell is going on? This doesn't make sense, but whatever is going on here, I can't risk dragging Emmy into this. But I need to confront her. Fuck! I have to find out what she knows and how she plays into everything. I can do it quickly and then send her on her way.

I open the door and look up the stairs.

There's no one there. Did I imagine it?

I run up to the top of the steps and yank the door open. It's dark outside, but I see a hooded figure shoving something into the back of a black sedan.

Is that Emmy?

My mind is reeling and the pieces of what I'm seeing don't add up or make sense. Before my mind actually processes the reality of the situation the sedan drives away. I sprint to my Jeep, and I follow it.

I stay far enough behind so they don't know I'm tailing them. I've never seen this car before and I can't tell who the driver is, but I'm confident someone was shoved into the back seat—unwillingly.

I follow for miles before we turn down a rugged forest road that says *No Outlet.*

I turn off my lights and let the sedan get further down. It should be easy to find them. I wait about three minutes before turning my lights on and continue down the bumpy path.

I catch a glimpse of a cabin in the distance. I get out of my car and run the rest of the way.

When I reach the property, the light from the cabin window illuminates the hooded driver as he pulls a body out of the back seat. Ben. He hoists it over his shoulder and walks toward the cabin.

It's Emmy.

CHAPTER SIXTY-SEVEN

Hudson
Sunday, October 17, 8:01 p.m.

"Oh my God, what did you do?" I scream.

I'm instantly sick to my stomach at the sight inside the cabin. My brother is standing between two girls. One tied up on the floor and one tied to a chair. The one in the chair vaguely looks like Jovie, but the beautiful face plastered all over the news is not the face I'm looking at now. But it's her. It has to be. She's scrawny, just skin and bones. She must have been here for weeks as we feared. Her eyes are sunken with dirt covering her face. But she's alive.

"Jordan, what did you do?"

Jordan doesn't seem fazed by my question, like I just asked what he wants for dinner, not why two girls are tied up.

His eyes slowly shift to mine and turn dark. His demeanor doesn't match up with the Jordan I know.

"Thanks for coming, brother of mine. We will get to them in a minute," he says, nodding to the two girls. "I knew your guilty conscience would leap into action at a chance to help me. I mean, you kinda owe me for fucking up my life."

"What?"

"Don't play dumb, Hudson. I know what you did."

My face begins to heat up as the guilt from my two biggest regrets in life simultaneously punch me in the stomach—following Kade and my affair with Nadia.

"I—I don't understand," I stutter.

"Nadia. You dimwit," Jordan says as spittle flies from his mouth, dropping to little speckles on the wooden floor.

His words catch me off guard, hitting me like a sonic boom and shattering me into tiny pieces. He couldn't have known about our affair. We were so careful. I tuck my head into my chin, avoiding his piercing glare. My words are soft as they leave my mouth. "You know about Nadia? For how long?"

"I knew from the first time you fucked her. I followed her. I knew she was screwing you for months."

"Why didn't you say anything? Why did you let me suffer with the guilt?"

"I mean, why not? It was fun to watch you squirm. I wanted you to marinate in your dishonesty and betrayal."

I raise my hand to my mouth to cover the vomit that's threatening to spew out. The whole reason I followed Kade was to keep that secret safe. No, no, no this can't be happening. Jordan knew everything this whole time. I swallow hard, pushing everything back down. "I, I, I'm so sorry for that, but what does that have to do with these poor girls? Why are they here—with you? What did you do?"

I let my head drop limp and I close my eyes, scared of the answer. I need to know, but I'm afraid of the truth.

"Look at me, when I'm talking to you!" he shouts.

I can't bring myself to open my eyes, and I know Jordan has moved; he's right behind me now, his breath hot on my skin. Chills trickle down my spine as his fingers twist the hair at the base of my neck. He yanks my head back. "Hudson, you're a fucking pussy. You made a mistake, so fucking man up. Open your eyes! See what you caused!"

I obey out of fear and slowly let my eyes flicker open. They sting from the tears that are welling up. I'm physically sick as my eyes drift to the two girls. He still hasn't answered my question.

Jordan steps out from behind me and casually strolls the room, weaving in and out of the two girls.

"It's really an interesting story, Hudson, but we must go back to the beginning. My fucking ex-wife. You know the cheating whore. I sensed she was catching on to my malfunction. Although it wasn't as fully developed as it is now, but I needed time alone to figure things out. I let her stray so she wouldn't dig into my issues, but I didn't think it would be with you. My *fucking* brother."

"I get that I did wrong by you but look what you're doing! These girls have nothing to do with any of it."

"I was going to punish you sooner, but when Ben wanted new members, I thought it would be the perfect way to fuck with you, so I dragged you to the club. Disappointingly, Ben wasn't pleased with my choice. After the first meeting, he wanted to kick you out of the club, but I talked him into using you. How do you think Ben knew your secret?"

The room is spinning.

"Hudson, I know what you did, how you followed Kade later that night. Thanks for that, by the way. Evie and Jessica were fun to play with. I know you didn't follow Kade the night of Jessica but your help with Evie kicked things into motion. Mateo was the lucky one to get that extra credit, or so I've been told."

My stomach lurches at his admission. No. This can't be right. No. Not Jordan. No. He's not capable of murder.

"You were the one who killed them? Not Kade?" I question, hoping I heard him wrong.

"Guilty." He laughs. "Nothing is wrong with me, Hudson. I'm just being myself. I'm living my true life. I'm playing Ben's game, and by the looks of it, I'm winning. Come on, haven't you always suspected I had a dark side?"

"What? No. You're my big brother, Jordan. I would never have thought that about you. Ben must have brainwashed you."

"Oh dumb, lazy and stupid Hudson. The signs were all there. You just missed them. I blame our parents. The verbal abuse, the threatening language—it takes a toll on a person. I never felt good enough for anyone, but then Nadia came along. She changed me and she changed the way Mom and Dad looked at me, but after a while, I needed more. Nadia got angry with me, as I sought out new things to curb my boredom, but nothing satisfied me. I had urges that I wanted to act on, but I couldn't. I felt broken and damaged, like there was something wrong with me.

"Then my little whore of a wife actually did it, she sought the comfort of another man as I was busy rediscovering myself. I let it happen, but I didn't realize the toll it would actually take on me. My life began to spiral out of control. I was depressed and didn't know how to fix myself. That is until I met Ben. He was my savior. He pealed back all my layers and helped me see who I was truly meant to be. He saw how my urges were festering inside and he knew the only way to make me whole was to feed my malfunction. For the first time, I felt alive. I owe the man my life."

"Jordan, you're not making any sense. Sure, Dad was an ass, and he has a temper, but I think you're remembering our childhood incorrectly. You never had a darkness. Ben's brainwashed you. This is not you. The man standing in front of me is not my brother."

"But Ben said it's always been there—waiting to be seen by someone, waiting to be released."

"Ben is using you for his own sick pleasure. Can't you see that?" I run over to the girl tied to the chair. "I'm untying her, Jordan. You aren't well. We can get you help, real help, but I'm getting these girls out of here now!"

"Oh, I wouldn't do that if I were you," Jordan says as the corners of his lips curl upward.

"Fuck you!" I shout.

"I'm just looking after *that* one." Jordan nods to Jovie tied to the chair. "She belongs to Ben. She's not for me to kill. It's *this one* you should be worried about right now," he says with a devil's smile, directing his attention to the girl lying on the floor.

"Well, it doesn't look like you're doing a good job looking after her. She needs medical attention, now," I shout.

Jordan ignores me as I try to untie the girl's rope, but I can't get my fingers to untwist the knots. I'm shaking and panicking. I don't know what Jordan is going to do to me—to us.

"But this little cookie, she's mine." Jordan smiles and walks over to the girl on the ground. The girl lets out a muffled shriek through her taped mouth. She scooches her tied up body across the hardwood floor to get further away from Jordan, but he uses his foot to slide her back into place.

A burst of cold air invades the room, stopping us in our tracks. Jordan and I look at each other in confusion, then over to the door where Ben is walking in with a body hanging lifeless over his shoulder.

"Emmy," I gasp. I knew I shouldn't have let her go alone. My stomach churns with guilt. "You monster, what did you do?" I shout to anyone willing to answer. Because they are all monsters.

"What are you guys doing here?" Ben demands. "This is not part of my plan. You were supposed to take care of my pet. What is *she* doing here?" His eyes are pinned on the girl lying on the ground, scared to death.

"Ben, you said to get creative."

"Yes, but this isn't your target, Jordan. Where is Sasha?" Ben shouts.

"You teased me, Ben. I got bored with Sasha, and I wanted to play with Ivy instead," Jordan responds. His confidence is shrinking in front of Ben.

"Ivy," I gasp. Of course, I recognize the girl from the news report. My brother is sick and not in his right mind. How did I not see the signs earlier?

"What's he doing here?" Ben is now diverting his attention to me as he effortlessly tosses Emmy's tiny body onto the couch. She hits the sofa hard and her head rolls into the crack between the cushions.

"He's part of my finale, Ben. I mindfucked my own brother. You said I've been good, so I thought I could have a little fun tonight. I figured the cleverer I was, the better chance I had at winning."

"Jordan, you fuck-up. You're ruining everything!" Ben yells.

When Ben doesn't clap or pat Jordan on the back, he shrinks into himself like a little dog, scolded.

"Has anyone seen Max during this whole charade?" Ben demands.

Max! Where is he? My eyes dart around the cabin impulsively. He was meant to be meeting Ben here, but I can't see any signs that he's hiding out, waiting for the perfect time to leap in and save the day. I'm sickened at the thought that perhaps he didn't make it here. Nothing is going as planned tonight. I'm afraid this isn't going to end well for any of us.

"Tie him up," Ben says to Jordan.

I try to run, but I've never been able to outrun my older brother. He pushes me down onto the floor, straddles me, and wraps the string around my wrists. He pulls tight and then sets me on the ground near the girl in the chair.

I'm squirming around, trying to free myself when I see something moving outside. Something ran past the window.

I have a glimmer of hope that we aren't all going to die here tonight. Ivy, Emmy, Jovie, and I need a miracle right now. Maybe that miracle is Max.

CHAPTER SIXTY-EIGHT

Max
Sunday, October 17, 8:10 p.m.

The door opens behind me, and I fall backward into the hallway. Before I have time to react, I'm being picked up and shoved back inside the room with a hand covering my mouth.

"Don't scream," a voice whispers into my ear.

I nod my head, but I'm not sure I can make that promise.

"I'm going to take my hand away now. Don't say a word."

I nod again. The hand slowly releases from my mouth, leaving a salty taste on my lips. I slowly turn around, my heart beating fast against my rib cage as if it might explode.

My body sags with relief when it's a familiar face—Kade.

He lifts his pointer finger to his lips, and I obey.

In his hushed voice, he whispers, "Max, we need to get Jordan and Ben away from the hostages. I'm going to rush Ben, and you take down Jordan."

"I can't take Jordan. I just saw how easily he grabbed Hudson, and I'm practically identical in size. Kade, I can't," I whisper back.

"Yes, you can. We need to save them. Emmy's out there."

A lump rises in my throat.

"Emmy?" I question.

"Ben brought her," Kade says.

Shit. Shit. Shit.

"On the count of three. You got this."

I shake my head no. I can't do this. I can't.

"Yes. Max, now is your time to be the hero." Kade grabs me by the shoulders and stares straight into my eyes. "You *can* do this."

I nod.

I'm not a coward. I can save them. I can do this.

I take a deep breath and allow Kade to start the count down.

"One." I nod

"Two." Kade nods

"Three!"

Kade takes off first, and I follow. We rush into the room. Jordan's eyes widen as I plow into him. I slam his body to the floor. His head makes a loud thump as it meets the hardwood. The surprise attack worked. I feel his panicked breath under the weight of my body. I clench my hands around his biceps to keep him locked on the ground. Jordan thrashes in an attempt to free himself.

But everything in the next moment happens so quickly.

A gun is fired.

I'm distracted by visions of me holding a gun in Cal's house. The memories flicker through my mind and feel so real. I'm paralyzed with fear—the familiar noise that haunts me echoes through the cabin.

Jordan takes advantage of my distraction, and reality quickly brings me back to the room when he takes his moment and flips me around, reversing us. He has me pinned under his body, holding my arms above my head.

Have I been shot?

No, I don't think so. I don't feel anything wrong. But now I'm fearful of who might have been shot. In the corner of the room, an open cabinet with a spot for a missing rifle is left open. Who has the gun?

I manage to twist my head and a surge of panic shatters me.

Kade is face down on the floor. His arms are stretched above his head, and his legs are twisted and lifeless. Blood begins to soak its way through his tan coat. Kade is losing a lot of blood. I can't tell if he's still breathing. "Kade!" I scream. Kade doesn't move.

Ben is standing over him with a hunting rifle.

"Kade!" I shout again, my voice bouncing off the cabin walls, shaking every cell inside of me.

Ben moves on from Kade now that he's no longer a threat. He begins to circle Jordan and me with the gun in his hand.

Emmy. Where is she? I scan the room until I spot her body slumped on the couch. I can't tell if she is alive.

Hudson's eyes are wide with fear as he sits next to Jovie with his hands pinned behind his back. Jovie is frightened and looks like she might pass out. Ivy's tied up next to me and appears to be in shock. I wish I could pull the tape from her mouth. I didn't like her, but I never wanted to see this happen. I fear none of us are getting out of here alive. Kade was our best chance.

This has to be a nightmare. I squeeze my eyes tight, and when I reopen them, nothing has changed. The room is exactly the same.

Ben's voice cuts through the cabin, and shivers run down my spine. "Max. This evening is not going as I hoped it would. I wanted an intimate gathering. Jordan ruined it for us, but you get the gist."

"Look, it's Jovie," he says sadistically, pulling up her head up so I can get a better view.

"Ben, stop it," I shout. "You're hurting her."

"The infamous Jovie. Max, she's not who you think she is. She is just like the rest of the mindless girls you hate. Practically just like her sister. Void of any real connection and feelings. A fake bitch."

"So what? That doesn't mean she deserves to die."

"Well, that's your decision, but we will get to that in a bit. This is all for you, Max. Don't you see that now?"

"What are you talking about, Ben?"

"I guess I should back the story up, but I think you'll catch on quick. Years ago, I started a club for men in the town of Tillicum Valley. You know the place, Max."

Oh, my God. No. No. No.

"See, it started with three founding members. My childhood friend Cal, my baby brother Mark, and myself. Do any of those names ring a bell?"

No. No. No. This can't be happening.

"Ding, ding, Max. Think about it." Ben double taps my forehead with the butt of the rifle. "Ringing any bells?"

Cal. My friend Cal. No.

"Cal came up with this brilliant idea—you're going to love this."

There is no way Ben knows Cal. No.

"He saw how one of his friends was being pushed around by a girl. And he thought it would be fun to mess with her and show his friend how bad she was for him. To show him that she couldn't be trusted. And then once it ended, this guy would see how horrible this woman was to him, and a new member would join our club. Well, things didn't go as planned. This friend went the wrong way and shot Cal. Can you believe that, Max?"

My skin is burning, and I'm dizzy. No, this can't be true.

"But see, Max, I still thought Cal's friend could be fixed. He just needed a little guidance. It wasn't his fault that he shot Cal.

It was the girl's fault. She pushed him to his limits. But the guy up
and left town, so we followed him. I really like Clear River. It's a
nice place to escape to. Wouldn't you agree?"

"Is, is Cal, OK?" I find the words and the courage to ask.

"Ah, so you are starting to put things together," Ben taunts.

"Cal, is here too?" I question.

"Oh, Cal. He's doing better than ever. He's a good little soldier,
and he's become quite the hacker since he was laid up for so long
with a shotgun wound. It's amazing what you can learn when all
you have is time and a laptop. Do you know how easy it is to hack
someone's Socialite account, among many other things?"

Relief floods me. I didn't kill Cal. He's not dead, but I did shoot
him. I feared the worst for years, but never could I have fathomed this
outcome. They've been following me—my every move.

"Chrissy? Is she OK? Where is she?"

"Funny that you seem to care now. But she's fine. She never left
Tillicum Valley. She never came looking for you. If that's what
you wanted to know. Sorry to catfish you, Hudson," Ben says with
a laugh.

Hudson's bloodshot eyes are filled with terror and tears.

This is all fun and games to Ben. He's using real people as his
playthings. He's a bully who exploits people's weaknesses to get
what he needs for his own sick pleasure.

"It's funny because if Chrissy only knew what you really did
for her. . . You finally stopped being a coward, Max. Well, at least
for a brief moment. You shot the guy to protect her, to fight for
her, but she doesn't even know what you did, because you didn't
go back. You ran like a pussy. Cal called me right away, not the
police. I took him to the hospital, where he told them he shot
himself in the leg, and the fools believed him. See, we weren't
done with you yet, Max. We knew this would be a longer game,

and we were so excited to play it. See, I really hate unfinished business and the game of revenge is so much sweeter, especially when a hunt is involved."

"You're all sick!" I shout. Jordan presses his weight into my chest further, squeezing the air from my lungs.

"Once Cal finished rehab and could walk again with the assistance of a cane, Mark, Cal, and I moved to Clear River. You were easy to find, Max. We set up a new club that aimed to help men just like you. And Mark—you know my little brother Mark, the bartender?"

The cane at the bar; it was Cal's. I bet he rushed out of there the second he saw my face. I bet Mark got a good laugh at my expense and to think I liked him. I'm going to be sick.

"Mark does an excellent job at keeping tabs on the members. He really took a fancy to Kade."

"Why did you get Kade involved?" I ask.

"He was your boss and the only person you seemed to like in this town. We used him to get to you. Things didn't go according to plan, so we improvised. Then Kade started to stray. We couldn't have him lose focus. Not when we were so close to you. We needed Kade to stay in the game. We needed to keep him close, so we had a little fun with him."

"Do you know how crazy you sound?"

"Those poor girls didn't have to die. If only Kade had been loyal," Ben continues with no remorse for his actions.

"You're fucked in the head!" I scream at Ben.

Wait, is that Kade's foot twitching? He's still alive. Ben doesn't seem to have noticed, which is good.

"I have this little dilemma. Your dream girl, Jovie, is here. I told you to be patient my friend, and look, didn't I say I would help you get her? Once we cleaned her up, she'll be good as new.

But Emmy, your partner in crime, got in my way, so she's here now as well. I know you care for her too."

Ben's smirk morphs into a villainous smile.

"Welcome to your finale, Max Jennings."

CHAPTER SIXTY-NINE

Max
Sunday, October 17, 8:19 p.m.

"Wake up, you traitor." Ben slaps Emmy across the face.

Emmy's eyes flicker open and widen with a horrified shock. She squeals and rocks her body fiercely against the couch.

"Stop it!" Ben yells, shoving the butt of the rifle into her cheek.

Emmy's movement ceases but I can still see her body quiver as her eyes fight to stay open.

"Max. It's time to pick. Who are you going to save?"

"Ben, this is not a game. These are real people. You can't do this." I reply.

"Come on, don't be boring. You've got to pick one," he taunts. "Will it be Jovie? The funky dream girl?" he says with the gun pointed at Emmy's head. "Or will it be Emmy? The coworker slash partner in crime?" Ben says, moving the gun to Jovie's head.

Both girls' eyes light up with terror, tears streaming down their cheeks.

"No, Ben, you don't have to do this. I'm sorry for what I did to Cal."

"You still don't get it, do you? It's not about Cal, Max. It's about so much more. All girls are bad. They're selfish, controlling, manipulative bitches, who need to pay for their sins. I tried to help all my club members see this, but some of you assholes just don't get it. Cal tried to show you this in Tillicum Valley—with Chrissy. Then once you fled, I couldn't let you disappoint me. You became a new version of the game. You were my pawn in this rat race, and I hate losing. Really, I do. No one gets away from me. But tonight, you're here, and it's the end of our little competition. Do you feel mindfucked yet?" Ben says, letting out a menacing laugh as he pushes the gun into Jovie's temple.

"Ben you're seriously insane." I shout. "Please stop this! We can talk this out."

Ben repositions himself between the couch and the chair, directly in the middle of the two girls. He's freely pointing the rifle back and forth between Jovie and Emmy.

"Max, you have one final opportunity to make me proud." Ben jeers. "Which girl will it be? I'm going to let one live and you will win the game. I'm giving you more than you deserve—you ungrateful shit."

"What about me?" Jordan asks.

"Jordan, we will talk later. Now, let Max have his moment."

"But Ben, I thought I was winning," he whines. "You said we were brothers; I did all of this for you."

"Jordan shut the fuck up. This is not your moment. Come on, Max. You need to decide. If you can't pick one, I will shoot them both."

I release a noise that startles me. Almost feral. "No, I can't. I won't!" I scream.

"You have three seconds, Max."

"Ben, shoot me. Let them live. It's all my fault they're here," I plead.

"It doesn't work that way, Max."

Ben cocks the rifle. "One."

"No!"

"Two. I'm serious. Pick one, or I shoot them both."

A vision of Emmy's eyes twinkling in my bedroom cling to my memory. Automatically, my eyes move to the couch.

"Emmy. Emmy. Emmy. Save Emmy!" I shout.

Everything happens in slow motion. Jovie's eyes close, she lets out a whimper. She tilts her head down again. She's preparing to die. Ben repositions his gun toward Jovie's beautiful face. His finger is on the trigger, slowly tugging it back.

In that dreadful moment, the legs of the table near me rattle, and the ground shakes below me. Kade has pushed himself up from the floor, howling like an injured animal.

Ben releases the trigger.

Kade throws his muscular, blood-soaked torso into the air, catching the bullet in his chest that's intended for Jovie. The shell exits his back, and blowback blood spatters Hudson and Jovie.

"No!" I scream as his body crashes down, smacking hard against the floor. Blood slowly fans out from his wound and into the cracks of the flooring. "Kade," I whimper, but he doesn't move.

Ben readjusts himself, repositioning the rifle, but this time in my direction and with no explanation. I'm pinned under Jordan and can't move.

I close my eyes. I don't know what's going to happen next. Ben cocks the rifle. I take a deep breath, preparing for my death when sirens ring through the cabin.

I manage to pry my eyes open just in time to see Ben leaping over the couch. He turns and runs down the hallway. The back door slams shut, and with it, a sense of relief veils over the room. Even the weight of Jordan on top of my body loosens.

Armed police officers storm the cabin. Several more officers pass by the window, and I catch a glimpse of a muscular figure.

Owen?

"Hands on your heads, no one move!" an officer demands.

Jordan and I obey. Everyone else is tied up.

"He ran out the back," Hudson shouts. "Get the monster that did this!"

A single gunshot pierces through the cold mountain air.

"Suspect is down."

EPILOGUE

Max
Sunday, April 17, 7:00 p.m.

It's been six months since the night at the cabin. I still can't believe all of that actually happened. Sometimes I wake up in a cold sweat as that night replays in my head. It always ends with a flicker of light from the rifle followed by a loud cracking noise as the bullet zips through the barrel—images and sounds that will forever haunt me.

"Max, you're in your head again," Emmy says. "Time to close up shop, it's already seven. Can you get the lights?"

"Yes, sorry. Today's been harder than I thought it would be. I can't stop thinking about that night," I respond.

"I get it. It's been on my mind all day, too," Emmy says, flipping the open sign over to closed. "Hudson, will you get the lock?"

"I still can't believe Owen was one of our heroes that night," Hudson says, twisting the lock.

"Right! Who would have thought Owen would have been the one to save us? Once he put two and two together, he realized his target was Kade's ex-girlfriend; he was done playing the game. He didn't want any part of that. If Owen hadn't gone to the club to confront Ben, he wouldn't have seen him shoving our sweet Emmy into that car. "I pause, giving Emmy a long kind smile. "Then he saw Kade follow Ben, so he assumed you were his next victim, and Ben was part of the murders," I say, gulping down the lump that's making its way up my throat. Thinking about Owen's bravery chokes me up every time.

"I owe Owen my life," Emmy says as the three of us walk to the backroom to gather our jackets and get the last set of lights. "I mean, he was wrong about Kade but right about Ben. Thank goodness he kept following them and had the smarts to turn around and notify the police, or things could have turned out so much worse—for all of us."

We don't talk about what happened with Jordan. It's too hard on Hudson. He still blames himself for not seeing the signs sooner. Jordan was arrested that night for the murders of Evie Simmons and Jessica Biles and the kidnapping of Ivy and Jovie Peterson. He's also since been charged with the murders of Erica Sweeny, Holly Ashen, and Josie Penner, the other women who were murdered. It turns out Jordan was a blabbermouth and told Jovie all his secrets while he was torturing her at the cabin over the five weeks she was held captive, and Jovie shared everything she could remember with the cops. Jordan must have assumed Ben would kill her, and he'd get away with everything. He might also be connected to a string of murders in neighboring towns that were unsolved but fit the time frame. Jordan has since publicly issued remorseful statements, but crutching on Ben as a cult leader, saying he had no control over his actions. I don't think a jury is going to be sympathetic toward him. I personally believe Ben made him think a certain way, but I heard Jordan in the cabin, and I think he enjoyed every minute of it. He deserves whatever he has coming to him.

As for the other members, Mateo, Ezra, Decklan, Bobby, and Ethan jointly planned on walking out and quitting after Ben laid down the rest of the rules. They didn't care what Ben threatened them with. They formed their own alliance. Good thing they weren't in as deep as the rest of us with Ben and his evil plans. Well, as far as I know.

"Sometimes I wish Ben would have been caught instead of killed that night," Emmy says coldly. "I wanted him to pay for his sins."

"He had his chance to stop, but he kept running, and the officers had no choice but to take the shot. He chose the coward's way out," I respond.

"He sure as hell did," Hudson adds. "I'm kind of disappointed that nothing happened to Cal and Mark. They were as much a part of the club as Ben was, but the authorities couldn't prove that."

"Which is bullshit. Cal was a hacker. Of course, he cleared all the evidence. He's not stupid. I personally think that Mark was afraid of his brother and was simply Ben's eyes and ears outside the club," I respond. I still feel bad that I shot Cal all those years ago. I shouldn't have run, but I did, and it cost me a lot. I will always have one eye over my shoulder, afraid both of them will come back and seek revenge, but so far, I've been lucky. I'm also fortunate that Emmy doesn't hate me for that huge secret I've kept from her.

"Ben's story is a little depressing, though. Living with a meth-addicted mother who abused him," Emmy says. "Then to end up with Cal's family who clearly didn't help him the way he needed help."

I nod in agreement. "It is kind of impressive that he built himself up after everything he went through, but he chose the wrong path once he got there. He chose a revenge rampage, and his mommy issues were at the root of it all. I guess we will never know what was going on in his messed-up head. All we do know is that he fed on the darkness in people and used them to fuel his hatred."

"In some sick and twisted way, it brought the three of us together," Emmy says, looping her arms through both of ours as we strut down the hallway to the back door of Epic Records. "I still can't believe we bought this place—it's ours—the three of us."

Emmy's right about it bringing us together, and it turns out that the three of us had a lot in common. So much so that Emmy, Hudson, and I moved into the apartment above the store. Plus, it felt safer for us at first. We were getting used to being together. We experienced so much trauma and loss we thought we should stick together.

"Emmy, we're grateful that you used the money you got from Ben to get us started. You know, once this store is making a profit again, Hudson and I will send you back to school," I respond.

"I know. You guys are the best. We couldn't let our hero's legacy die. He loved this store. It was the right thing to do," Emmy says with a kind smile.

Thinking about Kade always tugs at my heart. He was one of our heroes that night and he saved Jovie's life. Jovie and Ivy moved to California, and it turns out, Ben was right; Jovie wasn't who I hoped she was. Of course, she wouldn't speak to me after what I put her through, so I finally looked her up on Socialite, and she works for a social media startup that uses 'vintage' songs to create catchy videos for teens. Her profile is filled with images just like her sister's page. But none of that matters now. I'm happy she and Ivy are safe. I've since deleted the Socialite app on my phone.

"My phone is vibrating," Emmy says, unlocking her arms from ours. "Jake and Jed are going to meet us for drinks." She grins as she looks up from her phone.

The three of us walk out the back door together like we do most nights since we took over the store. Owen is waiting for us in the alleyway. He's dressed nicely and has a date with him. He's been seeing a therapist to undo the damage Ben did to him. He's faring much better with an actual licensed therapist. It's nice that we've gotten to know the real Owen, the man who alerted the police.

"Hey, Owen," I say, waving at him.

"Hey guys, it's good to see you," he responds as he kicks at the rocks below him. "I still can't believe it's been six months, bro."

"I know, man, it's been hard. But tonight we celebrate the life of our friend, Kade," I respond.

The five of us walk down the alleyway and turn toward the Rose Tavern. Emmy smiles a sweet smile. "Hey guys, I've been thinking. Do you think we should rename the store Kade's Records?"

"I think that's a great idea," Hudson responds.

I flash them a wide smile. "Me too, Emmy. I can't believe we didn't think of that sooner."

"Well then, Kade's Records, it is. Come on slowpokes, pick up the pace. Everyone is already at the Rose Tavern waiting," Emmy says in her cute, bossy voice.

I lean in and give her a soft kiss on the cheek. "OK, let's go, bossy pants. We don't want to be late."

For the first time in my life, I'm truly happy and I can be myself without fear. And I finally saw what had been in front of my eyes the whole time. I'm deeply and madly in love with my funky record-store girl—Emmy.

THE END

ACKNOWLEDGMENTS

This novel wouldn't be in your hands if it weren't for the village that helped, encouraged, and pushed me along the way. I have so many people to thank for assisting me in bringing another novel to life.

First, my amazing and supportive husband, Jeremy. My rock. My ride-or-die. My author career wouldn't be possible without your support, love, and encouragement. I must have driven you nuts as I overthought every decision with this novel, and for that, I'm sorry, and I owe you big time! If it weren't for you guiding me back to my center, I don't think I would have ever finished *The Liars' Club*. I love you, babe!

Next, my Critique/Accountability Partner, Author Stacey Spangler. You helped keep me on track with my goals. I will forever be grateful for our weekly chats, zoom calls, encouraging messages, and feedback. You've been an enormous asset in my writing journey.

I can't have my acknowledgments without thanking another Critique Partner of sorts, my friend, Alexis Coffey. Your endless insight and attention to detail have been crucial in pushing this novel over the finish line. I appreciate you and all your time and your espresso!

A special shout-out to my friend Tess Burga. Thanks for reading everything I write, even the gnarly first drafts. I'm grateful for your enthusiasm and encouragement. It keeps me going, and so do our coffee walks.

A huge thanks to Author Nichole Heydenburg, my super Beta Reader and Instagram buddy. Your insight and feedback helped mold this book into what it is today.

I want to thank the amazing authors and Bookstagrammers I've met on Instagram. It's been such a welcoming and fun community. A shout-out to the Thriller Babes. It's wonderful having a supportive group of authors to chat with and ask questions; the dark humor is also refreshing! Another huge shout-out to Nikki @onnikkisbookshelf for her amazing support in the Indie author community and for introducing me to so many awesome Bookstagrammers! I'm so glad we connected!

I have to give thanks to my new author friend, Frank Zafiro. Thanks for letting me ask you a million questions about the law and procedures. (Any mistakes are my own.) I also appreciate your advice on publishing and marketing!

I must take a moment to thank my fantastic editor, Rebecca, at Rebecca Millar Editorial. I appreciate all your time, feedback, and advice. You always ask the right questions and push me to see things differently. Thank you for challenging me.

Next up is my talented Cover Designer/Formatter, Natasha Mackenzie, aka Miss Nat Mack. I'm always blown away by what your creative mind comes up with! You are truly a gem in your field and brilliant at what you do! Thank you for another stunning cover.

I must give thanks to my family for their unwavering support—my mom and Don, Dad and Emily, and my sisters Sarah and Rachel. Thanks for reading, giving feedback, and handling my meltdowns. A special thanks to my mom in the meltdown department. Your encouragement always propels me back into action. Sarah, thanks for busting through the final version and giving me feedback and encouragement.

As I neared the completion of my novel, it was brought to my attention that the phrase, 'fake it until you become it' was used by psychologist Amy Cuddy. I want to let my readers know that my negative use of this phrase was never meant to undermine her positive message and was simply a coincidence.

I want to say thank you to my incredible Street Team! You guys are the best!

And lastly, to you, the reader. Thank you so much for choosing to pick up this book. I'm forever grateful that you gave it a chance. I hope you enjoyed it as much as I loved writing it. Thank you so much!

ALSO BY JAMIE LEE FRY
THE PRETTY ONES

ABOUT THE AUTHOR

Jamie Lee Fry is an adventure blogger turned psychological-thriller writer. She released her debut novel, *The Pretty One*s, in 2021. When she's not hunched over her desk creating thrilling stories, she's exploring the forests of Oregon with her husband, Jeremy. She has two Papillons, Daphne and Dexter, that go everywhere with her, including stand-up paddleboarding and kayaking. Jamie never says no to a good adventure, as long as mountains and waterfalls are involved. Jamie also enjoys a strong cup of coffee, baking, and documenting life with her camera. She is currently working on her next novel.

CONNECT WITH JAMIE:

@Author_JamieLeeFry

www.authorjamieleefry.com